CLOSE TO YOU

CLOSE TO YOU

A Nikki Barnes Mystery

Joan Albarella

Mystery and Suspense Press

New York Lincoln Shanghai

CLOSE TO YOU
A Nikki Barnes Mystery

Mystery and Suspense Press
an imprint of iUniverse, Inc.

For information address:
iUniverse, Inc.
2021 Pine Lake Road, Suite 100
Lincoln, NE 68512
www.iuniverse.com

ISBN: 0-595-27303-3

Printed in the United States of America

My love and appreciation go out to Meg Davis and Karen Whitney for all their support and talent. I also wish to remember Pearl for teaching me so much about life, death, and unconditional love.

PRELUDE

▼

A hooded shadow, almost unseen in the darkness, slipped out of room Eleven and quietly pulled the door closed. He paused, just for a moment, to silence the swinging Three Hearts Motel insignia. The sinister shadow figure then turned and slipped noiselessly past the row of neatly parked cars. The figure cautiously scanned the narrow parking area and motel driveway.

Just then, a purple Jeep with glowing white lights eased out of a parking space further down the row and raced down the long motel driveway. The back tires spit out loose gravel, as it moved onto the poorly lit county highway.

The shadow figure emerged again and raised a gloved hand to signal the last parked car in the row. The car, headlights off, backed cautiously out of the parking spot and continued backing down the driveway until it stopped abruptly. The driver threw the passenger door open, and the intruder slid in. The car tires slowly crunched the gravel, as it crept quietly toward the highway and eased into the concealing darkness.

The desolate night was invaded again when a noisy, young couple burst out of room Twelve. Arms around each other, they kicked the door shut together and laughed at their cleverness. He carried a boom box, and she dragged along a heavy book bag.

They pushed and pulled each other across the short walkway to their parking space, and got into a mud-covered pick-up truck. He turned on the engine, and the truck's broken muffler boomed a loud greeting from the rear of the vehicle. The ear shattering noise was intensified when they rolled both windows down, and the truck radio exploded with the sound of decibel deafening country music.

The brash driver threw the truck into reverse and screeched backwards onto the driveway. Not missing a beat, he shifted to first and forced another screech from the rear tires. He raced to the end of the driveway and spun out onto the asphalt pavement. The dark and the highway swallowed up the pickup and its noisy occupants.

The screeching truck tires jarred Talia Carter's violated consciousness. She was helplessly spread-eagle on the bed in room Eleven. She heard the scratch...scratch...scratch of the broken Three Hearts insignia, swinging on the outside of the door. The metal insignia was responding this time to the vibrations of the truck zooming past her room.

Talia couldn't move. Her body was too heavy...breathing was difficult. Her mouth was parched...no saliva left...her body was on fire and all her fluids were used up from fighting the fire.

She silently screamed at her body for help, but it wouldn't respond. Overwhelmed with her own fearfulness, she used sheer willpower to roll her naked body over the side of the bed. Her body was numb, and she helplessly hit the floor with a heavy thump. She felt no pain...she felt nothing in her body at all. Her face rested on a mound of her own clothing.

"Must crawl forward...toward the door...toward the telephone on the floor."

She summoned all of her mental abilities, as she maneuvered one inch at a time, toward the phone. Halfway there...moving somehow...she still felt nothing...couldn't swallow...couldn't breathe... needed to call Charity...tell her what happened...tell her..."I love you."

CHAPTER I

▼

Nikki Barnes saw the Sunday afternoon, May sunshine streak through her office window, and she felt it dance on her face. She happily leaned back in her desk chair and opened the tri-fold brochure. Disney World in the spring! It was "A wish Ginni's heart made" for at least the last three years. Now, this dream was coming true. In exactly one month, she and Ginni would leave their sleepy college community of Sheridan, New York...and the continuous stress of a medical practice that covered the St. David University Memorial Medical Center and Sheridan's community Mercy Hospital...and...and....

Nikki could go on and on with the reasons she and Ginni needed to get away, but there was really no one who needed convincing...except the two of them. On Saturday, Nikki took the final step and booked the airline and hotel reservations. She deliberately put down a deposit.

She leaned back further in her chair and studied the cartoon map in the open brochure. She spontaneously smiled as Minnie Mouse pointed with both hands to the Polynesian Resort Hotel, the fantasy paradise where she and Ginni would forget about everything but fun for ten glorious days.

Nikki's phone suddenly rang with its usual high-pitched scream, and even though she was used to the sound, it still made her jump. This quick movement popped her desk chair back into an upright position. She put the brochure down on her desk and picked up the phone in one quick move.

"Hello, Reverend Barnes' office." Nikki used the title "Reverend" much more than "Professor" lately. She actually worked under both titles at the University. She was a professor in the Arts and Letters department, where she taught courses in Bible Study and Ethics. She was also the Episcopal chaplain and did counseling at the student infirmary at the adjacent Memorial Medical Center.

She seemed to feel more like a Reverend lately. It could be her disenchantment with the University's new standards, which were more about money than students.

"Hey, Rev," a gruff, familiar, almost out of breath, voice said. "It's me, Max. I really need your help on this one."

Nikki smiled. She couldn't help but smile. Max Mullen was her friend, an Army buddy from the time they served together in Vietnam. She was a Second Lieutenant, Communications Specialist, and he was a Corpsman. They met when Nikki started doing Pastoral Care at the 90th EVAC Hospital where Max worked.

Now, he was a Sergeant in the Sheridan Police Department, and the University area was part of his patrol. After years of not being in touch, their two lives had unexpectedly intersected again, and they worked together to solve several murders.

A slight tingling on the back of Nikki's neck told her this phone conversation may put them back together for a similar reason.

"What is it, Max?" Nikki quickly asked. "What's wrong?"

Max didn't hesitate but did lower his voice and cryptically replied, "I'm over at the Medical Center...ya think, ya could get over here? Talia Carter just got brought in. I know she's one of your students...you work with her on that student organization. She's in a coma...not gonna make it. I'll fill ya in when you get here."

"Talia Carter! My God! What happened!"? Nikki responded. She realized Max must have been using a phone in a public area and couldn't tell her too many details. "I'll be right over," she said, as she instinctively opened the lower left drawer of her desk. "I'll meet you at the main information desk. Goodbye Max."

"See ya," Max answered, before he hung up the phone.

Nikki took her black short-sleeved, clerical shirt and white clerical collar out of the drawer. She was wearing jeans and a tee shirt. The jeans had to stay, because there were no spare slacks in her office.

She quickly changed into the clerical shirt and adjusted the plastic collar into place. Then she threw on her dark-blue blazer and brushed back her short, curly, blonde hair. She rushed out of her office toward the back entrance of Hayes Hall.

She crossed the back parking lot in a half-run, keeping up her pace down the short path and around to the front of the Medical Center. She saw Max though the glass doors. He was pacing back and forth in front of the Information Desk.

A little out of breath from her short sprint, Nikki didn't try to talk. She walked up to Max and gave him as big a hug as she could. His now middle-aged belly had expanded and Nikki's arms could barely wrap around him, but she still made that old-friend contact.

Max gave her his light-up-a-room smile and hugged her back, unintentionally pinching her with his large, western belt buckle. The steel buckle was a twentieth wedding anniversary gift from his wife, Rosa, and had become a good luck piece. He insisted on wearing it every day.

Nikki broke from the friendly embrace and stepped back. She looked up into his deep blue eyes and realized almost three months had passed since she last saw him. He looked a little sad…something more than just concern about this case.

Nikki put her hand on Max's arm and kept it there. "What's wrong, Max? So, what's going on?"

Max looked deeply into her grey eyes and led her toward several empty chairs along the sidewall. They sat next to each other, while Max took the little spiral notebook out of his inside jacket pocket. He flipped through a few pages, and Nikki knew they were getting down to business…police business.

"An ambulance just brought in Talia Carter. They had a call from the manager and owner of the Three Hearts Motel, way over in Benefield. Seems the cleaning lady…" Max paused, looked at Nikki and added, "Really the owner's mother…Three Hearts is one of those sleazy motels for university students and one-night stands. Anyway, she went into the room and found Talia Carter…totally nude…sprawled out on the floor."

He looked up at Nikki again. "I guess this wasn't an unusual sight for the older woman, and she tried to shake the girl awake. When that didn't work…and Carter started to convulse…she called 911."

Max flipped another page, studied it for a minute, and went on. "A police car answered the call with the para-medics. One of the officers found her wallet and student ID card. He called the University, and they said to bring her here."

Max again made eye contact with Nikki. "She was already in the coma when she got here. They're working on her, but…"

Max shook his head slowly from side to side. "Doesn't look good. They're trying to reach her family, now."

Nikki's thoughts split like two diverging paths. One path went directly to prayer…an automatic response, asking the higher power to take care of Talia.

The other path led her to retrace her personal connections to the dying student. She knew Talia Carter from the Gay and Lesbian Student Organization at the University. Talia was the president, and Nikki was the faculty advisor.

"Has anyone contacted Charity Daniels?" Nikki quickly asked. Charity Daniels was vice president of the gay and lesbian group and Talia's partner.

"Charity Daniels is Talia's…" Nikki hunted for a politically correct phrase. "Charity is Talia's partner…her significant other. They live together, somewhere in one of the off-campus apartments."

"She's already in there," Max said, pointing toward the Urgent Care Suite of the Center.

He got up and stretched his short, stubby legs. "Carter had an emergency card in her wallet. Listed Daniels as who to contact...also penciled in her brother's name and number, under Daniel's name."

Max checked back to his notes. "The brother's name is Ted Browning. Maybe you know him. He's a part-timer, Assistant Professor right here at St. David's."

Nikki thought for a moment before she got up. She was puzzled by this last information. How could she work so closely with Talia and Charity for almost a year, and have neither of the students mention that Ted Browning was Talia's brother.

Nikki understood of course that a gay sister was not always a welcome addition to an Assistant Professor's vitae, but still, both Talia and Charity knew Nikki could be trusted with this information. Perhaps they thought Nikki might slip at some faculty meeting or gathering. That was the only place she would ever see Ted Browning.

Nikki finally stood up. "I think I should get in there and see if I can be of some help." She took a few steps toward the Suite hallway.

"Just a minute, Rev." Max tapped Nikki's arm again. "There's something else...I can't be sure yet...but I think you should know this."

Nikki turned back to Max, curious about what he wanted to share with her. "What is it?"

"The patrol officer who found Carter," Max lowered his voice and came closer to Nikki. "He's seen cases like this before...at least two others. But those girls were already coming around when they called the police."

Max scanned the waiting area before he went on. "This is all very hush, hush. No one wants to start a panic or anything."

A twinge of red started moving up his face. He tightened his mouth and grit his teeth. "At least that's what my Chief said when he gave me orders to keep this quiet."

"What Max?" Nikki whispered, knowing that Max was getting more upset. "What are you being forced to keep quiet?"

"Benefield has had two...this will make three...cases of GHB date-rape." Max tried to relax a little. His contorted face went back to almost normal. "Here in Sheridan, we think we've had another four. It's hard to prove because the drug metabolizes out of the body so quickly, but from all the girls' reports, it looks like GHB."

"GHB...gamma hydroxybutyric acid." Nikki said the words slowly, as if reading them in a medical book. "So, why all the secrecy? GHB has been the topic of almost every talk show on television, and all the major newspapers have carried articles about it."

"It hasn't happened on this campus...or in this town." Max bit each word. "Or that's what Dean Haslett and my Chief want the parents and prospective students to think."

"That's the most ridiculous piece of thinking I've ever heard," Nikki's anger joined Max's and she forgetfully raised her voice. "How can we warn students? How can we protect them, if we don't let them know what's going on?"

"I'm with you, pal," Max answered, while he signaled with his hand that she should lower her voice. "I've gone through all the arguments with the Chief, but Dean Haslett has more influence than I do."

Nikki ended her outburst and nodded her head knowingly. "That's Haslett, all right," she hissed disdainfully through her tightened jaws. "Sometimes I think his only concern for the students here is for their tuition."

Max nodded in agreement and tried to be reassuring, "We followed up all four cases. One girl was two months pregnant before she even called us. Whenever we got to the questions about who were you with that night...none of the four could remember anything. I know the GHB causes memory loss, but we couldn't get much from any of them. They remembered being at parties on campus or with friends at bars...and they didn't want to get those friends in trouble."

Then Max added sarcastically, "The evil police might call some parents who don't want their kids drinking. Once we started asking some hard questions, no one wanted to talk. We just couldn't get a lead from any of them. Even the pregnant girl decided to talk to her boyfriend, instead of pursuing a police report."

"Can you be sure that it was date rape?" Nikki asked. "Maybe these girls just had second thoughts after an all-night drinking party."

Max shook his head again. "I don't think so. Two of them called from the hospital, that's how sick they felt in the morning. Plus, two attending physicians told me it didn't look like hangovers."

He looked directly into Nikki's eyes and added, "Something's going on with GHB. The Benefield troopers feel the same way, because all three of their cases are related to the Three Hearts Motel."

"Have you found any links to the cases here in Sheridan?" Nikki asked.

"From the little the girls will tell us," Max began again. "It looks like all of them spent some time at Tailfeathers Saloon."

Max shrugged his shoulders. "That's not much of a clue, since that's probably the most popular student hangout in town. Their dart tournaments bring in students from most of the adjoining towns as well. Not to mention the business people and other professionals who join those tournaments too."

He stopped talking and rubbed his chin thoughtfully. "If the Carter girl dies…this is gonna be a hard one to solve."

Nikki brought him back to the present situation. "Come on, Max. Let's get in there."

She led the way into the connecting corridor. They passed several adjoining hallways and turned right at the last one. This short hallway opened into a large waiting area. URGENT CARE was spelled out in gigantic red letters across the back wall.

Nikki scanned the twenty or so faces huddled in groups around the room. She recognized several students and most likely their parents, or the parents of friends brought in earlier. There were also several university employees present. A secretary from the English Department gave Nikki a little wave, as she hiked a young girl into her arms. A science professor waved a bandaged hand, and a bookstore clerk gave a small nod as she held a washcloth to her forehead.

Nikki never realized how busy the Urgent Care Suite was on these quiet Sundays. She spotted Charity Daniels just as a nurse led her into the next hallway. Charity seemed to be crying, so Nikki headed for the same hallway.

Just as she reached the entranceway, a tall, muscular, Hispanic woman, in a neatly pressed brown trench coat, stopped her. "Do you have some identification," the woman asked.

Nikki noticed the slight hint of an accent, and she turned to face the woman. "Just who are you?" Nikki asked instead of a reply.

The woman flipped open a badge and answered, "I'm Detective Ramos of the Sheridan Police, and I must ask you again to show some identification and tell me what your business is here."

Nikki quizzically turned around and looked for Max. To her knowledge there was only one woman in the Sheridan Police Department, and that was Betty Long, a rather matronly, crossing-guard type. When did they hire this thirty-something Hispanic with long black hair swept up with a tortoise-shell comb, and matching large, black eyes?

Max had been waved over to the Information Desk when they first entered the waiting area. He finished a short conversation with the Head Nurse Practitioner in the suite and furrowed his forehead in concern, as he caught Nikki's confused expression.

He bustled across the room and stood next to Detective Ramos. Hesitantly, he began introductions. "A...Detective Ana Ramos...this is Reverend Nikki Barnes, Professor at the University, Chaplain over here at the Center...advises us on a lot of cases."

He cleared his throat and then reversed the introduction. "Nikki...this is Detective Ramos." There was a long pause before he continued. "Detective Ramos is my...temporary partner."

Nikki did a double take and let her mouth drop open. "What happened to Henry?" The words just popped out of her mouth.

"Sorry..." Max began again, apologetically. "Been so much happening at work, I just forgot to tell you. I haven't had time to even make phone calls."

He was obviously upset and stumbled badly over his words. "Henry...well, it was so sudden...I mean, he's only fifty-four years old."

Nikki touched his arm and tried to get him back on track. "What happened to Henry?" She asked softly.

"Henry had a heart attack," Max said, nearly choking on the words. "Had a bad one. Was home working on his car. They did four bypasses..." Max paused and regained his composure. "He's gonna be fine. He even looks good now. But the doctors want him off for a while...and Henry wants to use up some of his sick time. Says he wants to take a whole year off...says he wants to finally clean his garage."

Max awkwardly gave a half-grin. "That Henry, he's got some sense of humor."

Nikki began to think out loud, "I'll have to get over to see him." She made a mental note, then slowly turned back and extended her hand to Detective Ramos. "So, this is Henry's replacement." Nikki shook the Detective's hand and said, "I'm glad to meet you. Please call me, Nikki."

The Detective said nothing and pulled her hand away quickly. She looked at Max for the next instructions, so Max took the lead and said, "Nikki knows the Carter girl and the Daniel girl. She's our university liaison and a personal friend of mine. She's coming in with us."

He turned to Nikki. "I've got some bad news though...Talia Carter is dead. They just took Charity Daniels in to see her body."

"That makes this a possible homicide," Ramos said firmly but quietly.

"I think it's a murder," Max answered, directing his remark to Nikki.

Nikki looked at Max and then at Detective Ramos. "Let's get inside. I think Charity might need some comforting...and I want to say a prayer for Talia."

CHAPTER 2

▼

The Emergency Treatment Room was only twelve feet long by twelve feet wide. Talia's lifeless body still had an intravenous drip attached to one arm. Several colored wires reached out from the top of her hospital gown and were attached to a turned-off monitor. Her eyes were closed, but her troubled expression seemed to be that of someone caught in a perpetual nightmare.

Charity held Talia's hand and then raised it slowly to her lips in a goodbye kiss. She placed Talia's hand back on the bed...overcome with grief. Tears welled up in her eyes, and she began to sob openly. She leaned over her lifeless lover and wrapped her arms around Talia. Still weeping, she buried her face in the gown covering Talia's breasts.

Nikki, Max and Ana Ramos witnessed this poignant scene, as they reached the room. Nikki motioned for the others to wait while she entered. She took a few steps toward Charity, but the younger woman was oblivious to anything but her loss. She was totally focused on Talia.

"What will I do without you, baby?" Charity said through her sobs. "What will I do? How did this happen? I don't understand." Her sobs began again. "I don't understand."

Nikki moved next to Charity and put an arm around her. "I'm so sorry," she whispered.

Charity finally realized who was next to her and turned to Nikki. "She's dead. Talia's dead. What am I going to do?" She buried her face on Nikki's shoulder and sobbed some more.

Nikki patted her gently and offered condolences. "I'm so sorry, Charity. Remember, Talia's okay now, and you'll be okay too. You haven't been left all alone. We won't let you be alone."

Then Nikki held Charity tenderly in her arms and promised, "We'll find out how this happened. I promise you, Charity. We will find whoever is responsible for this."

Charity stopped crying, moved a short distance away from Nikki, and wiped her eyes on her long, dangling sleeves. "What do you mean, find who's responsible?" Noticeably puzzled, she shook her head and wiped her runny nose on the same sleeve. "What do you mean? What really happened to Talia? I don't understand any of this."

Nikki touched Charity's arm and asked, "Are you up for answering some questions? Maybe the police can help make some sense out of all this."

Nikki took a long look at Talia's body and turned back to Charity, "I'm going to say a prayer for Talia. Would you like to pray with me?"

Tears started to pour down Charity's cheeks again, as she nodded yes and moved toward the hospital bed. Nikki put her hand on Talia's cold forehead and softly said, "Dear God, open your arms for our sister, Talia. She has had a difficult journey for these twenty years, and now it is time for her to rest and rejoice in your company. Hold her close to you and bring her peace."

Nikki paused before removing her hand from Talia's body. Then she opened both her hands, holding them palms up while she prayed, "Remember your daughter, Charity, Lord. Bring her comfort and hope. Give her the strength she needs for this time of transition. Amen."

Nikki turned and gave Charity another hug. They broke the embrace slowly, and Nikki asked, "Are you ready to leave now. We can talk better in the Common Room."

Charity composed herself and nodded 'yes' again. She leaned over the body and kissed Talia on the cheek. Nikki gently led her out of the room, and they followed Max and Detective Ramos down the hall to the doctor's Common Room.

*   *   *   *

The Memorial Medical Center's Common Room was a long open area. Two worktables surrounded by straight-back, wooden chairs had been placed next to each other in the center of the room. A row of beverage machines occupied one wall, while a row of file cabinets and a small computer desk were placed against the opposite wall.

Max sat heavily on one of the chairs already pulled away from the worktable. Ana Ramos pulled out another chair next to him and sat down, automatically folding her hands as she leaned her elbows on the table. Nikki pulled out a chair across the table from the two detectives and motioned for Charity to sit down next to her, which she did.

Max cleared his throat and took out his little notebook with his pen attached to the spiral binding. He looked up at Charity and sincerely offered his condolences. "I'm very sorry about your loss, Ms. Daniels."

Charity's lips started to quiver, but she held back the tears and softly answered, "Thank you."

Max flipped foreword a few pages in his notebook and looked up at her again. "Do you have any idea why Talia Carter was at the Three Hearts Motel in Benefield?" he asked.

"A motel in Benefield?" Charity echoed his question. "That can't be true. That's not right. She wasn't at a motel, and she wasn't in Benefield."

"Do you know where she was last night?" Detective Ramos asked.

"She went to Letchworth State Park. Her brother and sister-in-law rented a cabin there for the weekend. They had some car trouble, and Ted called Talia with the directions on how to get there. She was going to give him and his wife a ride home from some gas station where they left the car."

Max kept writing, as he asked, "And you didn't go with her? Didn't you get worried when she didn't come home last night?"

"No! No! It wasn't like that!" Charity got more and more agitated as she tried to explain. "I wanted to go with her. I told her we could take my car. It's a newer car...I didn't always trust her car."

Her voice started to crack, but again she pushed back the sorrow that was almost choking her. "I always worried that she might get in an accident or something." Charity's exhaustion showed as she buried her face in her hands momentarily and added, "I guess I didn't have to worry about that."

Detective Ramos wanted more information. "So, why didn't you go with her?"

"She wouldn't let me!" Charity almost screamed back. "She told me someone had to go to the 'Light Up the Night Vigil' against sexual assaults. I told her I'd rather go with her, but she insisted that an officer from the Gay and Lesbian Organization needed to be present...needed to light a candle representing the group. She wanted me to do it."

Charity stopped talking and looked from Detective Ramos to Max. She placed both of her hands on the table for support and slowly asked, "Just what did happen to Talia? What did she die from? No one has told me anything except she was in a coma when she was brought in. What happened to her?"

Max looked at Ramos, then at Nikki. He knew how awkward the silence was, but Nikki took the initiative and spoke first. "It looks like Talia was drugged with GHB. Only, whoever did it gave her too much, and it was a lethal dose."

Charity was on her feet in a heartbeat. "What? What are you saying? You mean she died from the date-rape drug? But why?...How?"

Nikki stood and tried to calm Charity down. "We have to wait for the official lab reports...but it looks like that might be the case."

Nikki again put her hand on Charity's arm. This time, Charity pulled her arm away. "You mean Talia was murdered. She was murdered in a motel room in Benefield." Charity shook her head and started pounding her forehead with the palm of her hand. "I can't believe this! I just can't believe this!"

She stopped mid-sentence. The full realization of what happened seeped into her brain, and she glared across the table at the two detectives. "What else did he do to Talia? What else happened to her?"

"Please...sit down, Charity," Nikki spoke softly and tried to encourage Charity back into her seat.

"No. I don't want to sit down!" Charity continued to stare at the detectives. "I want to know what happened to her! What else happened to her?"

Max slowly stood up and in a gentle voice said, "Please, sit down, Ms. Daniels...and I'll try to explain what we have pieced together so far."

Charity gave him her attention and slowly sat down. Max sat too, and in the same quiet voice started explaining the case. "We think Talia went to the Three Hearts Motel with someone. They may have been drinking, but we won't know that until all the toxicology reports come back. We do strongly suspect that the someone she was with gave her a lethal dose of GHB."

Max took a deep breath and began again, "A preliminary report shows that Talia had intercourse with someone, either consensual or forced. The motel cleaning lady found her early this morning, totally nude and already unconscious."

"That isn't true!" Charity raised her voice again. "That's a lie! She was forced...forced into the motel room...and forced to have sex. She was probably already drugged. She wouldn't go to a motel room with anyone. For God's sake, she wouldn't have sex with a man. She just wouldn't." She dropped her head onto her crossed arms, which were resting on the table.

"Can you be sure of that?" Detective Ramos wanted clarification again.

Charity's head shot up. "I'm positive! Talia would not have sex with any man. She didn't like men. She had reasons to hate them from the time she was a child, and she would not have sex with a man."

Max repeated Ramos' question, "Can you be sure she wouldn't go to the motel with anyone?"

"I'm positive!" Charity shot a questioning look at Nikki. "Tell them Reverend Barnes. Tell them! You know about Talia! She told you about the abuse...the baby. She hated men...and...and...she loved me. Please tell them."

Nikki put an arm around Charity's shoulders and tried to explain to Max and Ramos. "Talia did talk about a lot of abuse as a child. Her mother was a prostitute and some of the johns would get the mother drunk and then go into Talia's room. She was raped by several of them, over a period of three or four years."

Now Nikki's voice started to shake. Retelling this sad story hurt as much as it did the first time she heard it. "Talia was pregnant when she was twelve years old. Her mother forced her to abort the baby. That always haunted her...and that was when she finally ran away from home. Talia always said, she hated men."

"She wouldn't sleep with a man," Charity repeated her statement, turning again to Nikki. "Tell them she wouldn't sleep with a man."

Nikki took her arm away from Charity's shoulder and looked at Max. "I don't think Talia would sleep with a man. She would have to be forced against her will...raped."

Detective Ramos broke the resulting tension in the room by again addressing Charity. "Can you remember anything else from last night? Didn't you get worried when Talia didn't come home?"

"I got a call from her, just before I left for the vigil," Charity tried to explain. "She was at the gas station with her brother and his wife. The country roads out there were so dark she decided to stay with them and leave in the morning when it got light. She said she'd be home for brunch. We always go to brunch on Sunday at the Little White House Restaurant."

Charity's voice became dull and flat. "I was waiting for her to come home, when Urgent Care called to tell me she was here. I thought she was in an accident. I…"

Her voice trailed off, and she sat staring at the table. Max gave Nikki a knowing look and said, "Maybe you should get Ms. Daniels a ride home now. We can ask her more questions tomorrow."

He looked at Charity again and then back to Nikki, "Maybe you should see if she has a friend, or a parent, or someone who can stay with her for awhile."

Nikki got up, and said, "That's a good idea, Charity. I think you've answered enough questions for now. Let's go out to the nurse's station. Is there someone I can call? Someone who could stay with you for today?"

Charity didn't move; she just continued to stare at the table. Finally, she mumbled in an emotionless voice, "I need to make some arrangements. I promised Talia I'd take care of things if anything happened to her. She wants to be cremated…and the ashes are to be buried on her mother's grave."

She gave a sarcastic laugh at the last remark. "Can you believe that? She forgave her mother years ago, when her mother was dying of cancer. Talia went to see her and forgave her, and she wants to be buried with her."

Charity suddenly stood up and shook off some of the shock she was feeling. "I do have a lot of things to do now." She looked at Nikki. "Don't worry about me, Reverend. I'm okay. I'll call Betsy Frank. She'll stay with me for a few days. She'll help me with the arrangements."

"You can call me, day or night, Charity," Nikki hoped she was being reassuring.

"I will. I will call you. I know Talia would want you to do the funeral. I'll call you later tonight." Charity leaned in and hugged

Nikki. Then they walked down the long hallway together to the waiting area and the phones.

The Common Room was still filled with the heavy emotions of the preceding conversation, when Max closed his notebook and returned it to his pocket. Turning to Ana Ramos, he said, "Now, we need to find the brother and check out the story Talia Carter told her partner."

"You sound like you don't think the story is true," Ana Ramos remarked.

Max looked at the empty seat where Charity had been sitting, and pensively said, "I want to believe the story. I want to think Talia Carter was faithful to her partner, even if it means she did hate men...but I'm not so sure. At this point, I'm not sure what to believe."

CHAPTER 3

▼

Nikki returned to the Common Room and replied to Max's questioning look. "Carol Turner, the Nurse Practitioner, was waiting for Charity when I got to the Reception Desk." Nikki explained. "Carol was taking care of Talia when she died, and she wanted to spend a few minutes with Charity…to see if she needed any counseling. Carol will call Betsy Frank to come and take Charity home."

Nikki sat back down at the table and faced the two detectives. "So, what happens now?"

Max gave her a smile and forty-eight hours of tiredness showed on his face. "We have to be real careful with this one."

This last remark got both Nikki and Ana's full attention.

"With the way the Chief and Dean Haslett feel about the whole idea of date-rape…" He paused before continuing his explanation. "We have to make sure we can prove that GHB was used to kill Talia Carter."

He rubbed the unshaven stubble on his chin and went on, "I think the Practitioner's report and the supervising doctor's report will be confirmed by the toxicology and other lab reports. I'm calling it in as a homicide."

He turned to Ana Ramos, "Unless you have a different call, I think it's time we get the forensic boys in on this."

"I agree with you," Ana Ramos replied. "I think all the indications are that she was drugged and raped, and the amount of drug was a lethal dose."

Max pushed back his chair and stood up. "I'll go make the calls...first to the Chief, of course. Then we better stick around and wait for the lab boys...and hopefully Carter's brother will show up, so we can question him. We need to piece together the last day of that young girl's life."

With this last comment, Max gave Nikki a sad look and moved next to her. He affectionately patted her arm and left the room.

Nikki thought deeply about Max's last comment. She silently prayed for Talia...and Charity. Her deep concentration was finally broken when she looked up and saw Ana Ramos staring at her. Nikki smiled at the intensely serious detective.

"Is something wrong?" Nikki finally asked, trying to open a conversation. "Is there something you want to ask me?"

Ana Ramos broke from her stare and started studying her fingernails. "No. I'm sorry. I didn't mean to stare. I guess I better join Sergeant Mullen and wait for forensics to arrive."

Before she could get up, Nikki stopped her, "Well, you may not have any questions for me, but I have quite a few for you."

Nikki had Ana Ramos' full attention. "I don't think Max ever mentioned there was a female detective in the Sheridan Police Department. I'm sure I would remember something like that."

Ana Ramos relaxed a little in her chair. "I'm sure you would, since Betty Long, the old Chief's sister is the only official woman cop in Sheridan. She's been here a hundred years, taking care of the complaint desk Monday through Friday, nine to five. Just say 'Hello' to her, and Betty will gladly fill you in on all kinds of precious information. She'll also add that respectable women do not take men's jobs or spend long days in police cars with married men. I think her words were, 'Tempting them with extramarital indiscretions'."

Nikki couldn't help it. This last comment went right to her bent sense of humor and the strain from the events surrounding Talia's death needed very much to be broken. So Nikki started to laugh. She tried to muffle it by putting a hand to her mouth, but it didn't help. She laughed so hard tears started to roll down her cheeks. Two whole minutes passed before she gained some composure and wiped her eyes.

"I know. I know." she laughed and talked at the same time. "I've said good morning to Betty and heard the same story. She told me that even though I was a priest, I showed a lack of propriety riding around with Max…at night…when we were working on a case."

Nikki started laughing again, and Ana Ramos smiled too. Some of the tension finally left the room. Nikki composed herself a second time and asked, "Now seriously, how did you end up in Sheridan?"

Ana Ramos made a tough call and decided to trust Nikki. "It's a short but rather painful story. I trained at the Buffalo Police Academy. My only goal since I was a young girl was to become a cop and work for the Buffalo Police Department. I thought my dream came true when they hired me right out of the academy. Of course, my degree in Criminal Justice and good grades, and excellent physical training also helped me get the job."

She leaned in closer, and Nikki felt the heaviness of the emotions in what she was saying. "I was a well-trained cop, and I loved what I was doing. The Police Department paired me up with a twenty-year-veteran. He had several awards for bravery and meritorious service. I knew his reputation and was proud to be working with him."

Ana was silent for a moment, as she thought back and remembered those first years. "After two years…and after getting a few medals myself…I just couldn't ignore what was going on."

She looked up at Nikki again and asked, "Do you know what 'the silent blue line' means? Have you ever heard of the Police Code of Silence?"

Nikki's answer was unemotional and straight forward, "Police never tell on each other. Not even if they commit crimes or break the law in any way. If you do tell, you suffer terrible consequences."

"It's all true," Ana replied. "The Code of Silence is stronger than any officer, judge, or jury. You can't break the code. I knew that going into the profession, but I never thought I would have to make the choice I was forced to make."

Ana fell silent again, but Nikki wanted to hear the rest of the story. She knew from her counseling experience that purging this sad history might be good for Ana. "What happened?" Nikki asked quietly.

"My partner...," Ana started slowly. "My partner, the hero who saved women and children...well, he beat his wife on a regular basis. You have to understand. I don't get involved in domestic matters. I mean, what happens behind your closed doors is your business. I can live with that. I don't want anyone nosing into my life either, but you see..."

Her eyes were almost pleading now. "He was over six-feet-three inches tall and weighed about two-hundred and fifty pounds. She was maybe five-feet, and she had a bad limp from when she had polio as a child. I knew he was hitting her because he would talk about it. Afterward, he would be all apologetic, telling me how he didn't mean to. He had all this built up frustration over all the crime on the streets. I didn't say anything. I would listen. I figured he gave her a drunken slap or two. If she wanted to take it, then it was her business."

Ana twisted a little in her seat. "Yeah, there was alcohol involved. We stopped for a beer at lunch and then a few beers or whiskey before we signed off for the night. I wasn't a drinker, but you had to be one of the boys. I would fake a beer, twice maybe three times a day. My partner, he would have two or three to my faked one, and he always added a few shots at the end of the day."

Silence again. A long stretch of minutes passed, until Nikki asked, "What happened?"

"He called me at home, about an hour after we went off duty. Asked me to get right over to his house. He was in some trouble. When I got there, he came to the door with a beer in his hand and led me to the kitchen. His wife was in there, lying on the floor in a pool of blood."

Her voice dropped to almost a hush. "She was just a mound of black and blue bruises and blood everywhere. 'She gave me some lip.' That was what he said to me. 'She really asked for it this time,' he said."

"I couldn't believe what I was hearing. I went over to her and tried to get a pulse. There was one, but it was pretty faint. I grabbed the phone to call 911, but he stopped me."

"'Now let's get our story straight.' That was what he said to me."

"'Get our story straight!' I started screaming at him. I mean I was really in a panic. 'I think she's dying!' I kept repeating that, but he wouldn't listen, and he wouldn't let me call for help."

"'She fell down the stairs. That's all we say. She fell down the stairs, and we both saw her fall.' He kept repeating that until I agreed. Then he let me call for an ambulance."

Nikki saw Ana shiver, as she continued the story. "Well, I couldn't do it. I stood there watching this little, crippled woman bleed to death, thinking about the Code of Silence and my future. But I couldn't do it. He was nothing more than a drunken bum who bashed his wife around. We arrested guys like him at least once a week."

She looked up at Nikki again, "To make a long story less complicated, when the ambulance arrived and the paramedic asked what happened. I told them he hit her, and I walked out. I went home…and my life has never been the same."

Nikki looked at Ana for a moment, "How did you end up here…with Max?" Nikki asked.

"After I filed the formal complaint against him, my brothers in blue made my life hell. The case never got to court because his wife, and this is the irony, she insisted she fell down the stairs. I wouldn't take back my complaint, but the Internal Investigation found no wife's complaint, no wrong doing on the part of my partner. I was transferred to a desk job the next day. Then there were the phone calls at all hours of the night, dead animals in my mail box, anything to harass me. But I was determined not to just walk away from my career. I kept thinking it would all quiet down. After all, no charges were filed…nothing happened to him…but I broke the Code."

She sat back in her chair before finishing her story. "So they decided I was the perfect candidate for the police exchange with Sheridan. It's some kind of educational grant program to share expertise by having an officer from one department work for another Police Department for an unlimited amount of time."

"Max just happened to have an opening for a partner, so you got the job," Nikki added.

"No," Ana answered quickly. The anger and caution moved back into her voice. "I know he's your friend, but he didn't just voluntarily take me on as a partner. I still think he doesn't really want me or even like me. My reputation as a snitch followed me to Sheridan, because Buffalo isn't that far away. So my first day here, no one would even speak to me. No one would volunteer to work with me. Max holds a rank, so he had to assign me to someone. Rather than force one of his boys to work with a bitch like myself, he took me temporarily until his partner returns."

Pain mixed with anger crept into her expression, as she added, "I don't think he realized Henry would be out so long. Or that we would actually have to work together on a murder case."

Ana stopped talking and looked at Nikki for some acknowledgement.

Nikki again took some time to think before she spoke. "I think you did the right thing, and I think you are true to your profession. I know that doesn't help when you're blacklisted and harassed, but you must know deep down, that what you did was right."

"It cost me my friends and my career. It turned everything I thought police work stood for into crap," Ana shot back.

"Don't say that," Nikki quickly responded. "It just isn't true. You took a stand for justice, and that is what a good police officer does. I also think if you didn't do the right thing, you would be just like your old partner, and you're not like him...and you don't want to be like him."

Nikki added one more point, "I also think you shouldn't underestimate Max. I worked with him and fought with him in Vietnam. He's a good guy. He believes in justice too."

Ana Ramos stood, ready to leave the room and the conversation. "I'm not so sure about that. The war was a long time ago. Max Mullen is a cop now, has been for years." She walked toward the door.

While Nikki watched Ana leave the Common Room, she wondered if Max really was the same sensitive guy she remembered, someone who looked out for those who needed help. She wondered if maybe he had changed...maybe he had to pledge allegiance to the Code of Silence.

CHAPTER 4

▼

"This was supposed to be a lovely, lazy Sunday," Nikki mumbled to herself, as she pulled into the parking lot of the Mercury Club. She had planned the day so that there was plenty of time to finish grading papers at her office, get home for a quick shower and change of clothing, and get to the Mercury Club for a drink with Ginni before the program started.

All her well-timed plans fell apart when Max called her about the murder of Talia Carter. She barely had enough time to throw on some black slacks and black loafers. The black cleric shirt had to stay, but she added a grey, tweed blazer. When she looked into the hall mirror, she had to agree with her reflection, she did look like an Episcopal priest. Ginni would hate the outfit.

How many times had Ginni said, "If you have to dress like some English vicar, could you at least wear some color? That all black outfit makes you look like you're going to a funeral."

Ginni even bought Nikki a half-dozen cleric shirts for Christmas. They represent most of the colors in the rainbow, including red, green, purple, pink, powder blue, and yellow. Too bad Nikki didn't have time to iron any of them. She suddenly started to laugh. Her mind full of concern was being replaced with a picture of both Ginni and herself avoiding any ironing. It was the one household chore, neither of them liked to do.

Just thinking of her partner, Dr. Virginia Clayton, brought a smile to Nikki's face. They first met when Nikki was helping Max with a murder case at the Memorial Medical Center. For a short time, during that case, Ginni appeared to be one of the main suspects.

However, Nikki knew from the first time she saw Ginni that she was falling hard, and love finally knocked her over. They had lived together ever since. Nikki put up with the crazy hours Ginni worked in the Family Medicine Suite at Memorial Medical Center and her on-call work in the Emergency Room at Mercy Hospital. On the other hand, Ginni had accepted Nikki's various duties at the University and her extra-curricular detective work with Max. Well, she hadn't totally accepted the detective work.

Nikki shook this last thought from her mind and walked into the ballroom of the Mercury Club. About thirty tables, with six guests to a table, were spread out around the large room. The stage was set up as the dais with two long tables for dignitaries on each side. A standing microphone was in the space between the tables, and a large banner which read, "The Sheridan United Women's Clubs" was draped across the base of the stage,

"A rather pretentious name for a group of small town clubs," Nikki muttered quietly to herself. "Of course, women are allowed to be pretentious once in awhile. Men have been doing it for years," she concluded.

Lunch was already being served, so Nikki made her way through the parade of servers to where she thought Table Six might be. She tried to hurry because she knew this day was very important to Ginni.

Ginni was to receive one of the Distinguished Women of Sheridan Awards. Something Nikki agreed she deserved. Ginni also wanted Nikki to meet an old and very special friend of hers, Taylor Fleming, who was also receiving one of the awards.

Taylor Fleming was Commissioner of the County Office For the Handicapped. She and Ginni met in undergraduate school at the University at Buffalo and had maintained their friendship ever since. Ginni went on to medical school, and Taylor received her doctorate in Business Organization. She was working as a vice-president for the Reynolds Tobacco Company in North Carolina when she was involved in a terrible car accident. Both of her legs had to be amputated below the knee, and she almost died of her internal injuries.

Since the accident, she went on to become a nationally known activist and advocate for the handicapped. Her confrontational style and outspoken demeanor gave her a reputation as a foe to be reckoned with.

Nikki never met Taylor, but she had read articles about her and had heard tales from Ginni about Taylor's battles and conquests. The County appointed her Commissioner just to get her off its back. As Commissioner, she had to fix the historical and political problems she found, and the word was she did that very loudly and well.

Nikki located the table and gave a wave to Ginni, who was nervously scanning the entire room, looking for Nikki. Ginni smiled back and waved, self-consciously combing her fingers through her short, reddish-brown hair. The furrow in her forehead and the intensity of her large, green eyes told Nikki she was in that neutral zone between anger and concern, a zone Ginni often went to with Nikki.

"Sorry I'm late," Nikki said quietly, as she leaned down and gave Ginni a quick peck on the cheek. "Something came up at the Medical Center."

Ginni's forehead furrow started to relax. "I was afraid something would come up. Did Dean Haslett call you over to the Center?"

Nikki anticipated Ginni's reaction and started to fumble over her words. "No...no...it wasn't the Dean. It was Max. He called me over about a student."

Ginni's eyes got bigger, and she pursed her mouth ready to speak. She hesitated a moment and all that came out was, "Max…on a Sunday?"

Nikki jumped in and directed the conversation away from the present inquiries. "Yes, I'll tell you all about it later. I think I better sit down now."

Ginni got Nikki's hint and tried to relax again. "We saved you a seat, right next to Taylor. Nikki, this is Taylor Fleming." Ginni motioned to the woman next to her who sat in a wheelchair, which was pushed close to the table.

"It's a real pleasure to meet you," Nikki said shaking Taylor's hand and instantly noticing what a strong grip she had. "Ginni has told me a lot about you," Nikki added, trying to release her hand from a handshake that was lasting too long.

Nikki finally got her hand back and walked around the wheelchair to the empty chair next to Taylor. As she sat down, Ginni continued the introductions at their table. To Nikki's left was Sister Mary O'Donnell, President of the Metro-churches Justice Coalition. Nikki was also a member of the Coalition. Next to Sister Mary was Carol Larchmonth, CEO of Mercy Hospital, and next to her, on Ginni's right, was Dr. Sheba Reinstein, the new pediatrician at Memorial Medical Center, who Ginni had taken under her wing.

Nikki felt comfortable at the table, since she knew everyone a little, except Taylor Fleming. She felt this was an opportunity to get to know her too. While the salads were placed on the table, Nikki snuck a good look at Taylor. Her wheelchair sat lower to the ground than the rest of the chairs, so she appeared smaller than she really was. Her dyed blonde hair was long and shiny. It came to her shoulders and had just enough curl to make it fall softly into place and complement her elliptical, perfectly proportioned face.

Taylor was wearing a long, sleeveless black dress that draped to the footpads of the wheelchair. The dress was cut in a low V, so that a small amount of pale-white cleavage showed when she bent over to eat.

She also wore a choker-type necklace of black pearls, which matched her small, black-pearl earrings and bracelet. She finished her ornamentation with five silver rings; one for each finger.

Nikki couldn't help but notice the fine muscles in Taylor's upper arms. She knew that double amputees used their muscles a great deal lifting themselves in and out of their wheelchairs, and for just generally getting around. Their hands and arms seem to develop extra strength.

Whatever the reason, Nikki thought to herself. *Taylor's upper body workouts have given her a most attractive and fit appearance.*

Taylor caught Nikki staring at her and smiled. She put her fork down and rested both her hands in her lap, which was hidden by the tablecloth. "Well, it is nice to finally meet you, Reverend Barnes," she said in a low, seductive voice.

"Oh, please call me Nikki. I'm just Nikki to my friends," Nikki squeaked out nervously, not knowing why this woman seemed to make her fluttery.

Taylor just smiled. Then she licked the moist, red lipstick she was wearing and connected her piercing almost lilac-colored eyes with Nikki's. "You must be so proud of Virginia," she continued in the same sensual voice.

"I…I…am very proud of her," Nikki stammered, as she tried to recover the composure that seemed to be slipping away. "And congratulations to you, too. I hear you'll also be receiving one of the awards."

Taylor gave a little, open-mouthed laugh, broke eye contact, and returned to eating her salad. Nikki started eating her salad too, but she couldn't help notice, from the corner of her eye, that every bite Taylor took was deliberate and precise. More like a sexy dance than just eating.

Nikki deliberately pulled herself back to the salad, which was quickly replaced with the main entree; the obligatory stuffed chicken breast, twice-baked potatoes, and mixed vegetables. She wondered how often she had seen this particular entree arrangement at banquets and social gatherings.

She pondered the difficult culinary decisions of banquet halls and nibbled on her chicken. Suddenly, she felt a hand on her thigh just above her right knee. She swallowed the half-chewed forkful in her mouth and looked at Taylor. Taylor didn't look up, just continued her food ballet. Her left hand still looked as if it was resting on her lap under the tablecloth. Nikki knew otherwise.

The mistress-of-ceremony started explaining how they would begin the program while everyone continued the meal, since they wanted to end in a timely manner. The warm hand was still on Nikki's knee, and she didn't know what to do. She sat frozen, like a punch-bowl ice statue.

The United Women's Club's President had just introduced everyone on the dais and thanked everyone on the committees. She introduced the Supervisor of Sheridan, who also thanked the committees and all the people on the dais.

The invisible, hot hand was moving slowly up Nikki's leg toward her now twitchy crotch. She shot a look at Taylor and coughed for attention. She didn't get anyone's attention. Most of the table was listening intently to the Governor's representative, who had just declared the day Sheridan United Women's Clubs Day. Taylor also sat totally absorbed in the reading of the proclamation.

Nikki continued in frozen perplexity. This was not the place to create a scene. This was also very confusing. Just what was this woman doing? Nikki finally put her own hand under the table and grabbed Taylor's hand…two inches below the goal line.

Taylor still sat staring at the stage. She appeared enraptured by the dull speaker.

Nikki continued struggling with the strong hand on her upper leg. She felt like she was arm wrestling one of the University boys. Taylor was very strong and managed to twist her hand in such a way that she and Nikki were in a mutual grip, holding hands.

Taylor then moved her third finger just enough to brush back and forth on Nikki's palm.

This is too much! Nikki's heard herself screaming somewhere inside her head. She shot up out of her chair, and Taylor released her hand instantly.

The entire table looked at Nikki, who was now standing. "Excuse me," she quietly muttered, as she quickly left the table and headed for the woman's room. She made her way to the sink and started dabbing her face with cold water.

"What is going on?" she quizzically asked her own reflection in the mirror.

Before she could answer, Ginni burst into the empty women's room. "Are you okay, Nikki?" Ginni asked with deep concern in her voice.

"No...no. I'm not okay." Nikki sputtered, wondering how on earth she could explain what just happened to Ginni.

"Well, what's wrong?" Ginni asked apprehensively, nervously biting her lower lip.

Nikki decided to just spit it out, "Your friend, Taylor Fleming, has been feeling me up under the table...and when I tried to stop her...she grabbed my hand...and...and...She brushed her finger on my palm...and you know what that means."

Ginni crossed her arms. A reddish blush moved up her bronze-toned face, and she gave Nikki a long, aggravated, look. "What did you just say?" She demanded clarification.

"She felt up my leg...gave me a finger..." Nikki's exasperation could be heard in her voice, as she demonstrated the finger in her hand. "There's something wrong with that woman!" Nikki finally concluded.

Ginni took a deep breath and let it out slowly. "Nikki...I don't know what is going on under the table." She said this in her best doctor voice. The one used especially for those suffering mental fatigue. "I do know that in a few minutes I am going to get an award that helps me reaffirm that what I am doing means something to people. This is important to me, and I want you to be there with me when I get the award."

"I know this is important," Nikki never wanted to distract Ginni from her important moment. "I'm really sorry I even mentioned this...I just don't understand..."

"Nikki," Ginni talked doctor talk again. "I am sure something happened at the table, but do you think it can wait until I get my award?"

Nikki started to answer, thought better of it, and just nodded her head.

"Good," Ginni said, knowing the patient would now take her medicine and go get the tests. "Let's get back to the table and see if they've called my name yet."

Nikki obediently followed Ginni out of the women's room and back to the table. Everyone at the table, including Taylor, looked at them again as they returned. Ginni sat back in her seat, and Nikki moved hers as far as possible away from Taylor. This put her very close to Sister Mary, who just gave her an odd look.

Taylor asked Nikki for her untouched ice-cream dessert. Nikki pushed it over to her, and Taylor kept both hands on the table from that point on. Nikki still didn't move any closer to Taylor. She got up, as instructed the day before by Ginni, and took pictures of Ginni receiving her award and Taylor receiving hers.

The program finally ended with everyone present breaking into informal groups for congratulations and friendly chats. Nikki didn't wait for any friendly chats with Taylor. When the last speech finished, she hurriedly walked out the door to the car. She didn't even tell Ginni where she was going.

Nikki sat in the car for twenty minutes waiting for Ginni. When Ginni finally left the luncheon and walked toward the car, she was beaming with joy and proudly holding her plaque, Nikki didn't have the heart to open up the whole Taylor thing again.

Instead, she planted a big kiss on Ginni's cheek and said, "I'm so proud of you. I think I got some good pictures too. These little throw-away cameras work pretty good."

Ginni tenderly ran her two fingers over the white streak in Nikki's hair, and then she took Nikki's face in her hands and gave her a sweet, loving kiss on the lips. "Thanks, Nikki. This does mean a lot to me."

Ginni sat back and fastened her seat belt, while Nikki started the car and pulled out of the lot, heading for home. They drove slowly past a sporty-looking dark, green Mercedes, and saw Taylor Fleming just opening the driver's side door. She saw them too and waved.

Ginni returned the wave, and Nikki looked quickly away. "Oh, by the way," Ginni began. "Taylor said she was just fooling around with you. She really has quite a sense of humor, don't you think?"

Nikki slammed on the brakes. "Sense of humor?" she repeated questioningly.

"I tried to explain to her that priests don't always appreciate jokes with sexual connotations," Ginni explained matter-of-factly, as she rubbed the award that had all of her attention. "Taylor promises never to tease you again."

Nikki tried to put everything that happened today into some perspective. She couldn't, but she knew Ginni was happy and that might be enough for now. She started driving again and managed to say, "I'm glad she's your friend and not mine."

*   *   *   *

It only took ten minutes for Nikki and Ginni to both agree on where to hang the praiseworthy plaque. Nikki stood on a kitchen chair, hammer in hand, nail in mouth, ready to prepare the living room wall for a major decoration. She eyed the right spot and proceeded to tap the nail into the wall.

Ginni was still hugging her prize, as she walked over and handed the plaque to Nikki. Nikki hung it on the nail and an almost audible sigh could be heard in the room. Both women took a moment to admire the award.

Nikki, over-dramatically, cleared her throat and in a very formal voice read the award, "The Sheridan United Women's Clubs name Virginia Clayton, MD, one of the Distinquished Women of Sheridan."

Then Nikki gave Ginni an energetic applause, complete with whooping and whistling. She jumped down from the chair, wrapped her arms around Ginni and kissed her deeply and passionately. "I'm so proud of you, Ginni," she whispered.

Ginni stepped away, still holding Nikki's hand and made a grand curtsy. "Thank you. Thank you, all my fans and members of the Sheridan Women's Clubs. I would like to thank my family, my tax lawyer, my lesbian, priest lover, and all the little people who have made this award possible."

Laughing, she walked back into another embrace with Nikki, and they both again stared silently at the award. The silence this time was suddenly broken with a loud, "Meow!"

Both women turned to find Fluffy, Nikki's rather senior, grey around the whiskers, mostly black with a white bib, adopted cat, sitting in the doorway that separates the living room from the dining room.

Fluffy was also admiring the new wall hanging. She stared at the award for a few seconds, and then looked at the two women. "Meow!" was her timely, if not repetitious, response.

"I think she's proud of you too," Nikki added.

"Thank you, Fluffy," Ginni answered, breaking the embrace and walking over to the cat. "I certainly appreciate all of the support you have shown over the years." She bent down and petted Fluffy's head. The cat returned an appreciative purr.

"What do you say…" Ginni addressed her adoring fans, "we head to the kitchen and grab a few cat treats. I may even rustle up some coffee for the less discriminating."

Ginni led the family into the kitchen and put a few cat treats on Fluffy's floor mat. Then on automatic pilot, she went through the various steps needed for a pot of freshly ground coffee.

Nikki returned the chair turned step stool to its proper place at the round, oak, kitchen table. As if in a pantomime, she sat in the chair, let her jacket slide off and onto the back of the chair, slipped out her plastic cleric collar, and unbuttoned the two top buttons of her black shirt. Her whole body then seemed to relax into the warmth of this familiar room.

Ginni placed two empty mugs on the table and sat across from Nikki. "Okay, that's enough about me." She smiled at Nikki. "So why did Max call you over to the Medical Center?"

Nikki was taken a little off-guard by the change in topic, but realized from Ginni's smile, that her partner was always aware of what was going on...or wanted to be, especially if it involved police sergeant friends and sudden calls to Medical Centers.

CHAPTER 5

▼

Nikki sipped from her steaming cup of coffee, trying to fully comprehend the fact that one of her students had been drugged, raped, and killed. She looked up at Ginni, sitting across the table from her and suddenly felt warm tears blurring her vision and trickling down her cheeks.

Ginni reached across the table to touch Nikki's hand. "What's wrong? What is it, Nikki?" She felt the seriousness of the situation, so she continued to hold Nikki's hand while she waited for a response.

Nikki slowly pulled her hand away and took a tissue out of her jacket pocket. She wiped her eyes and quietly began, "Max called me over to the Medical Center because Talia Carter was brought in by the paramedics. She was found unconscious in a motel over in Benefield."

Nikki needed to stop again, to replay the morning events in her head. The priest in her was composed and in control at the hospital, but now the teacher and friend was struggling with the shock and grief of the situation. "She was given GHB...and she was raped." Nikki's voice quivered with sorrow and anger.

"My God!" Ginni gasped, hardly above a whisper. "Is she all right? Can she remember anything?"

"She died," Nikki said flatly. "She didn't make it...too much of the drug...that's what Carol Turner said." Nikki started to cry. She buried her face in her hands and tried to stifle her shoulder-shaking sobs, but it was no use. Finally, giving in to her emotions, she let the tears and sobs flow freely.

Ginni quickly got up and went over to Nikki. She didn't try to stop the flowing emotions. She just stood next to Nikki, gently rubbing her back as she cried.

"That poor girl never got a break in life," Nikki choked out the words, finally feeling her emotions calming down. She again reached in her pocket for another tissue, but Ginni already had them ready.

Ginni let Nikki compose herself while she pulled a chair up close to Nikki's. "Do the police know who did it?" Ginni asked, as she pushed a loose blonde curl back off Nikki's face.

"No," Nikki shook her head. "No. Max thinks they've had more date rape cases, but the Dean and Police Chief are hushing them up."

Nikki felt the calm returning to her being, and she smiled at Ginni. "I guess I needed that. Charity Daniels, Talia's partner, is calling me later to work out the funeral details. I want to have it together when she calls."

"Nikki?" Ginni gave her a very serious look. "I have some other bad news for you. I just heard it this morning. Ted Green called me in for a consultation. He's a heart surgeon over at General Hospital, and he just casually asked me how Henry Ostrow was doing. I told him we hadn't talked to Max or Henry for several months."

Ginni leaned closer and again took Nikki's hand. "I don't know if Max told you this morning, but Henry had heart surgery. It was very serious...he almost died. Henry may never be able to return to the police force."

Nikki put her hand over Ginni's and gently squeezed it before she answered. "Not a day for good news, is it?" She forced a smile, and Ginni smiled back. "Well, according to my buddy, Max, Henry is on the mend but wants a year off to clean his garage."

This last comment was so out of place with the previous conversation that Ginni started to laugh. This was a break they both needed, so

Nikki joined her. Between laughs, Nikki added, "Poor Max. He now has a very pretty but butchy policewoman from Buffalo as a partner. She's Hispanic and hated by all the other officers because she blew in her wife-beating ex-partner."

Ginni stopped laughing. Her expression froze, and her eyes grew large, as she tried to absorb everything Nikki was saying.

Still giggling and oblivious to Ginni's concern, Nikki just went on. "Poor old Max. No one would take her as a partner, so he had to. He looks so lost without Henry."

"Nikki?" Ginni became very serious again. "I hope you don't plan to replace Henry as a temporary partner for Max."

Nikki stared at Ginni, then smiled. "I'm no competition for Detective Ana Ramos, believe me. Max just wanted my input since I knew Talia."

"Max never just wants your input," Ginni's gentleness was changing quickly to sternness. "I don't want you getting involved with murder, again. I know you are concerned about the students, but let the police do their job. Promise me Nikki, that you will not put yourself in any danger? Promise me?"

Without hesitation, Nikki raised her right hand, as if taking a pledge, and answered, "I promise. I will not put myself in any danger. I will avoid all date rape situations and let the police do their job."

Then she leaned in and kissed Ginni.

Ginni kissed back, pushed slowly away, and looked Nikki right in the eyes. "Why am I not convinced?"

*   *   *   *

Nikki carefully made her way up the dark, narrow, wooden steps that led to the open deck entrance of Talia Carter and Charity Daniel's upstairs apartment. Betsy Frank's phone call earlier in the evening was the reason for Nikki's unplanned visit to the apartment. Charity had been inconsolable for most of the day, and Betsy was afraid that in her depression, she might hurt herself.

"I think she might kill herself," Betsy uttered into the phone in her tiny, almost squeaky voice. "I'm not kidding, Reverend," she nervously continued. "I think you should come over and talk to her. I mean, she's not in any danger right this minute, but she's so upset. I thought a walk might take her mind off Talia for a while, so I sent her on an errand, to look for an open store and buy some milk. It gave me a chance to call you…I think you should come over."

Nikki could just picture Little Bet. That was what everyone in the Gay and Lesbian Organization called her. Little Bet was only four feet eleven inches tall, but she had the biggest heart in all of St. David University. Whenever anyone was sick, Little Bet made the chicken soup and brought it over. She also provided free babysitting service, free tutoring, even free laundry service. She was bright, and feisty, and filled with what Nikki called love for her fellow man or woman, as the case may be.

If Betsy Frank didn't feel she could handle Charity, then Nikki wasn't sure she could either. But she knew, she needed to try. She thought about putting her cleric clothes back on but decided against it. Instead, she changed into something less formal and hopefully friendlier. She pulled on some worn jeans, threw her blazer over a St. David tee shirt, and jumped into her car.

Nikki lost some time getting to the apartment when she hit all the red lights on Main Street. She finally reached Brownwood Road where Charity lived, but she wasn't sure whether to turn right or left. Right turned out to be wrong, so more time was lost. Almost twenty minutes passed before Nikki reached the apartment.

As she continued to climb up the dark, creaky, stairs, she hoped that Betsy had managed to sooth some of the pain in Charity. It seemed odd that no lights were on inside the apartment. Nikki could understand forgetting to turn on the outside light, but some of the inside lights should have been on.

Nikki's heart began to pound a little louder and faster. Her breathing quickened, and she knew the stairs were not that steep. She finally reached the deck and knocked on the door. No lights came on, but she heard a sound from inside. Footsteps…maybe?

Nikki knocked again, this time louder and longer. No one came to the door. Nikki tried one more time, as she called out, "Betsy! Charity! It's Reverend Barnes. Nikki Barnes. Please, let me in!"

No one answered the calls, so Nikki tried the door. She knocked with one hand and slowly turned the doorknob with the other. Then she pushed the door half open and again yelled into the apartment, "Betsy! Charity! Is anyone home?"

She stepped carefully into the long, dark kitchen. There were no lights on anywhere. A reflection from the first quarter moon shed just enough light for Nikki to see where she was going. She slowly made her way to the living room without running into anything.

Nikki's breathing was now in unison with the heavy banging of her heart. The hair on the back of her neck was wet and standing at attention. Her wartime instincts had kicked in. *There may be enemies in the bush…be careful…have your gun ready.*

Unfortunately, Nikki didn't have a gun with her. She left them both home…This was supposed to be a routine recon expedition…This area was safe…Nikki tried to shake off these memories, as she got closer to the living room.

"No area is safe…no recon is routine," she whispered this old warning and entered the living room. It took a minute for her eyes to adjust to the darkness, but when they did, she noticed something on the floor…next to the sofa…a pile of something…a person…a body.

A car passed the house and a short flash from the headlights pulsed into the room. "My God! There's someone on the floor!" Nikki's voice was barely a whisper. She carefully made her way toward the sofa and the body on the floor.

She reached the far end of the sofa, but the further she went into the room, the darker it got. She stopped and fumbled in her jean's pocket for a small box of matches she carried to light the candles in the Medical Center Chapel.

Nikki took out the matches and heard them shaking in her hands. The first one wouldn't light, so she threw it down and tried the second. The match spit a hint of light over several feet of the room. The body was nude...surrounded by pieces of clothing.

Nikki's instincts tried to kick in again. "Lights? Where are the lights?" she asked and answered herself, while the match flickered out. She tried to focus logically on what needed to be done next. She scanned the dark room again and with her peripheral vision made out a lamp on the table next to the sofa, only a foot away. She took a few short steps toward the table and felt around for the lamp.

Yes, she had it. She felt the base and worked her hand up to the switch. There it was...but this was when she let her guard down. Focusing on the lamp and not on the danger, she foolishly ended up in an ambush. Before she could push the on switch, the enemy was at her...hand to hand combat.

She tried to push the assaulting black figure away, but a knife...a thin knife pierced through her left hand. A kick to her abdomen sent her lungs into exhale, and she could no longer breathe.

Nikki got one quick look at the enemy...not the Viet Cong this time...not even the Cambodians. This was a murderer, dressed in black slacks and black turtleneck sweater. A black stocking over his head...distorted face...big, squeezed lips...flattened nose...stocking hair...no air...no air. A sudden pain hit the back of her head...a searing, smashing pain. Nikki gasped in the long-awaited air and felt her limp body land hard on the thin rug, just inches away from the other body.

She would fight to stay alive. Soldiers always fight. She moaned through the pounding pain at the back of her head and tried to get up...but she couldn't rally any strength. Another car passed the house and sent a quick flash of dull light into the room. This was just enough light for Nikki to see two black figures running hurriedly toward the kitchen. She heard quick footsteps and then the door slammed.

Nikki lost consciousness and slid slowly into a painful dream state. She fought to come back to wakefulness...must come back...someone was hurt...work to be done. Slowly and deliberately, she raised her hand and carefully felt the back of her head. It was wet and sticky. Maybe her hand was bleeding? She touched her face...wet and sticky...bleeding...have to get help...

Suddenly, Nikki heard footsteps again...the enemy returned...she would fight...she needed a plan...can't move...losing consciousness again.

*   *   *   *

The muffled sound of sirens...police cars...maybe an ambulance...closer now...louder now. Nikki tried to open her eyes again. Tried to fight her way back from the unconscious world that the pain in her head escorted her to. The darkness was gone, but the lights were too bright. Someone was rolling her over, putting small, cold pillows on the back of her head...on her hand...her face.

Nikki tried to speak, but no words came out. She wanted to tell them someone was hurt...was lying in a mound without any clothes on. That girl needed help. Nikki was okay. She was hit by bullets before...in Nam...In Country. Three different hits. She was okay. She was always okay.

"How's she doing?" Max asked nervously, still puffing from his run up the rickety stairs. "She gonna be okay?"

"Can't tell yet," the female paramedic answered, as she inflated the blood pressure cuff again. "She took a nasty blow to the head. Probably with that brick over there, and she has a deep puncture wound in her left hand. Must have tried to fight him off."

Max leaned intently over Nikki, willing her to wake up. "What about the blood on her face? Is her face cut too? That's a lot of blood."

"No face cuts," the second paramedic answered, while preparing Nikki to be lifted onto the nearby gurney. "Looks like most of the blood is from the head and hand wounds."

"She looks awful," Max mumbled, covering his mouth with his hand, trying to hold back the nausea he felt moving up his body.

"At least she's alive," Ana Ramos commented, as she moved next to Max. "The other woman isn't doing very well. Looks like she was sexually assaulted, but we got lucky this time. Reverend Barnes must have walked in on the assault. He didn't have time to rinse out the two glasses. There's a definite residue on one of the glasses, so I've called for the Sheriff's forensic team. They're on their way."

She paused while the second gurney was popped up. This one held the comatose body of Betsy Frank, blankets belted tightly around her, IV drips in both arms.

"They're taking her to Mercy Hospital," Ana went on. "Her wallet was right in her jean's pocket. The license says her name is Betsy Frank."

Max continued to watch the gurney carrying Nikki. The paramedics took a few moments to work it around the narrow doorway leading into the kitchen.

"Would you like me to wait for the forensic team?" Ana asked. "I could interview Charity Daniels. She found them, so I can see what she has to say about all this."

"I should really wait for the forensic team," Max hesitantly replied, his eyes still following the movement of Nikki's gurney. "Charity Daniels has a lot of explaining to do. She's involved in a murder and two attacks now, and none of them appear to be forced entries. Somebody knows this perp."

He looked up at Ana and finished his thought, "And this perp almost killed a friend of mine."

Ana spoke quietly but confidently, "I can handle this end of the investigation for right now. Why don't you go to the hospital with Reverend Barnes? I can meet you there."

Max looked at the kitchen and heard the strain of the paramedics carrying Nikki's gurney down the steep stairs. He looked back at Ana. "Okay, Detective Ramos. I would appreciate that. I need to make sure Nikki's okay. You sure you can handle this end?"

"I'm positive, Sergeant," Ana replied, somewhat bothered by his lack of confidence in her. "I have investigated murders before."

"Right. Right," Max answered, already preoccupied with getting to the hospital. "I'll meet you later at Mercy Hospital."

He started for the kitchen and just before he reached the door, he turned back to Ana and said, "Thanks. I appreciate this Ramos." He turned and hurried through the small kitchen and down the stairs.

Ana stepped aside, so the second gurney could move through the living room to the kitchen and stairs. "At least he trusts me this much," she muttered under her breath.

Then she moved toward the far corner of the living room. Sitting on the floor, hugging her pulled up knees was Charity Daniels. She was biting her lower lip and rocking aimlessly back and forth. Her eyes were locked on a pile of books that fell, when one of the bricks was removed from her makeshift bookcase.

She kept her eyes focused away from the mound of Betsy's clothes, lying next to the books, and the puddle of dark liquid next to the clothes…seeping into the rug.

Charity started to hum. It wasn't really a song. She just hummed music, dissonant music, not really comprehensible. Like this room…like her life right now…dissonant…not really comprehensible.

CHAPTER 6

▼

Nikki forced herself to wake up from a long, troubling dream. From somewhere outside her dream, she heard an old Gregorian chant. "Tantum ergo…Nikki…tantum ergo, Nikki." There was definitely something wrong with the last word in the chant.

She tried to open her eyes, but the lids were too heavy to lift. She finally stopped struggling and listened to the chant again. "Tantum ergo, Nikki."

"No," Nikki thought to herself. "Those are not the words."

Still unable to open her eyes, she tried again to listen carefully to each word. This time she heard the right words. "You promised…Nikki! You promised, me. You promised…Nikki."

Ginni was singing the incantation. "You promised me, you wouldn't get hurt. Look at you. You're a mess!"

These last terms of endearment opened Nikki's eyes. She was free-floating on some major medication but did recognize Ginni, who sat next to the bed holding her bandaged hand.

"I…didn't…break…my…promise," Nikki in a drugged slur chanted the response from her prone position.

Ginni jumped in her seat, unprepared for Nikki to wake up so soon. She got to her feet and leaned over Nikki, kissing her gently on the forehead. "Nikki, I was so worried about you. What did you just try to say?"

Nikki tried to form the same sentence again. This time, she chanted out the words, as if she was preparing the Communion Elevation during a church service.

"I…didn't…break…my…promise…," Nikki chanted.

Ginni just shook her head and stifled a small laugh. "We're not in church at the moment, Nikki. You can just talk normally."

Nikki tried to understand what normal was at the moment. This took a few seconds of deep, drugged thinking and some mouth muscle control. She finally whispered, "I didn't break my promise, Ginni. I just went to arrange the funeral. The murderers were in the house…someone was on the floor…I got hit on the back of my head. Ouch!"

The memory of the attack brought back some of her head pain.

"Everything is okay now," Ginni murmured reassuringly, as she patted Nikki's shoulder. You're going to be fine. You were stabbed in the hand and hit on the head with a brick." She leaned over Nikki again and tried to ease her own fear with some humor. "They thought a hit with a brick could bring you down, but they didn't know how hard that head really is."

Nikki got this one and smiled back at Ginni. "Could you crank this bed up a little?" Nikki asked. "Boy, I'm really dry. How about a little water?"

Ginni pushed the button on the side railing of the hospital bed and brought Nikki up to an almost sitting position. Then she poured some ice water into a Styrofoam cup, added a straw, and held it while Nikki took a few long sips.

"Better than beer," Nikki smiled.

"Like you drink so many beers," Ginni replied, as she put the water cup down on the bedside table. She leaned in closer to Nikki and asked, "Are you ready to see Max? He's been up here for hours, even rode with you in the ambulance. He's very worried about you…and

I'm sure he has lots of questions for you. Are you up to answering them?"

Nikki slowly turned onto her side. Her whole head felt like a swollen melon, but at least the cobwebs were leaving her brain. "I'm not sure if I can remember everything, but I'd love to see Max."

Ginni left the room, and Max entered almost immediately. He quietly approached the bed and handed Nikki a small bouquet of artificial crocuses. The white, purple and yellow polyester petals looked very fake. "How ya doin pal?" Max asked in almost a whisper. "I know ya like flowers, so I got these in the gift shop."

Nikki was so overcome by the sincerity of this gift and by the totally disheveled look of her old buddy, that she almost cried. "I'm fine, Max. Really. I have a terrible headache, but they have me loaded with pills. A few days and I'll be back to my charming self."

Nikki smiled at her own joke, then got quiet and serious. She needed to ask a question but dreaded the answer. "Who was on the floor, Max? Who was she? And will she be alright?"

Max rested his arms on the bed rail, making it squeak a little under his weight. "Are you sure you're up for this?" He asked. "They're gonna send you home tomorrow. We can talk then."

Nikki reached over with her bandaged hand and touched his arm. "I'm okay, Max. I really need to know. Who was it?"

"Betsy Frank is dead." Max answered, with an overwhelming emotional tiredness in his voice. "Looks like she was killed the same way as Talia Carter. She lapsed into a coma while the paramedics were working on her and died in the Emergency Room. They're running some toxicity tests now. Plus, her murderer left behind a glass with some possible residue. We'll know for sure if it was GHB this time."

Max paused before continuing. This gave Nikki time to digest what he was saying. "You must've caught him before he could clean up the glasses," Max added.

Overcome with grief, Nikki said nothing. Then the anger she kept locked away…away from her everyday life, crept foreword and shoved the grief out of her emotions...pushed the pain of her injuries away...and made her sit up straight and alert.

"Who...?" She hesitated. "Who would kill Betsy Frank? She never hurt anyone in her short life. Who is this bastard, and how do we get him?"

Max was taken off guard by Nikki's anger and apparent recovery. "We don't know who he is. We don't even know how he got in, or how he managed to drug her with no struggle. Not a mark on her body except the cuts on her thighs...so she didn't even put up a fight."

Nikki tried to think back, tried to remember the sequence of events, but the medicine was clouding her thinking. "Betsy called me around eight o'clock." She stopped and rubbed her temples, trying to clear her mind. "She was worried that Charity might hurt herself. I got over there within twenty minutes...I got lost or I would have made it sooner."

She looked up at Max. "I could have been there...maybe stopped the attack."

"What could you have done?" Max answered. "This guy manages to get them to take the GHB. He doesn't seem to force it down their throats. Maybe he would have given it to you too."

Max paused again for another long minute. "Don't get stuck in the 'could haves'. Maybe we all could have done something different, but it didn't happen that way. He killed her, and he almost killed you. If Charity Daniels didn't come home when she did and call the police...Well, he might have just finished you off too."

"Charity came home?" Nikki tried to remember. "She was the returning footsteps. I must have blanked out after that. I remember the two attackers running out of the room. Then I heard someone coming back. I thought it was one of them, but it must have been Charity."

"You need to rest now, Nikki." Max pushed himself up to a standing position. "I'm gonna check in with Ramos and then get some sleep. I'll come over to your place tomorrow afternoon, and we'll talk some more. It'll be clearer to you tomorrow."

He gave her a half-smile. "Maybe you won't be seeing so many murderers tomorrow. We can talk about just the one."

Nikki forced herself to think back again to when she was lying on the floor. She opened her eyes and saw two figures running out. "There were two of them, Max. I'm sure of it."

She looked straight at him and repeated what she just said. "I saw two figures, all dressed in black, with stockings over their heads, running out of that room."

Max dropped his smile and gave her his full attention. "How can you be sure?"

"Because one of them stabbed my hand. I was face to face with him, looking right at that distorted face." Nikki pictured the attack as she spoke. "The other one hit me from behind. I never saw him...or her...until they ran out together."

Max came closer to the bed. "You think one of them was a woman?"

Nikki shook her head. "I don't know. I never got a good look, but something just now, made me think it might have been a woman." She made eye contact with Max again. "I think I was attacked by a man and a woman."

The two friends stared silently at each other, each trying to comprehend this surprising revelation. At that same moment, Ginni came marching back into the room. "Sorry you two, but it's way past visiting hours."

Nikki and Max broke their knowing glance and gave their attention to Ginni.

"As a trained physician and recent winner of the Distinguished Woman of Sheridan Award," Ginni tried to keep things light, "I am obligated to tell you that Nikki needs to get a good night's rest, so she can come home tomorrow. So Max, any questions you have will just have to wait until them. Say good night, you two."

Max leaned over and pecked Nikki on the forehead. "I'm real glad you're okay, Nik. See ya tomorrow."

Nikki touched his face and smiled. "See you tomorrow, too. Maybe then, I'll remember more."

Max gave Ginni a more formal hug and left the room.

"I'm going too," Ginni said, once more leaning over the bed to kiss Nikki. "I want you to rest. Fluffy will miss you tonight; she hates when you don't come home." Ginni started for the door, but turned back, "And Nikki, so do I."

Ginni pushed the door open, waved goodbye, and left. Nikki fumbled around for the button on the side of the bed and lowered herself back to a reclining position. All the lights were turned down in the hallway, and the hospital was suddenly very quiet.

Nikki closed her eyes and thanked God for saving her life. She prayed for Talia and Betsy, for Ginni, Max, and Fluffy. Then just before she slid back into a drugged sleep, she heard herself say, "Help me get those bastards!"

*   *   *   *

Max leaned heavily on his elbows and crushed several short stacks of manila folders on his desk. His red eyes and bristly chin revealed the telltale signs of lack of sleep. He flattened his arms momentarily to grasp his hot coffee mug with two hands. Then he slowly brought the steaming nectar up to his mouth for a quick, cautious sip. He put the mug down again and opened one of the files in front of him.

Ana Ramos sat in one of the chairs opposite Max's desk. She watched his overtired movements in silence. Her rested body affirmed her decision to get at least five hours of sleep the previous night. Now, she was more alert and better able to analyze the crime and the clues.

Max is too close to one of the victims, too involved with the people in this case, she thought to herself.

Max looked over at Ana. "Why don't you go get Mr. Browning and his wife," he said.

While she went to the waiting area of the police station, Max pulled another chair up next to his desk. He thought about the closeness for a minute and slid the chair about two feet away from his.

Ana reentered the room and the Brownings followed behind her. Ted Browning was thirty-seven years old, six foot three inches tall and had black well-groomed, curly hair. His well-chiseled face and light complexion complimented his deep, brown eyes. He was dressed like a typical professor of his age; grey slacks, shirt and tie, and proverbial tweed jacket with leather elbow patches.

His wife, Lindsey, was thirty-five years old and a rather classic example of the young professor's spouse. She was shorter than her husband at five foot seven inches tall and had the same light complexion. She kept her long, dirty-blonde hair pulled back with a beige silk scarf. The color of the scarf was picked up in her ankle-length wool jumper. Her loafer-style pumps coordinated nicely with her husband's cordovan loafers.

Ana motioned the young couple to sit in the two chairs facing the desk. Then she noticed that Max had pulled an extra chair next to his. Pleasantly surprised by the inclusion, she walked over and sat next to the Sergeant.

She had already introduced herself to the Brownings, so she handled the introductions. "Mr. and Mrs. Browning this is Sergeant Mullen."

Max gave a cursory nod and pulled a yellow legal pad full of questions closer to the edge of his desk. He looked at the two people sitting across from him and said, "I'm very sorry about your sister. You have our condolences…and I want to assure you that we will do everything to find her murderer."

Ted Browning pushed some lose strands of his stylish black hair off his forehead. He gave Max a puzzled look. "Murderer? No one told me my sister was murdered."

His voice was nervous, and he measured every word. "I thought my sister died from some kind of seizure or heart failure. No one said anything about murder."

Max sat back in his chair, trying to fight his tiredness and be delicate at the same time. "At first, we didn't know what the cause of your sister's death was." Max tried to frame each word with care. "Last night, another young woman was attacked in a similar way and murdered. This time, evidence was left behind, and an eye witness was there."

Ted Browning began to sweat, visibly showing his growing anxiety. He wiped his palms on his grey corduroy pants, and then nervously rubbed his grey silk tie. "I...I didn't know she was attacked. Do you mean she was sexually attacked?"

Max looked at Ana, and she accepted his invitation to explain the circumstances around Talia Carter's death. "Not all the forensic evidence is in yet, but we suspect your sister was given the drug, GHB. You may know it as Liquid Ecstasy. She was apparently given too high a dose."

She waited for what she said to sink in. Ted Browning and his wife both listened intently. He unbuttoned his tweed jacket and fiddled with one of the leather buttons. His wife sat motionless.

"This drug not only affects the memory center of the brain but can also put the respiratory center to sleep," Ana continued. "And when too much of it is mixed with alcohol, there's often a deadly result. In many cases, it is slipped unknowingly into a drink. Your sister, like many victims of the mixture of GHB and alcohol, first had seizures, then went into a coma and died."

"Are you sure this is what happened?" Ted Browning asked again.

Max answered this time. "She died before all the drug metabolized out of her system. GHB is a fast metabolizing drug, but with the new toxicity equipment the Sheriff's Department has, we were able to determine that there was a toxic level of GHB in your sister's blood."

The silent Mrs. Browning finally spoke. In a flat monotone, she asked, "Who would do this to Talia? Who would want to kill her?"

Ana made eye contact with Mrs. Browning. "He may not have wanted to kill her. Maybe he didn't realize that he was giving her a lethal dose, or that mixing it with alcohol would be deadly. Whatever the reason, he did rape her."

Ted Browning's face twitched and his shoulders belied a small shiver, which he tried to control.

"That brings us to some questions we need to ask you," Max tactfully interjected. "Can you tell us where you were Saturday evening? And when you last saw your sister?"

Lindsey Browning stared at her hands, which were resting in her lap. Ted Browning rubbed his silk tie again, and then delivered his explanation, much like he would deliver a lecture. "Lindsey and I went to Letchworth Park for the weekend. It was a celebration of sorts. I just got a full-time position at the University of California at Berkeley."

He paused before going on, "We were just outside of the park, about five miles from the cabin we rented, when my car just cut out. It wouldn't start. We walked back to a gas station we passed on the main highway, a good two or three miles from where the car died."

He stopped and swallowed hard, obviously fighting a dry mouth. "I didn't take my cell phone with me. You know, we didn't want to be disturbed. We just wanted to enjoy nature and not be interrupted."

He swallowed hard again. "The gas station was getting ready to close for the weekend, but the owner said he would tow my car in. But he couldn't fix it until Monday. Then he let me use his phone, and I called Talia. I asked her to come and get us because I didn't want to get stranded out there and miss my classes on Monday."

Max jumped in with a question. "Did Talia say she would come and get you?"

"No," Browning answered very matter-of-factly. "She said she couldn't help us. She had to attend a "Light Up the Night Vigil.""

Max shot Ana a quick glance. "So, Talia couldn't get you. She was going to the vigil."

"Yes," Browning answered. "That's what she said. She had to represent her organization at the vigil."

"What did you do next, Mr. Browning?" Ana asked.

"We really couldn't think of anyone else to call. We're both new to Sheridan," Browning continued. "So, I asked the station owner if he could drive me to a car rental place. He said there wasn't any nearby, but he would rent me a loaner car that he had."

"What's the name of this service station?" Max asked, as he got his pen ready to take down the information.

"I think it was called A-1 Service," Browning answered coldly.

"You do have a receipt for the loaner and the work on your car, don't you, Mr. Browning?" Max continued his line of questioning.

Browning squirmed in his seat. "Now just a minute. Why do I have to have a receipt? Just what are you saying?"

Ana intervened. "We aren't saying anything, Mr. Browning. It's just important to establish where everyone close to Talia was on Saturday evening."

"Then why don't you talk to Charity Daniels," Lindsey broke her silence.

Max looked up from his writing and asked, "What should we talk to Charity Daniels about?"

Lindsey looked straight at him and answered, "Why not ask her where she was that night? Why she couldn't go to the vigil instead of Talia. Why Talia felt she had to always keep an eye on her partner."

"What do you mean, 'keep an eye on her partner'?" Ana asked quickly.

Lindsey moved her gaze from Max to Ana. "There was definitely trouble in paradise. Talia wouldn't come and get us because she was afraid Charity would disappear with her new boyfriend. That's the reason she didn't come for us."

Max made several quick notes on the yellow pad and looked up at the two Brownings, before he calmly asked, "Is there anything else you think we should know?"

Both Brownings hesitantly shook their heads "no".

"I'll get your statement typed up and ask you both to come back tomorrow, whenever you can and sign the statement." Max slid back in his chair again.

"Oh...Mr. Browning, we would appreciate a copy of those receipts." Max gave a fake smile and added, "Just a formality, mind you."

Max slowly stood up, and the Brownings got up too. Ana walked over to them and escorted them back down the hallway.

As they left the room, Max sank back down into his chair. "Just what is going on...I wonder." he mumbled to himself.

CHAPTER 7

▼

Nikki drove through the late afternoon drizzle and grumbled to herself. "A whole day wasted in the hospital." Steering the car with one hand, she gingerly felt the swollen area at the back of her head and delicately ran her finger over the five stitches holding the wound closed.

She wondered if she made the right decision when she told Ginni to "Just go to work and try to finish up early. Then you can dote on me all evening."

She felt less confident than she did in the hospital and more aware of her pain. So Nikki decided not to head straight home, but to seek out the company of a caring friend. She didn't feel like being alone right now.

Max was first to come to mind, but he called before she was released and sounded super tired. Like a good soldier, she told him she didn't need a ride home. If one of his officers could bring her car to the hospital, she was up to driving herself.

"Why don't you go home and get a few hours of sleep." Those were her exact words. "Then come over to my apartment tonight, because I want to hear all about the interview with the Brownings."

Max didn't divulge any information on the phone. He just said, "Some interesting facts came up, and they put a new twist on this investigation."

That was when Nikki knew something pertinent or something weird came out of the interview. She was lucky that Max shared information with her. He realized that she cared about this case not only because two of her students had been killed…but because she was almost killed too.

A shiver involuntarily went down her spine, as she made the turn from Girard Street to Main Street. She slowed down and cruised past the several buildings that made up Sheridan's Main Street.

Nikki passed the hardware store, the large convenience store, which posed as a supermarket, the coin-operated laundry, toyshop, card shop, sneaker and tee shirt shop, dog and cat groomer, newspaper stand, and bakery/restaurant. The Fait Accompli Bakery and Eating Emporium was Nikki's destination. She found a parking space right in front of the restaurant, glided her black Saturn into the space and parked. As she turned off the car, she checked her appearance in the rear-view mirror.

"Not a pretty sight," she said to her reflection. Her left cheek was brush-burned from when she hit the rug, and both of her cheeks seemed to have residual swelling. She resembled a blonde chipmunk with war paint on one cheek.

Nikki addressed her reflection again, "My face won't matter much, once she sees the shaved patch and stitches on the back of my head."

This realization sent Nikki rummaging through the papers, books and odd articles of clothing on her back seat. "That's it," she said to herself, holding up a very worn St. David University cap. She proceeded to put the cap on backwards, so that the rim hid her stitches. This however, left the sizing tab in the middle of her forehead…further accentuating her swollen cheeks.

Nikki looked into the mirror again and shrugged her shoulders. "This will just have to do." She got out of the car and walked toward the restaurant.

Barrett Fairburn, one of Nikki's past tutorial students was the owner of the "Fait Accompli Bakery and Eating Emporium". Nikki smiled as she remembered Barrett's outlandish clothes and bad attitude.

They seemed to hit it off right away. *It was our mutual interest in good food*, Nikki thought, as she continued strolling down memory lane. *I was really shocked when Barrett told me she was in love with me. I mean...I never felt that way about her...I cared about her as a student, but I was already in love with Ginni.*

As Nikki reached the restaurant door, she noticed a heart chalked onto the sidewalk with the word "Love" written across the middle of it. *That reminds me of all those letters and cards Barrett sent me, and the way she chased me around with pies, and truffles, and all sorts of goodies. It's just a good thing I could help her convince her millionaire father that she was better suited for the Culinary Institute than a Business Degree from St. David's.*

Nikki knew there was an ulterior motive in her support for Barrett becoming a chef. The Culinary Institute was far enough away from Sheridan to give Barrett the time she needed to realize her romantic love for Nikki was not reciprocal.

The real irony of that whole situation was when I saw the family photo in her house and realized that Barrett's mother was Trang. Nikki shook her head in disbelief. *I helped Trang escape to Malaysia during the war.*

Nikki instantly tried to erase some of the memories that just crept back into her being, by taking a deep breath and entering the bakery. *Barrett always makes me think of Trang. I wonder how she's doing on that business trip to Vietnam? It's been almost three years since she left...ran away really. She just didn't want to answer any more questions from the police.*

The day Trang left, Nikki promised Barrett that she and Ginni would always be there for her. That was a promise Nikki still tried to keep, but today Barrett could help Nikki. She was hungry and a little lonely...or maybe just feeling vulnerable.

"Barrett always has a way of cheering me up," Nikki affirmed, as she stepped into the restaurant. "I love these upscale little bistros," Nikki went on talking to herself. She gently ran her hand along the long, curved counter that reached from the right of the door to the opposite wall.

That's a nice touch, she thought, noticing the high-back, dark-wood stools tucked under the counter. "And look at that!" she whispered like a kid in a candy store. She paused for a moment and watched the sun-rays, coming in from the storefront window, bounce off the sheen of the mahogany countertop.

She took a few steps further into the restaurant and realized the hissing sound and subtle smell of vanilla, coffee, and cocoa were coming from four huge chrome espresso and cappuccino machines along the left wall.

Nikki walked down the two steps to the main seating area. Twelve round, glass-top cabaret tables of two different sizes were arranged next to each other with two or four cushioned, iron chairs around each table.

No one was in the restaurant, and Nikki realized she had arrived between the lunch crowd and the supper group. She found a small table next to the wall and sat down.

Barrett heard the scraping of a chair and signaled for her waitresses to continue their break. She walked casually out of the kitchen through the curved archway into the restaurant. Recognizing Nikki, she gave a small wave and made her way over to the table.

"Is this a new look for you, Nicolette," Barrett said sarcastically, pointing to the cap.

Nikki couldn't help smiling at Barrett. She was the only person in all of Sheridan who insisted on calling her Nicolette.

Then Barrett leaned over, bringing her five foot-eleven-inch frame closer to Nikki. "What happened to you? Are you okay?" She asked, her dark, almond-shaped eyes getting wider.

Nikki tried to think of a smart comeback, but her mind wasn't up to the task. "Actually, I was hit on the head with a brick," she lamely commented.

"You were what! Oh, my poor, poor Nicolette!" Barrett exclaimed, so concerned that she instinctively touched Nikki's head.

"Ouch!" Nikki yelped. "Don't touch my head. Everything hurts right now."

Barrett's hand recoiled instantly and she said, "I'm sorry. Who did this to you? When did it happen?" She took the seat opposite Nikki and started scrutinizing Nikki's face.

Nikki put her elbows on the table and rested her puffy face on her entwined fingers. She wasn't up to a long, detailed explanation, but knew Barrett deserved an answer.

"One of my students was raped and murdered," Nikki began slowly. "I went over to her flat to help her partner arrange the funeral. The murderers were in the apartment…they killed another student…and cracked me on the head." Unexpectedly, Nikki heard her voice crack as she retold her account of that night.

Nikki wouldn't cry though. She swallowed hard and stifled the tears that tried to escape. This wasn't the time or place for her tears. She was still a good soldier.

Barrett got up quickly and moved to Nikki. She leaned over again and gave her old professor a spontaneous embrace.

Nikki returned the hug, while she explained, "I've been in the hospital all night. Haven't eaten a decent meal since Sunday afternoon…and that one wasn't really very good."

Barrett broke the embrace and enthusiastically responded to the hint. "I've got just the thing for you. First, you need a nice hot cup of vanilla coffee. While you sip that slowly, you can pause every now and then to dunk a few chocolate biscotti. Then I will make you the best mushroom and havarti cheese omelet you ever tasted, with a side order of fresh-baked focaccia with dried tomatoes and garlic butter."

Nikki felt slightly uncomfortable for liking all the attention but still replied, "I think that would really help me feel better."

Barrett now resorted to her usual flirtation. "You love my cooking don't you, Nicolette? Admit it. You love my cooking."

Nikki smiled again and shook her head. "I do love your cooking," she readily admitted the truth.

"Oh boy!" Barrett seemed amazed, as she moved to the cappuccino machine. "You really did get hit hard, because that's the first time, you ever admitted loving anything about me."

She poured the coffee, put three biscotti on a small saucer, and returned to the table. Placing both in front of Nikki, she added, "I'm a patient woman. Someday, you'll get tired of a doctor who can't cook, and I *will* be available. I do believe the way to a woman's heart is through her taste buds."

Nikki tried not to take what was being said too seriously, as she nibbled one of the biscotti. Then she answered, "I'm not sure if my love of food will ever be more pressing than my need for medical attention."

Barrett just smiled and turned dramatically before heading for the kitchen.

Nikki sat alone in the restaurant and sipped the vanilla cappuccino slowly. She let the hot liquid warm her whole being. Holding the cup to the side of her face, she allowed the heat to permeate the hurt throughout her body and in her psyche. She studied the clusters of grapes on the gold wallpaper and stared at the white icicle lights hanging from the ceiling.

Finally, she closed her eyes and thought of the two young women who were brutally murdered. She said a silent prayer for each one, asking God to hold their hands until their journey ended in light. Her eyes opened to the hanging lights again. Maybe this was a sign that they were okay now.

While Nikki waited for Barrett's return, several groups of patrons entered the restaurant. Two male college students took a table up front and immediately became engrossed in their textbooks. Three elderly women shoppers selected a table in the middle of the room and surrounded themselves with shopping bags while four women in business suits chose the mahogany counter for coffee and bagels.

Marsha, Barrett's head waitress, moved smoothly between each group. She got beverages, took orders, made suggestions or gave explanations. Nikki watched this waitress-ballet with deep admiration. Marsha finally realized Nikki was watching and glided over to her table to refill the cappuccino. As she arrived at Nikki's table with the revived vanilla scented liquid, Barrett also arrived from the kitchen with a full tray in her hands.

Nikki looked up at Barrett, who seemed much taller with her pleated and starched, chimney-high chef's hat on. Her long hair was shorter now, just below her ears, still one layer, pulled behind her ears, so the hat fit perfectly.

A pressure built in Nikki's chest. She was so proud of Barrett, so aware of what Barrett had to overcome to be the success she was now. Nikki felt warm tears trickling down her face.

"What's wrong, Nikki?" Barrett quickly put the tray down on the table and knelt next to Nikki. "Is something wrong?" she asked, touching Nikki's shoulder.

Nikki brushed the tears away with her hands and explained, "No, I'm fine. Really, I'm fine." Nikki tried to regain her composure. She smiled at Barrett and added, "Maybe, I'm really hungry."

Barrett spontaneously bounced back up and said, "Okay, tough woman. Here's the best meal in town."

Nikki was dined in style, and Barrett spent the next hour keeping her company, while her second chef saw to the other customers. Nikki moaned with joy and mumbled compliments with almost every bite. Barrett kept the conversation going by telling funny stories about incidents in the restaurant. She was the perfect tonic for what ailed Nikki.

"This vanilla cappuccino is a great ending to a great meal," Nikki sighed and drained her cup.

She finally pushed herself away from the table, and Barrett escorted her to her car. Just as Nikki was about to get into her car, Barrett lifted her off the ground in a compassionate bear hug.

"So you'll go right home and rest, right Nicolette?" Barrett asked, as she put Nikki back on the ground and released her hug.

"That's my plan," Nikki answered, as she slid contentedly behind the wheel. She started the engine and rolled down the window. "Thanks for the wonderful food and the company."

Barrett stepped away from the car and waved. Then she turned and walked back into the restaurant.

Nikki pulled away from the curb and turned toward home.

CHAPTER 8

▼

Nikki drove her car into one of the two designated parking spaces for the townhouse she shared with Ginni. Next to her, in the other designated spot was Max, sound asleep, with his 1986 Chevy Cavalier seat slightly reclined. His chin was resting on his chest and bobbed up and down as he breathed slowly in and out. His open suit jacket revealed his two-day old, crumpled white shirt clinging uncomfortably to his belly, which was squished against the steering wheel.

Nikki turned off her car and stared at her old buddy. "He didn't go home and rest," she said, as she shook her head. "He probably worked straight through the night and then came here to check on me." She finished her self-explanation.

She got out of her car and walked over to the Cavalier. Not wanting to startle Max, she tapped lightly on the driver-side window. Max, still in a slight sleep-daze, opened his eyes and gave Nikki a grin. Then he moved his seat to an upright position.

He rolled down the window and sleepily asked, "How ya do'in, Nikki?"

"I'm feeling much better," she enthusiastically replied. "What are you doing here? I thought you were headed home for some sleep?"

"I'm on my way," Max answered, as he tried to stretch his arms in the undersized car. "I just wanted to stop by and check on ya, before I head home. I told ya on the phone, we learned something new from Ted Browning…"

He paused before asking, "If you're up to it, I'd like to run it past you."

Nikki opened the car door for Max, and said, "I just had a great meal, and now I'm ready for action. Come on in. I'll put on some coffee, and you can fill me in."

Max rolled up the window and got out of the car. He hiked up his pants and adjusted his big western belt buckle, so it didn't cut into his belly. "Great meal," he commented through a yawn. "Ya must have stopped at that crazy student's place." He started for the front door with Nikki. "She's a good cook," he continued. "Always was."

Nikki laughed, remembering again how Barrett chased her around with food when they first met. Many times Nikki passed the desserts on to Max. But when Max started investigating a murder at the Medical Center, he thought Barrett's behavior was very suspicious because she turned up wherever Nikki happened to be.

He was sure Barrett was involved in the murder, until Nikki proved otherwise. *Max may have thought Barrett was a possible suspect in those days, but he always enjoyed her food,* Nikki silently concluded.

"I could use some of her fancy desserts right now," Max pulled Nikki back to the present.

"I think Ginni left something for me to eat," Nikki tried to reassure him, as she opened the door and led Max to the kitchen.

Fluffy, who heard Nikki's car enter the parking space, met both of them at the door and followed them into the kitchen. Max took his usual seat at the head of the small table, and Fluffy immediately jumped into his lap. Max knew this drill and proceeded to pet his other old friend.

Nikki turned on the coffeemaker and checked the refrigerator for food. Ginni had indeed prepared for Nikki's return home. On the top shelf of the refrigerator was an unopened can of chicken noodle soup, nicely chilling, and what appeared to be a Deli pastrami with Swiss cheese sandwich.

Not even asking Max if he wanted the sandwich, Nikki unwrapped it and put it in the microwave to warm. She placed the sandwich on a plate in front of Max and said, "This is one of my all-time favorites, so enjoy it, Max."

Max lifted an edge of the rye bread, "This is one food the two of us agree on, unequivocally, but what about you? Not even a bite?"

"I'm not hungry," Nikki explained, as she patted her stomach. "I just finished a four course meal, but let's keep this between you and me. Chef Ginni must never know that last night's take-out was not what healed me. Do we have a deal?"

She held out her hand, and Max gave it a firm shake. Then he tackled the sandwich with total enthusiasm. Fluffy never moved, having no interest in pastrami, she felt no need to relinquish her comfortable lap lounge.

Max was halfway through his sandwich when his attention went back to the case. Nikki sat across from him and sipped her tea, while she patiently waited for Max to share some information.

He took a big gulp of coffee and put his cup down. "We interviewed Ted Browning and his wife. Very typical, young professor, already climbing. He just got offered a job on the west coast. His wife is typical too, but a little more of a cold fish than he is."

"I never even said hello to him," Nikki commented spontaneously. "Talia never mentioned she had any relatives that were still alive. I wonder why she never mentioned him? She must have known we would run into each other."

"Maybe she didn't want you to know he was her brother," Max answered. "Maybe she wasn't on good terms with him." He tried to keep the thought process going.

Nikki rubbed the rim of her cup with her finger. She thought and talked at the same time. "I knew about Talia's mother being a prostitute. I also knew she was raped by the johns, and about the pregnancy and abortion. Why wouldn't she mention an older brother?"

"Sounds like the older brother didn't help her when she needed him," Max continued. "Charity Daniels said Talia hated all men, that probably included her brother."

"They must have been friendly enough…," Nikki directed her comment to Max. "For the brother to call her to come and get him when his car broke down."

Max took his little notebook out of his inside jacket pocket and flipped it open. "According to Browning, Talia couldn't go get him because she was going to the 'Light Up the Night Vigil'. So he rented a loaner car from the gas station guy who towed his car in and drove home."

Max flipped a few more pages. Then he looked at Nikki and shook his head. "Here's another thing. Mrs. Browning said Talia couldn't go get them because she had to go to the vigil to keep an eye on Charity…who has a boyfriend."

"What?" Nikki asked, puzzled by this new information.

"Mrs. Browning said," Max checked his notebook again, bit the sandwich, and talked with his mouth full. "There was trouble in paradise."

Nikki was too dumbfounded to speak. She just looked at Max and waited for more information.

Max flipped his notebook closed and took another bite of the sandwich. "I called Charity Daniels. She's staying with her aunt in Buffalo since the attacks at her apartment."

The pause Max took here again revealed his deep concern for Nikki. He said nothing, but Nikki answered anyway. "I'm fine, Max. I'm too hard headed to be hurt by a brick."

Max smiled at the attempted humor and got back to the case. "When I called Daniel's aunt, some guy…a young guy, answered the phone. Told me the aunt was out of town for two weeks visiting her sister. Said his name was Bill Hanson."

Nikki sat up straight, "Bill Hanson? Bill Hanson is one of my students. He's president of the student government and a well-liked guy."

"We haven't checked him out yet," Max said, as he finished the sandwich and licked the last bit of Thousand Island dressing off his fingers. "He put Charity Daniels on the phone, and I'm meeting her tonight at 8:00, for a little chat. We're meeting at the Gay and Lesbian Organization office in the Student Union."

"I want to be at that interview, Max. Please?" Nikki pleaded. "I need to hear what she has to say. So much of this is just not fitting together. Can I go with you?"

A worried look came over Max's face, and he asked, "Do you feel up to it, Nikki?"

"I feel fine," she answered without hesitation. "I can rest all afternoon." Not waiting for a no answer, she added, "I'll meet you in the Student Union at 7:45."

Max started to protest but knew with Nikki it was of no use. "Okay. Okay. If you get that rest."

He gently picked Fluffy up off his lap and placed her on the floor. Slowly standing back up, he brushed the breadcrumbs off his jacket and said, "I'm heading home for a few hours sleep myself."

Nikki walked him to the door, and just before Max turned to leave, he gave her a big hug. The pressure of that belt buckle made her wince, but she only showed him a smile.

"Remember," Max said seriously. "You got stitches. No bending, no heavy lifting."

Nikki smiled and gave him an affirmative shaking of her head. He smiled back, pushed the door open, and headed for his car. Nikki gave him a wave, as he drove away.

She walked back into the living room and sat next to Fluffy. Petting her other old friend, she said, "This case just doesn't make much sense, maybe a little sleep will help my thinking."

She took an Indian blanket from the back of the sofa and pulled it up over her and Fluffy, as she laid down for a nap.

*   *   *   *

Nikki stood outside Hayes Hall and watched the setting sun turn the sky from baby blue to pink. The colors finally disappeared into the grey of dusk. She gave a deep sigh and whispered a prayer of thanksgiving for all the wonders of nature. She added a second prayer of thanksgiving for all the protection God gave her, so she could appreciate these wonders.

She finally turned and entered Hayes Hall. The hall lights came on automatically as she entered. The newly renovated first floor had bright yellow walls, new blue carpeting, and bright full-spectrum lights.

Nikki walked slowly to her new office, anticipating the pleasure she felt in her new surroundings. She loved the oak desk and matching chair, and although the room was small, she now had a large window with a view. There was also a small patch of grass in front of the window, which was home to a flowering crab tree. This was Nikki's private meditation area. She could just open her window and be part of this patch of nature.

She also enjoyed the privacy of her new office location. The office to her left was usually empty, since it was reserved for guest lecturers and one-day dignitaries. That office had been empty since Nikki moved to the first floor.

The office to her right was also empty. Professor Hurd was on a two-year sabbatical, studying Mormon educational systems. *A perfect research theme for the bookish Professor Hurd*, Nikki thought to herself.

The two offices across the hall from hers belonged to the Baccomo sisters. Both were professors in the Graphic Design Department, and both spent most of their time in the graphic studios and computer labs. Nikki had only met the two, heavy-set, grand dames twice since she moved into her new office.

Nikki's attention moved back to the work at hand. She sat at her desk and started shuffling through the various papers she planned to take home. "Here's my folder with the grant information. Oh no! It's due next week!" She kept up a dialogue with herself. "Okay, I need to fill out these final grade forms for Carol Drake and Ryan Bobish, and the year-end report for the Dean, and my Professional Development Report."

Nikki neatly packed all the papers and folders into her Kenneth Cole attaché case. The expensive case was a sentimental gift from her old friend, Linda. Nikki kept it close by because of the positive energy and love connected with the gift.

As she left her office, Nikki stopped to lock the door. She unexpectedly heard a strange, high-pitched, buzzing sound coming from the guest-lecturer's office. Without warning, that door flew wide open.

Nikki's senses went on alarm. She dropped her attaché and put her back to her door. She readied her keys as a weapon, and her mind immediately planned an escape route...but she didn't need to run...yet.

Taylor Fleming, the overly-friendly, handicapped friend of Ginni's, who also just won a Distinguished Woman of Sheridan Award for her work as Commissioner of the County Office For the Handicapped guided her motorized wheelchair out of the office. As she turned to close and lock the door, she spotted Nikki.

"Reverend Barnes," Taylor began, flipping her long blonde hair back over her shoulder. "Now, this is a coincidence." She powered her wheelchair closer to Nikki and added, "I didn't realize your office was in this building. I didn't even realize you taught this late in the year."

Nikki, still frozen, squeaked out a reply, "I...don't...teach now." She tried to relax, moving her shoulders away from her door. "I just needed to get some papers. Finishing up the year-end paperwork. Teaching is done for the year. No more teaching," Nikki babbled.

"I see," Taylor cooed, moving even closer. "Too bad, we could have been close neighbors." She smiled at her own power to unnerve Nikki. "I'm teaching a special two-week course for Social Work students. It's an awareness and sensitivity seminar on dealing with handicapped persons." Taylor locked on Nikki's eyes and stopped talking.

Nikki, unsure of why this woman made her nervous, gained back some poise. "That sounds very interesting," she said in her most professional voice. "I'm sure our students will get a great deal of helpful information from the seminar."

Taylor cocked her head to one side and studied Nikki's outfit. The sneakers, jeans, black tee and black blazer didn't get much attention. The baseball cap turned backwards got much more.

"Ginni always said you were a 'casual' dresser," Taylor remarked, not taking her eyes off the cap. "But I didn't take you for a woman who likes hats."

At this point, Nikki realized she still had the cap on. She quickly whipped it off and held it at her side. "I didn't expect to run into anyone," she tried to explain. "I didn't think anyone would be in the offices. I don't usually dress *this casually,* but I was in a hurry. I have a meeting."

Before she could finish, Taylor spotted the bruising and swelling on her face. "What happened to you?" Taylor asked with genuine concern. "Are you okay, Reverend Barnes?"

"I'm fine. I'm really fine," Nikki stammered out, not wanting to go into a long explanation. "Now, I really must go. I'm almost late for my meeting."

With this last comment, Nikki bent down and picked up her attaché. Then, she walked around the wheelchair and headed for the exit door. Taylor flipped the power button on her wheelchair and turned, so her eyes could follow Nikki.

"Just a minute, Reverend," Taylor called after Nikki. "You might want to put that cap back on. That bald patch on the back of your head, the one with the big bandage, might get more attention than the hat."

Nikki turned back slowly and faced Taylor. She put the cap back on, but this time, she kept the rim in front and slid the back of the hat over the stitches. Now, the hat rested on the back of her head. "Thanks for the reminder," she said quietly to Taylor, still not wanting to give that explanation.

"I was hit on the head…with a brick," she finally explained.

"Maybe you really should consider giving higher grades," Taylor responded with a smile, as she wheeled closer to Nikki again. "No wonder Ginni worries so about you," she added. "You're a classic disaster magnet…but a really cute one."

Nikki felt too close to Taylor now…embarrassed…maybe intimidated…her face was starting to heat up. She was about to turn around and make that hasty exit, when she heard the door open behind her.

Detective Ana Ramos took a few confident but cautious steps into the hallway. She gave Nikki a cursory wave and moved closer to the two women. "Sergeant Mullen asked me to meet you at your office," Ana opened with an explanation. "He thought you might appreciate an escort."

Taylor Fleming gave the Detective her usual once over, starting with the sensible black pumps, moving up the tailored, well-pressed slacks, navy blue gabardine blazer, full lips with muted red lipstick, and finally, eye contact.

"I'm Taylor Fleming," she said, wheeling closer and extending her hand.

"How do you do, Commissioner, I'm Detective Ana Ramos." Ana answered, as she shook Taylor's hand and offered another explanation. "I recognized you from your pictures in the newspaper."

Taylor wheeled back about a foot and kept the eye contact with Ana. "Well, I am impressed," she said in her most seductive voice. "I thought Sheridan only had one policewoman, good old Betty Long. I see we are coming up in the world."

"I'm just here on an exchange program from the Buffalo Police Department," Ana commented, not dropping the eye contact either.

At this point, Nikki felt lucky to have Taylor's attention diverted to someone else. She regained her composure, and as her confidence returned, she realized Max was still babying her by sending an armed escort. Now her dander was up again.

"I don't know why Max sent you," she snorted at Ana, who was still oblivious to anyone but Taylor. "What's the matter with him?" Nikki went on. "Doesn't he think I can walk a few feet to the Student Union. I must make that trip fifty times a day when classes are in session," she continued indignantly. "It's not like I haven't been beaten up before...I mean, I can take care of myself!"

This last outburst finally tore Ana's attention away from Taylor and back to Nikki. "I'm sure the Sergeant realizes that you are a capable woman," Ana began as tactfully as possible. "He just didn't know how many things you needed from your office and thought you might need help carrying them."

Nikki started to mumble to herself again, "That's the lamest thing I've ever heard." Then she remembered the last thing he said to her when he left her house. "Now watch those stitches. No bending...no heavy lifting."

Just like Max, forever a hospital corpsman. Nikki smiled at this last thought, remembering how protective Max always was in Nam, when they both worked at the 90TH EVAC Hospital.

He learned so much about medicine, he could have been a nurse, Nikki's thoughts continued, as her pride softened into memories of their friendship.

She finally returned to the present. "Okay. Okay. Let's just get over to the Union."

Ana made a move to carry Nikki's attaché. "Oh no, you don't," Nikki protested, whipping the bag away from Ana's reach. "I can carry my own bag...and I won't hurt my stitches."

At this outburst of perceived unnecessary arrogance, Taylor jumped in, "The Reverend may not need your services, but I do," she cooed.

Both Nikki and Ana turned and looked at Taylor, who slowly added. "There's a terrible ledge by that doorway." She pointed to the entranceway before continuing. "I may need help getting my wheelchair over the bump." Taylor pursed her mouth and blew a little air out with the pronunciation of "Bump."

With this last obvious performance by Taylor, Nikki just let her mouth drop open. But Detective Ramos moved into action. "I'll be glad to help you," Ana said, quickly moving behind the wheelchair.

Taylor just gave Nikki a sly smile and flipped the chair control to manual, so Ana could push it toward the doors. The now famous, "Bump" appeared more like a slight incline, and Taylor and Ana were soon outside. Nikki tagged behind. She then embarrassingly got her attaché caught in the door and made it all worse when she caught her leg trying to get it untangled.

Ana was forced to leave Taylor and offer help to Nikki. "I'm fine, just fine," Nikki snarled between clenched teeth."

Ana backed off and held the outer door open. Nikki finally marched through and turned toward the Union. Ana paused for a moment to say goodbye to Taylor.

"Maybe we'll meet again," Taylor said quietly, as she offered her hand for a shake.

"I hope so." Ana answered softly, as she gently shook Taylor's hand.

CHAPTER 9

▼

Nikki, Max, and Ana grouped together outside the Gay and Lesbian Organization door on the second floor of the Student Union. Nikki impatiently looked at her watch, then up at Max. "Do you think Charity will show?" she asked.

"She's got no reason not to," he replied philosophically. "But you never know," he added.

Almost at the same time as his last comment, Charity and a male student climbed quickly up the large central stairway and headed toward the group of people waiting at the door. Her companion was at least five inches shorter than her five-foot-six height. He had short-cropped hair similar to hers, but his receding hairline was apparent even with the stylish cut. They both wore matching dark green turtleneck sweaters and light chino pants. He carried a stack of books and papers under his arm, while she fished in her pant's pocket for keys.

"Sorry, I'm late," Charity said, as she moved in front of the others to unlock the door. The male student, who was walking next to her, veered off and kept walking until he reached the next office.

Charity fumbled with the keys several times before she got the door unlocked. This gave Nikki time to recognize the other student, as he entered the Student Government Office. It was Bill Hanson, this year's Student Government President.

Charity flipped on the light switch and entered the office. She walked around the unmanned reception desk and moved to a second room, where she flipped on that light too. Max, Ana and Nikki followed her into the small lounge.

She finally sat nervously on the edge of one of the two cushioned chairs in the room. Nikki sat in a chair opposite her, and Max and Ana were forced to share the medium sized sofa to the left of Nikki.

Charity finally broke the long, tense silence that permeated the room. "I know I should have said something before. I just didn't think it mattered." She paused and swallowed hard. "I mean...I loved Talia...I will always love her." Her voice began to crack. "She knew that. She always knew that."

Charity stopped talking and waited for a response.

Nikki, in a calm but determined voice asked, "Why didn't you tell me that you and Talia were no longer a couple? That you had a boyfriend?"

"Talia asked me not to tell anyone," Charity answered, her voice still a little shaky. "She said she wanted to tell people. When the time was right for her. That's what she said."

Leaning forward in her chair, so she was closer to Charity, Nikki pressed on with her questions. "What does that mean? When the time was right."

"I'm not sure," Charity's voice was almost pleading now. "She didn't want me to move out of the apartment or tell anyone about Bill. She said the time wasn't right yet and too many people would be hurt...including her. So, Bill and I agreed not to tell anyone until Talia said it was okay."

Max didn't wait for Nikki to jump in again with another question. He quickly asked, "Wasn't that kinda hard on your relationship with Bill...and Talia?"

Charity looked directly at Max, as she answered. "Bill was okay with not telling anyone yet. He knew I was Talia's partner for almost four years. Bill knew how much she meant to me. I told him all about her…and what a terrible life she had growing up. He liked her too. He didn't want to hurt her either."

"How did Talia like Bill?" Max asked, taking out his little notebook. "Just how did she react to you breaking it off with her?"

Charity sat back in her chair and redirected all her attention to the ring she kept twisting on her left hand. "She was very hurt at first," Charity said in a barely audible voice. "Talia thought we would be together forever."

"So did I," Nikki jumped in on the questioning. "When did you meet Bill?"

"I met him last year," Charity relaxed a little. "He was a student escort and so was I. You know we would go as a group and escort students to their cars after dark. That's how we met. We all used to go for coffee and stuff when our duty was over. He knew that Talia was my partner…but we really hit it off. You know. He was so easy to talk to, and we had a lot of things in common."

She looked directly at Nikki now, and added, "He never tried to break us up. I never thought I would have feelings for guys again. I wasn't looking for that. It just happened." Her voice got very quiet, "I fell in love with him."

Several minutes of silence again hung over the room. Ana broke it this time with another question. "Did you say, you were involved with guys before?"

Charity looked up again and faced Ana. "Yes. I went steady with a guy in high school. We were going to get engaged before I went off to college." She studied the ring again and added, "I had some doubts about my love for Tim. That was his name, Tim. You see, I had a really close girlfriend all through high school too. Her name was Pricilla."

Charity's furrowed brow revealed the pain that these memories brought to her. "I never had sex or anything like that with Cilla…but I knew my feelings for her seemed more than just that of a girlfriend. And who could I talk to? My parents were practically planning the wedding with Tim. My school counselors were very Christian conservative. My whole town was either black or white, no grey areas…and definitely no gay areas."

She took a deep breath and let it out slowly. "I broke up with Tim…and just before I left for college, I heard he was dating Cilla." Charity looked over to Nikki and said, "So, I'm very glad I never told her how much I loved her. When I got to St. David's, I advertised for a roommate to share expenses for an off-campus apartment. Talia answered the ad. We moved in together, and I fell in love with her."

Max squirmed uncomfortably in his seat. As open as he tried to be, these coupling conversations made him a bit uncomfortable. "So, did Talia know you were bi-sexual?"

"No, it never came up," Charity answered, as she watched Max jot things in his notebook. "That was…not until I told her I was in love with Bill."

"When was that?" Max asked, looking up from his notebook.

"I told her about three weeks ago," Charity said, furrowing her brow again. "I got tired of sneaking around to meet Bill…and he asked me to spend the summer with him, at his parent's cottage at Lake George. I felt I had to tell her. I couldn't just walk out on her."

"How did Talia take that news," Max pushed on with the questions.

"I told you," Charity answered, showing her impatience with what seems to be the same questions. "She was hurt."

"Was she angry?" Ana asked.

"Of course, she was angry," Charity shot back. "Wouldn't you be angry if your partner just said she was leaving you?"

"Did she threaten you in any way?" Max continued the questioning process.

Charity looked perplexed at this question but attempted an answer. "I don't know what you mean. She was hurt and angry. No, she didn't say she wanted to kill me…or Bill. Talia wasn't like that. She wouldn't blame the break-up on me."

"Who would she blame it on," Nikki asked.

"You should know the answer to that one, Reverend Barnes," Charity answered. "Talia would blame herself. She always did. That was her greatest fault. That's what always kept her down. Kept her trapped in her horrible past."

Nikki wanted to understand what was being said, so she asked, "What do you mean?"

"Talia blamed herself for being raped as a child," Charity began slowly but assuredly. "She blamed herself for aborting her baby, blamed herself for not being the woman her mother wanted her to be, and blamed herself for not being a good partner."

With this last comment, Charity choked back tears and tried to explain. "Talia blamed herself for all the darkness she carried inside. She never let any light in on that darkness…maybe that's why when I met Bill…he was so full of light, of fun and wonder. Talia wouldn't let anyone in. I couldn't help her. I couldn't erase any of that pain. So, she even blamed herself for my leaving her…and maybe this time her self-fulfilling prophecy came true."

Max scratched behind his ear and silently read over some of his notes. Then he asked, "Was Talia close to her brother?"

"No." Charity seemed relieved at the change in questioning. "Not at first. She hadn't heard from him for years. Then he turns up on the same campus. You should've seen her the first time she saw him here. She turned white…almost fainted."

"When did she first see him?" Max asked.

"We were at the annual English Tea," Charity turned to Nikki, as she tried to explain. "You know, the one they give every year for students who have poems or essays in the college literary magazine."

She turned back to Max. "Talia had two poems published last year. All the English professors come to the Tea, even the part-time ones. That's how she saw her brother. They just stared at each other for a while. Then she started to shake all over and asked me to get her out of there. I just thought she got sick. But when we got outside…she was taking these big, gulping breaths…she looked like she was going to fall over. I sat her down, and she told me that Browning was her brother."

Charity tried to remember all the details. "After I got her home, and she seemed to calm down, I asked her what the story was with her brother and her. She shut the door to that one in a cold minute. There was no more discussion of her brother, not with me, not with anyone."

Ana gave Max a quick glance, and Max turned again to Charity. "So, when did Talia start talking to her brother?"

"I never knew they were talking until the other night," Charity said with a puzzled look on her face. "That's when she told me her brother and his wife were stuck out at Letchworth Park, and she was going to get them."

Now Ana needed some clarification. "How would the Brownings know you were dating Bill Hanson?"

Charity shrugged her shoulders, "I don't know. Talia must have told them. Bill and I didn't tell anyone. Charity wanted me to stay in the apartment until the end of the month. That's when our lease was up. I promised her that we would keep the relationship secret until we left for the cottage. Unless she said we could tell people or be seen together in public."

Charity stared at the ring again. "I thought that was the right thing to do. That I owed Talia that much out of respect for the years we were together."

"What about your boyfriend," Max asked. "Did he feel he owed her that too?"

"Bill's a nice guy," Charity looked right at Max. "He left that decision up to me. Bill was happy with me spending a few nights at his place. I told you, he liked Talia too. He knew about her past because I told him about her. He didn't want to hurt her anymore either."

"Wasn't he a little angry at the limitations Talia placed on your relationship," Ana asked.

Charity looked up at Ana. "He knew what he was getting into when he started dating me. I told him everything about myself…and about

Talia. He accepted the situation, just the way it was. He loves me, and I love him."

Anger started to seep into Charity's voice when she added, "Bill is not the type of person who would hurt anyone, if that's what you're getting at with these questions. He also has the same alibi that I have for the evening Talia was killed. We were with two hundred other students at the Light Up the Night Vigil…and almost all of the two hundred saw us and can verify the time we were there. We were both sitting on the outdoor stage or giving speeches for most of the evening."

Charity was on her feet, no longer hiding her anger. "Bill warned me that you might try to twist everything I say and make me a suspect. Well, I loved Talia…and this might be hard for you to understand, but I love Bill too. Bill told me to tell you, if you have any more questions, you can call the lawyer he's hiring for me."

She turned and stomped out of the lounge. Nikki shot up out of her seat and was right behind her. "Wait! Wait a minute, Charity, I don't think you understand."

Charity turned around and faced Nikki. "I do understand, and I'm a little disappointed in you, Reverend. I thought you would understand. That you would be a little open to all differences."

"I don't have any trouble with you being bi-sexual," Nikki tried to explain. "I don't even have a problem with you breaking off your relationship with Talia. We're just trying to find a murderer."

Nikki put her hand on Charity's arm. "Someone killed Talia and Betsy. They tried to kill me, too. We need to know everything, if we're going to catch this murderer."

Charity pulled her arm away from Nikki's touch, and said, "I gave Talia several years of my life. She really never gave me anything back. She couldn't. All she knew was pain, and all I ever felt from her was depression and rejection…But I didn't kill her and neither did Bill."

She pulled the door open and without looking at Nikki said, "Please close the lights and lock the door when you leave."

Charity stepped into the hallway and closed the door behind her. Nikki stared at the closed door for a few minutes, then turned and joined the others back in the lounge area.

Max waited for Nikki to sit down before he commented, "She certainly learned about getting a lawyer in a hurry."

"She said her boyfriend, Bill, suggested the lawyer," Ana added.

Nikki traced the slight crevice in her chin with her thumb and thought out loud, "I think Charity is frightened…she's carried a heavy secret around for several weeks now."

Nikki looked up at Ana and Max before going on, "I'm sure she didn't want to hurt Talia. Charity, like her name, appears to be a kind person, but don't be fooled by her nonchalant front. Telling her fellow classmates and the faculty at St. David University that she is no longer a lesbian, after fighting to be out and accepted…and now she's a bi-sexual in love with the president of Student Government…that would not be an easy task."

Nikki paused before adding, "Waiting for the right time was convenient for Bill and Charity as much as it was for Talia."

"What do you know about this Bill?" Max asked. "Could he be the killer?"

"No, I'm sure he's not the killer," Nikki answered in a flat tone. "However, I wouldn't rule out the fact that he might be involved in some way."

"How can you be so sure, he's not the killer," Ana asked inquisitively.

"He's too short," Nikki answered confidently. "He's only about five feet tall. The man I saw when I was attacked was at least six feet tall…and the woman with him was only slightly shorter."

"Woman?" Ana asked in a puzzled tone, as she turned to Max. "What woman? The report I got was only a male perpetrator. One male perp was assumed for both murders. Did you ever hear anything about a man and a woman?"

Max flipped back several pages in his notebook and read a few lines. He avoided Nikki's eye contact and looked at Ana. "We pretty much discounted the woman being there," he said slowly, trying to measure each word. "Nikki was hit so hard on the head...and both crimes appeared to involve sexual attacks...I just assumed...."

Max stopped talking and looked at Nikki. "I discounted the story of the woman you said was at the attack scene. I thought you were just seeing double or something." He dropped his voice and added, "I didn't consider the fact that a woman might help a guy do these attacks and murders."

He looked back at the notes in his book. "I think I was a little too close to the case at that point. I got too anxious to catch the guy and forgot to step back and consider all the evidence."

Max glanced back to Ana. "I made a bad call. I'm sorry. We need to add Nikki's information about the woman she saw to the report."

Ana stared at Max for a long moment, remembering all the times her partner in Buffalo made mistakes and forced her to go along with the cover-up. She didn't know what to make of Max, yet. She only knew she couldn't trust anyone, least of all, a fellow cop.

She turned to Nikki and asked, "What did this woman look like? The one you saw at the crime scene?"

Nikki instinctively touched the bandage on the back of her head. "I've tried to get myself to remember more about her, but it's a hard one." Nikki patted the bandage before going on. "I figure, she's the one that hit me from behind with the brick, because I can remember him. He was taking a few steps toward me."

Nikki closed her eyes and tried to recall the details of that night. With her eyes still closed, she continued. "He still had Betsy's camisole in his right hand. He had a knife or something in the other hand...ready to stab me...He was wearing black slacks, black turtleneck, dark gloves, with a black stocking over his face. I couldn't see anything but his eyes, and I couldn't make out the color. He was too far away."

She opened her eyes and blinked several times. "I put my hand up to deflect the knife or whatever weapon it was, and that's when I got hit from behind. That hit brought instant pain. You know the expression, 'I saw stars'? Well, I did...more like flashes of yellow light with this blue aura around the edges. I fell over right away. I couldn't open my eyes at all. I tried to. I struggled to try and get them open...to try and remember what was going on."

Nikki stopped talking and tried to compose herself. Her acetaminophen was wearing off and a terrible headache returned at a rapid rate. She began again, "I did make a point to listen for any clue I could. I figured if I couldn't see, I could at least hear something. There were muffled whisperings, pretty close to where I fell. That's how I knew there were at least two of them. Then I could feel some vibrations on the floor and hear them moving away from me."

She stopped again and looked up at Ana, "This is when I finally did get my eyes open. I could see the two shadows standing for a moment in the kitchen doorway. She was dressed exactly the same as he was; dark slacks, turtleneck, stocking mask, but she was shorter. I looked at both of them for maybe, a few seconds. My eyes just couldn't stay open. I heard the outside door close and they were gone."

Nikki rubbed her aching temple, and added, "The apartment was only quiet for a few minutes when I heard someone enter the kitchen again. I could hear whoever it was walking across the floor...I thought they came back to finish me off too, but then I must have passed out."

"That was Clarity Daniels, supposedly returning home," Max jumped in. "She's the one that found you and Betsy and called the police."

Ana was writing feverishly in the reporter's notebook she kept in the side pocket of her blazer. She looked up from her writing, and again addressed Nikki, "You said one of the attackers was a man and one was a woman. With the outfits they were both wearing, how do you know what gender they were?"

Nikki thought for a moment before answering, "The one that was facing me...that came at me...he was shaped like a man. I mean, he had muscular arms, bigger hands. He was taller."

"You're really not sure, are you?" Ana said.

"I guess, I just assumed because Betsy was nude..." Nikki searched for a reason for her belief. "I guess he was bigger, and I figured he was the attacker...so I thought he was a man."

She looked at Max for help. "I can't really be sure he was a man."

"What about the one that hit you?" Ana went on. "Can you be sure that one was a woman?"

Nikki shook her head as she answered, "When I saw her silhouette, she seemed to have more curves to her body. I mean by her waist and hips...and she was shorter with smaller arms."

"Can you be sure she was a woman?" Ana asked.

"No," Nikki answers sheepishly. "I can't be sure if either of them was a man or a woman, or two men, or even two woman. They were dressed the same."

"But you are sure there were two of them, right Nikki." Max clarified the question.

"Yes," Nikki didn't hesitate. "I'm sure there were two people at the murder scene."

At this point, a cell phone rang. Ana took hers out of her pocket and flipped it open. "It's not mine," she said, looking over to Max.

Max fumbled in his jacket pockets, looking for the ringing phone. "Dumb new equipment," he mumbled. "So damn small, I can't even find the thing."

He finally located the phone, flipped it open, and took several more rings before he pushed the right buttons. "Hello. Yeah, this is Sergeant Mullen. Yeah..."

As Max's voice got quieter, Nikki stood and looked at a side door that led to an adjoining kitchenette area. She whispered to Ana, "I'm just going to get some water to take a few pain killers." She opened the side door and left the lounge.

CHAPTER 10

▼

In the few minutes it took for Nikki to pop two more acetaminophen tablets and return to the lounge, Max and Ana had moved to the outer office. They both stood nervously silent next to the door leading out to the hallway. Max's face was whiter than usual, and Ana avoided all eye contact with Nikki.

"Was the call important?" Nikki asked, as she joined them by the reception desk.

Max moved a few steps closer to Nikki and put his hand on her shoulder. "I've got some bad news, Rev," he said, clearing his throat.

A cold shiver ran down the full length of Nikki's spine. Max never called her Rev, which was her nickname in Nam, unless something awful was about to happen. She braced herself for the worst.

"What is it, Max? What's wrong?" She felt her legs get wobbly and suddenly realized who the bad news might be about. "Is it Ginni?" she blurted out.

Max shook his head and answered, "I'm afraid something bad has happened to Ginni."

"My God! What is it?" Nikki was almost screaming at him now. "What's wrong with her? Where is she?"

"Nothing's certain yet," Max said, near tears himself. "The information is still sketchy."

"What's really wrong, Max," Nikki grabbed his sleeve. "What happened to Ginni?"

Max cleared his throat again and took a moment to swallow the lump that had formed there. He tried to speak but couldn't. Spontaneous tears filled his eyes, and he bent over and hugged Nikki.

Ana felt an obligation as a police officer to try and mediate the touching scene she was witnessing. She moved closer and calmly explained what Max couldn't find the words to say. "There's been another rape and murder. The officers answering the call suspect this murder follows the same MO as the Talia Carter and Betsy Frank murders."

Nikki broke from Max's hug and stared at Ana. "You don't mean…" she fought back the anguish. "Are you telling me that Ginni was raped and murdered? That she's dead."

"No." Ana answered in a strictly professional tone. "We don't really know what happened or who is involved."

Max regained his composure and followed Ana's professional lead. "All Officer Easton told me on the phone…," he began in a shaky voice. "Is that an unidentified female, around five-foot-eight, darker complexion…was found in the back of a stolen convenience store van parked in an empty lot behind the Harris Building. That's the building next door to Tailfeathers Saloon."

He stopped talking, exhausted from his own feelings and not wanting to report the next information to Nikki. Ana made a judgment call and continued the story for Nikki. "The woman was nude, apparently sexually attacked, some unidentified drink in a glass nearby. We suspect something mixed with GHB…left for us to find."

Ana now felt the need to take a breather from the intensity of the situation. She looked at Max's worn face, then at Nikki, and finally continued, "The two Officers were responding to a phone tip that came into the University Station. They haven't located any clothes or identification yet. Everything is gone…except a white lab coat with a small nametag on the pocket."

Nikki covered her mouth with her hand and tried to hold back the scream she desperately wanted to flail at the whole universe. She silently whispered, *God help me! Make this all go away, and please, please, keep Ginni safe.*

She removed her hand from her mouth and addressed Ana, "I don't believe the dead woman is Ginni."

Ana felt she should give Nikki all the facts they had so far. "The nametag says...'Dr. Virginia Clayton'."

"I still don't believe it!" Nikki yelled at no one in particular. "I don't believe Ginni is dead. I would have known. I would have felt some of her fear."

She turned to Max. "I want to go to the crime scene with you."

Max responded instantly, "I don't think that's a very good idea, Nikki. We don't know what we're going to see there. Even the Sheriff's boys haven't arrived yet. The officers have cordoned it off...but are trying to keep it low key because of the big crowd at the saloon next door. We don't want to start a panic..."

"I have to go," Nikki begged. "You can't keep me away from there. Please, Max, I have to see if it's Ginni. I need to be there if it's her."

Max started to protest again but was once more overcome with emotion.

"I don't see any reason why the Reverend can't come with us, Sergeant," Ana said softly to Max. Then she carefully added, "Perhaps she can help us with an identification."

Nikki didn't wait for the full effect of this last statement to sink in. She opened the door and led the other two down the stairs and out to the parking lot.

*   *   *   *

Max maneuvered his Cavalier down the narrow driveway of the Harris Building. He pulled up to the two Police cars with their white lights flashing. Nikki sat next to him in the same silence they had shared for the ten-minute ride to the small, empty parking lot. An old white van with an array of rust spots was in the middle of an area roped off with yellow crime scene tape.

Max got out of the car and walked over to open Nikki's door. She didn't wait for him to get around the car. She just threw open the door and quickly led the way to the back of the van. The first officer stopped her with his outstretched hand.

"She's okay, Easton," Max said, walking up to the officer. "She's with me. Came to identify the victim."

"Yes, sir," Officer Easton replied, as he slowly opened the back doors of the van. "We think we have a positive ID though," he added, reaching for a large plastic bag tucked in the back of the van. He turned around and took a white lab coat out of the bag. "We found this stuffed between the front seats. I guess someone was trying to hide it there."

Nikki took the lab coat and looked closely at the sewed on nametag. The tag read "Dr. Virginia Clayton." Spelled out in magic marker in Ginni's unmistakable script.

Nikki wanted to yell and scream and beat her fists on the ground until they bled. Instead, she held back her emotions and waited to see the body. She prayed to God…and her belief was strong. God brought her through Nam and through the seminary and parish work that almost destroyed her faith. God reunited her with Max and saved her life a dozen times. It was her faith that led her to meet Ginni and took away all the loneliness she lived with for so many years. So, God would help her through this too.

"I'd like to see the body," she said quietly.

Ana moved closer to Nikki and asked, "Are you sure you want to do this?"

"I'm fine," Nikki answered, as she handed the lab coat to Max. "I would like to see her now."

Max nodded to Officer Easton, who helped Nikki step up into the back of the van. He held a flashlight on the face of the nude corpse.

Nikki gasped and then started crying uncontrollable sobs. Her whole body shook with the sobs. A mixed sense of fear and sadness seemed to fill her being, as large tears ran down her face.

Max motioned for Easton to pull her out. "Help her out, will ya. Just get her outta there," he yelled.

Easton guided Nikki back out of the van and helped her jump back to the ground. She practically fell into Max's arms, still sobbing.

"I'm sorry, kid," Max held her tight and tried to fight his own tears. "It's gonna be okay. I'm so sorry."

Nikki finally slowed down her crying and hunted in her pocket for a tissue. Max realized what she was doing and gave her his big, white handkerchief. She buried her face in the handkerchief and finally quelled her tears. She wiped her eyes and her runny nose.

"I'm sorry, Max," she choked out each word. "I just couldn't help crying. I'm so sorry."

She stopped speaking for a moment and bowed her head in a silent prayer of thanksgiving. Max bowed his head too and kept his arm around Nikki.

Ana felt the awkwardness of this emotional moment and tried to bring some closure to it by asking, "Then the murdered woman is Virginia Clayton?"

"No," Nikki quickly replied. "No, she's not Ginni."

Max's mouth fell open. "What did you say?" he asked. "Did you say she's *not* Ginni?"

"Ginni isn't dead," Nikki repeated. She gave Max a little smile and added, "The dead woman is Dr. Sheba Reinstein, the new pediatrician at the Medical Center. Ginni must have loaned her the lab coat."

Ana wrote down this new information. "I'll go make some calls," she said quickly and started walking toward her car. "See if I can locate some family."

Max fumbled in his pockets and handed Nikki his cell phone. "Here, you better call Ginni and tell her to meet us here. We need to ask her some questions about that coat…and I think you need to talk to her right away." He gave Nikki a wide grin.

Nikki smiled back at him and made the call to the hospital.

CHAPTER 11

▼

While Max and Ana carefully combed over the crime scene, Nikki spotted Ginni's car pulling into the parking lot and ran the several yards of blacktop to meet her. Ginni drove her late-model, cream-colored Cadillac as close as she could to the flashing police cars. Nikki didn't even try to hide her excitement at seeing Ginni. She enthusiastically jerked open the car door, leaned into the front seat, and kissed Ginni passionately on the lips.

Ginni quickly broke from the embrace and kiss and pushed Nikki away. "Nikki? What's wrong with you?" she adamantly asked. "There are tons of people around."

Then Ginni took a long look at Nikki's drawn but smiling, face. "Why aren't you home resting? I thought that's what you promised me at the hospital."

"I did go home to rest," Nikki replied, leaning in for another hug.

Ginni gave her another quizzical look and said, "This is not home." She pushed Nikki out of the way and got out of the car. "This looks like a murder scene," Ginni started again. "A scene you promised me you would try to avoid."

Slightly on the defensive, but too happy to really care about anything, Nikki grabbed Ginni's hand and superficially explained, "I went home, but Max was waiting for me. He had some new information about Talia's murder. He wanted to tell me that Charity has a boy-friend...and Max said if I felt well enough, I could go with him when he questioned her."

Ginni scowled, but Nikki plunged on. "We met Charity at the Student Union, and then Max got a call about another murder...here..."

Nikki squeezed Ginni's hand tighter and started to choke on her words. "The woman was nude...no identification...but they found a lab coat at the murder scene...with your name on it."

Nikki grabbed Ginni and held her close. She started to cry and talk at the same time. "I was so scared...Oh Ginni...I thought I lost you...I thought the dead body was you." She stopped talking and sobbed deeply, while she buried her head into Ginni's shoulder.

Ginni held Nikki close and let her cry. She knew her partner had held those tears in for days now. She found herself gently rubbing Nikki's back and whispering, "I'm all right, honey. It isn't me. I don't know how they got my lab coat, but I'm okay."

Taking a deep breath, Nikki tried to get some moisture back into her mouth. She fumbled in her pocket for another tissue, but couldn't find one. Ginni quickly handed her a lace-trimmed handkerchief, and Nikki wiped her eyes.

Finally composed, Nikki looked in Ginni's eyes and quietly said, "The murdered woman is Sheba Reinstein. She must have been wearing your lab coat."

Ginni's mouth dropped open, and she shook her head in disbelief. "Sheba Reinstein. Why would anyone want to kill Sheba? I can't believe this is happening."

At this point, Max walked over and nodded to Ginni, "We need a positive ID, if you don't mind seeing the body. Gotta ask you some questions about your lab coat too."

"That's an easy one," Ginni put her arm through Nikki's and walked slowly toward the van. "Sheba was finishing her rounds around 5:30," Ginni began her explanation. "She spilled some betadine on her jacket and slacks. So she asked if she could borrow my old lab coat, the one I keep in my locker for emergencies."

Ginni stopped and tried to remember as much information as she could. "Sheba thought the betadine looked too much like blood. She didn't want to frighten anyone who might see her walking to her car. That's why she was wearing the coat."

Max finally looked up from his notes and motioned Ginni toward the yellow tape. He lifted the tape, so Ginni and Nikki could walk under it.

"This is Dr. Clayton," Max said to Easton and Ana. "She's here to identify the body." Easton stepped forward and helped Ginni step up and into the back of the van. Ana moved closer to Max and held out a water glass in a plastic evidence bag. "Not much liquid left," she remarked. "But there may be enough to leave some residue."

Max took the bag and carefully studied the few drops of liquid at the bottom of the glass. "You know what my guess is," he said, looking at Ana. She nodded her head in agreement.

"I think there's GHB in here...and I think we have a serial rapist and killer on our hands."

He handed the glass back to Ana and added, "Let's hope the Sheriff's boys can nail that down for us."

"Easton told me Officer Johnson was on the desk," Ana explained. "Johnson said he couldn't tell if the caller was a man or a woman. Muffled his voice somehow. Just said there was a body in a van behind the Harris Building."

Officer Easton helped Ginni jump down from the back of the van. Ginni walked back to Max. "No doubt about it," she choked a little on the words. "That's Sheba Reinstein. Her parents live in Seattle. I have their number on my pocket organizer in the car."

Ana moved foreword and extended her hand to Ginni. "I'm Detective Ana Ramos. I work with Sergeant Mullen."

Ginni took her hand, and Ana gave her a strong, quick shake before pulling her hand away. "When did you last see Dr. Reinstein?" Ana asked, while she took out her notebook and pen.

Ginni was somewhat put off by Ana's brusque approach but answered the question. "I saw her about 5:30, in the Common Room at the Memorial Medical Center. I still had two patients to see, but Sheba…Dr. Reinstein was finished with her patients."

Taking a deep breath, Ginni paused before going on. "As I told Max, she spilled betadine on her clothes and wanted to borrow my lab coat to cover them up while she waked to her car. That was the last time I saw her."

"Did she happen to mention where she was going?" Ana pushed on for more information.

"No," Ginni answered. "I guess I just assumed she was heading back to her apartment. I don't think she'd go anywhere with her clothes all messed up."

Max jumped in at this point. "Do you have any idea what kind of car she drives…or where we might find her car?"

"I think she drove an older BMW," Ginni answered, pushing some stray curls back into place. "I know she didn't drive a real expensive car, because she told me she's leasing until she can pay off her student loans. Then she wanted to buy an SUV." Ginni's voice got very quiet. "She really wanted to get one of those."

"Where is her apartment?" Max asked, softly.

Ginni's thoughts were pulled back to the present, and she answered flatly, "Sheba lives…lived…at 74 High Park Road."

"That's not far from here," Ana commented to Max, as she wrote down the address.

"No," Ginni replied. "She liked living close to the University. She taught an undergraduate course in Microbiology." Ginni paused again and let her thoughts drift off into remembrances of her friend.

"Sheba even played in some faculty/student dart tournaments, right over there at Tailfeathers," Ginni finished by pointing toward the saloon located in front of the next door parking lot.

Both Max and Ana shared a knowing look at this last piece of information. Nikki also made a mental note and thought, *Tailfeathers seems to come up a lot with people involved in these murders.*

Two more police sirens cut through the night, and the Sheriff's Crime Unit arrived, accompanied by two Sheriff's deputies. Max excused himself and headed for the Crime Scene Investigators. He flipped open his notebook and sent the two deputies to High Park Road in search of anything that might help. Since the Sheriff and the Sheridan Police were working together on these cases, Max had no problem delegating the work. Easton led the investigators to the van, and Max returned to the three women, who stood in silence, watching all the activity.

"I don't think we need you two any more tonight," Max said to Nikki and Ginni. "You can go home. I'll call you if we have more questions."

Nikki and Ginni turned to leave and overheard Ana telling Max, "I think I'm going to take a look around Tailfeathers. Do you need me for a few minutes?"

"No, go ahead," Max replied. "I'm waiting for the boys to call from High Park. If they don't find anything, I'll get a court order to look around her house. I don't think we'll get any more information tonight. When the Sheriff's boys are done with the van, they'll call for the morgue guys."

Ginni grabbed Nikki's arm again and quietly asked, "What's wrong, Nikki? You have that look on your face."

"What look?" Nikki asked back. "I was just thinking."

"About what?" Ginni asked again. "And the answer is probably, no. You shouldn't. It's getting too dangerous, so let's go home."

"I'd just like to look around Tailfeathers too," Nikki said, ignoring everything Ginni just said. "This is probably a good time. We could go in with Ana."

"Just what part of "No" don't you understand," Ginni exclaimed, stepping in front of Nikki and stopping her in her tracks. "We are not getting any more involved in these murders. So, please, let's just go home. Okay?"

This last body block by Ginni forced Nikki to approach the present situation in a different way. "I really need a drink of water," she coughed for effect. "My throat is so dry." Here she pulled on her neck for more proof of her discomfort. "I probably should take another pain pill, too."

Ginni, softened by each new gesture in this poor performance, inquired, "I don't suppose you'd consider drinking out of the bottle of water, I carry in my attaché."

"YUK!" Nikki made a horrible grimace. "That half-filled bottle has been traveling with you for about two weeks. I can't afford to pick up someone else's germs."

"They're my germs," Ginni countered. Then giving up, she added, "I suppose the only liquid worth having tonight is in Tailfeathers."

Nikki gave her a big smile and grabbed her hand. They walked carefully up the incline that separated the one parking lot from the other. They moved quickly and almost caught up to Ana, who was slowly making her way through the rows of parked cars, as she headed for the back entrance.

Not totally sure if Ana would appreciate the company, Nikki slowed down their pace and let Ana reach the outdoor patio before they did. Since it was still early spring, the festively lit patio was empty.

Ana was about to open the sliding door entrance, when a noise in the parking lot caught her attention. The high-pitched electrical sound was Taylor Fleming's wheelchair. She was navigating the wider spaces between the cars, which sent her on a great many detours before she reached the back entrance.

Nikki made Ginni stop walking, when she saw Taylor wheeling toward Ana. The Detective recognized Taylor immediately and patiently stood…smiling, while she waited for the Commissioner.

"I can't believe she's here too," Nikki whispered. "She must be following me."

"Who?" Ginni asked in a normal voice. "Who's following you?"

"Your old friend, Taylor Fleming," Nikki answered, still trying to keep her voice down. "She was in Hayes Hall earlier tonight. She's teaching some special seminar and has the office next to mine."

Ginni now had a clear view of Ana and Taylor. "You're right, it is Taylor," she said, excitedly. And without any hesitation, she yelled out, "Hey Taylor! It's me, Ginni! What are you doing here?"

Before Nikki could grab her or even try to stop her, Ginni took off for the patio. She went directly to Taylor, bent down and gave her a big hug.

"What are you doing here, Ginni?" Taylor laughed at the coincidence. "I heard this was the most popular bar in town, but I thought they meant for University types."

"What *are* you doing here?" Ana mimicked the words but in a much more serious tone.

By this time, Nikki reached the group but hung back and said nothing.

"Nikki needs a drink of water," Ginni explained, turning all her attention back to Taylor. "And Nikki just told me you're teaching a seminar at St. David. I think that's great. You'll be so close you can stop over for dinner…or lunch…or just anytime."

Nikki's face dropped at Ginni's last invitation, and Taylor didn't miss the change in facial expressions. She caught Nikki's eye and cooed, "I think that would be great fun…don't you Reverend?"

Nikki concentrated on staring at her sneakers. Rather than respond, she bent down and pretended to tie a lace that had not come undone.

Taylor laughed and diverted Ginni's attention to Ana. "You have met this new, strong detective, haven't you Ginni?" Taylor punched each adjective. She helped me out this afternoon. Lots of muscles. Her name is Ana Ramos. Detective Ana Ramos."

Ginni laughed at Taylor's flirting. "Yes, we met a little while ago," Ginni replied.

Taylor wasn't listening. She wheeled closer to Ana, "Well, if we're all going in for a drink, maybe you can help me with my chair again, Ana?" She paused for a beat and added, "I can call you Ana, can't I?"

"Sure," Ana answered, as she made her way behind the wheelchair. "Let me help you in."

"Then I'll buy the drinks," Taylor gushed.

Ginni just crossed her arms and laughed at Taylor's seduction of the Detective. Nikki finally felt safe enough to come up from her sneaker tying. She joined Ginni, who was still watching Taylor and Ana navigate the doorway.

"I think that Taylor is strange," Nikki carefully announced, after Taylor and Ana disappeared into the bar.

"Good," Ginni commented. "Try to keep that opinion of her." Then she laughed and took Nikki's arm. "Let's go get that drink of water you need."

CHAPTER 12

▼

Ginni and Nikki stepped simultaneously through the sliding glass doors of the patio entrance to Tailfeathers Saloon. The noise overload hit them with ear-deafening, disco-beat music blaring from extra-large speakers in every corner of the bar.

They made their way down a short, dimly lit hallway, which led to the large, circular, main room. The walls of the hall were plastered with notices of dart competitions and various entertainers due to perform at the Saloon.

The music boomed louder as Ginni and Nikki finally emerged from the cavernous hallway into the brightly lit main room. This pie-shaped room was divided into four large sections. To their immediate right was a sunken dance floor surrounded by a wooden railing. The ornate wooden railing was broken in six places by steps that led down to the dance floor. So dancers found the mirrored floor accessible, no matter where they were in that quadrant of the saloon.

A grey-haired, pony tailed, disc jockey adjusted various sound levels, while standing behind a glass enclosure just off the dance floor. The overhead lights in this area were definitely dimmer than anywhere else in the main room and from time to time, colored laser beams shot up from various spots on the mirrored dance floor.

"Don't you think it's too loud in here," Ginni yelled toward Nikki.

"What?" Nikki answered. "I can't hear you with all this noise."

Ginni just shook her head, grabbed Nikki's sleeve and led her away from the dance floor. They walked toward the bar area in the upper left quadrant of the room. The volume on the ear pounding music seemed to lesson as they moved toward the long brass bar. Unfortunately, every bar stool was taken, and patrons were standing two rows thick behind the stools.

"We've already lost Taylor and Ana," Ginni said in a now normal voice to Nikki.

"How can you find anyone in this crowd," Nikki groused.

Ginni noticed some empty tables in the section before the bar. She pointed to the area and said, "Let's just take a table and get you that water."

Nikki nodded, and they walked toward what was the mellowest section of Tailfeathers. The subdued lighting was augmented with battery-operated candles on each table. The music was still present as an undertone, but it was now joined by the hum of table conversations.

A waitress dressed in St. David sweatpants, sweatshirt, and a cap similar to Nikki's came over to their table. "What'll it be folks?" she asked pleasantly. "I like your hat, Professor Barnes."

Nikki recognized her as one of the students in her "Morality in Media" course. "Hello Elsbeth," Nikki said, as she smiled at the student. "I didn't know you worked here," Nikki added, trying to be friendly.

"Yep," Elsbeth cheerily responded. "Helps pay for my books…and I get to keep the uniform."

They all laughed at her humorous reply, and Elsbeth got her pencil ready, "So what'll it be?" she asked again.

"I'll have a big glass of ice water," Nikki said, suddenly remembering her aches and pains.

"I'll have a glass of red wine…a Merlot. If you have it," Ginni added.

Elsbeth bounced off to fill their order, and Nikki fished around in her blazer pocket for another acetaminophen. Locating one of the pills, she pulled it out and dusted off the surrounding lint. She placed the pill on the table and was momentarily distracted by a familiar voice. She did a half-turn and glanced at the two people sitting at the end of the bar, practically behind her.

Ginni saw her staring and asked, "What are you looking at?"

Nikki quickly turned back and said, "I can't believe it. Do you know who that is?"

Ginni strained her neck to get a look around Nikki, then answered, "No. Are we looking at the cozy couple?"

"That's who we're looking at," Nikki said, not looking back again. "The girl is Charity Daniels, Talia Carter's partner."

"Very interesting," Ginni mused, still staring.

"What makes it interesting is that she just told us she has a boyfriend, whose name is Bill Hanson," Nikki tried to explain. "That isn't Bill Hanson. That guy with the arm around her is Bradley Davis."

"Bradley Davis!" Ginni made a sour face. "Isn't Bradley Davis the guy that walked out of your class because ministers shouldn't be women and no one should be gay?"

Nikki gave her a knowing half-grin, "That's almost a direct quote."

Then Nikki turned and looked again. This time she caught the couple hugging and kissing. They came up for air and Nikki quickly turned back to Ginni. "I must have been hit on the head harder than I thought. She was just with us at the Student Union professing her love for Hanson."

Ginni looked over Nikki's shoulder again and said, "She definitely lied. They are in the longest tongue-lock I've ever witnessed."

At this point, the waitress returned with their drinks. During the time it took Nikki to swallow the pill and wash it down with some water, she remembered more about Bradley Davis.

"He's a fascist, jock-head, prejudiced, dumb, bully. What could Charity possibly be doing with him?" Nikki asked rhetorically.

"Well, whatever she's doing with him, she's now leaving to do more of it," Ginni answered.

Nikki turned her head away from the exit path, as Bradley and Charity walked past and headed toward the rear exit.

"You didn't really need to hide," Ginni commented, as she sipped some wine. "They only had eyes for each other."

Nikki said nothing, just sipped her ice water and tried to figure out what she just saw.

"Hey! There's Taylor and Ana," Ginni shouted, as she pointed to the last area of the room. "Let's go see what they're up to."

Nikki reluctantly got up and followed Ginni over to the dart competition area of Tailfeathers. They stepped down the one step that led into the well-lit competition area. Nikki glanced around at the dartboards hung every four feet on the back wall. Lines were taped off from the dartboards to a smaller circular bar at the opposite wall. Rows of people from each team lined up in these taped-off alleys waiting their turn to throw. The rest of the room was crammed with fans and on-lookers drinking and cheering on the teams.

Ginni pushed her way through a small group of fans, and Nikki followed. When they reached Taylor's wheelchair, Ginni tapped her on the shoulder. "What are you two doing?"

"There you are," Taylor warmly responded. "I thought Nikki was still out in the parking lot tying her sneaker."

They all laughed, except Nikki. She looked over at Ana, who was suddenly engrossed in watching one of the dart games. Nikki wondered what was catching Ana's attention, then she saw Ted Browning make a bull's eye. His wife was behind him waiting her turn to throw.

Nikki was about to say something to Ana, when someone yelled, "Look alive!…Watch out!…Stray dart!"

Taylor quickly turned her wheelchair to the left, and the incoming dart bounced off the steel part of her wheel. She turned back to face the tipsy player, who obviously lost the dart when he brought his arm back for a shot.

"So sorry about that," he slurred, trying to bend down and retrieve the fallen bird.

Ana beat him to the ground and quickly picked up the dart. "You need to be more careful," she said harshly to the younger man. "These darts could hurt someone," she added, about to hand the dart back to him.

Nikki looked at her own bandaged hand and then at the dart. Something clicked. "Wait a minute," she said quickly to Ana. "Let me see that thing?"

She reached over and took the dart out of Ana's hand. Then she held it in her bandaged hand and commented, "I'll bet these things are as sharp as a knife. They could really do some harm."

"Yessss," slurred the young man. "I mean, no…not really." He tried to explain. "I mean, they aren't really sharp like a knife…but you could give someone a bad puncture wound…with the point."

Then in obvious embarrassment, he added, "I'm real sorry about the dart flying over here. I'm really stupendously sorry."

Nikki took another long look at the dart and handed it back to him. He gave her an awkward bow and returned to his team.

Ana caught Nikki's eye. "Could give someone a bad puncture wound," she said, reading Nikki's thoughts. Then she added, "Let's get out of here," she added.

"Good idea," Nikki agreed, leading the group back to the one step that put them on the main floor.

Nikki went up the step with Ginni right behind her. Ana was next, but she stopped to carefully wheel Taylor backwards, up the step. As she turned the chair around, Taylor cooed, "Isn't she wonderful. Handles this thing like an old pro."

All four proceeded past the bar and the table area to the hallway leading back to the exit, where they entered. Once outside, they huddled for a caucus. "So, what's going on?" Ginni asked. "Why did we have to hurry out?"

Nikki clenched her teeth in anger. "It was a dart," she practically snarled.

"Yes..." Taylor added, trying to draw out more information. "That was a dart that flew into my wheel...and?"

Nikki held out her bandaged hand and pointed to the palm with the puncture wound. "He stabbed me with a dart. In the dark, I thought it was a knife, but it was a dart."

"There were some strange cuts on Talia body too, and I thought I just saw some on Dr. Reinstein's inner thighs." Ana added reflectively. "I think he used a dart on them too."

"What are you all talking about," Taylor finally asked. "Who used a dart? Does this have something to do with the murder you're investigating?"

Ana suddenly gave all her attention to Taylor. "Sorry, we're not trying to exclude you. When that dart came flying over, Nikki and I both realized that the person who tried to stab her was holding a dart not a knife. That's why no one could figure out what he used for a weapon. He took it with him."

"When did Nikki get stabbed?" Taylor asked innocently. "Have I been asleep or something? I mean, I just thought you were accident-prone. You know, hit with a brick. I didn't know you got stabbed."

Nikki was very annoyed. "I was hit on the head and stabbed in the hand," she sniveled.

"I never saw your hand," Taylor shot back. "All my attention was drawn to that crazy hat you wear."

Ginni felt this might be a good time for her to step in. "Nikki got involved in the murder of one of her students," Ginni patiently tried to explain. "When she went to help arrange the funeral, she found another student murdered. Nikki was hit on the head and stabbed in the hand."

Ana continued to fill in the needed information. "We think another murder is also related. Actually, we thought Ginni was the dead woman. This time we found some clothes with her identification tag on them at the crime scene."

Taylor sat in silence, taking in everything that was just explained to her. "I'm sorry, Nikki. I was just teasing you a little. I had no idea all this was going on."

She reached out and took Ginni's hand, as she continued. "Ginni, you must have been crazy with worry." She looked up at Nikki and added, "If you thought that dead woman was Ginni, you must have been…well, out of your mind with grief. I'm so sorry."

Taylor let go of Ginni's hand and made eye contact with Ana. "So, what's going on around here, Detective? Is there a serial murderer loose? Should I worry more than I am right now? Because if my legs could shake, they'd be doing it right this minute."

Nikki cringed at Taylor's black humor and quietly said to Ginni. "I think we better go now. I'd like to stop and see if Max is still at the crime scene. I want to tell him about the dart connection…and the motley crew we just saw in the saloon.

"Okay," Ginni said. Then she turned to Taylor and asked, "What about you, Taylor? Where are you parked?"

"Don't worry about me," Taylor answered. "My car's just over there." She paused a minute and added, "I'm hoping Detective Ramos will follow me home. I don't mind telling you, all this information has made me a little nervous."

She looked up at the silent Ana and asked, "Do you mind following me to my apartment? My place isn't too far from here. I could make you a cup of coffee…or something."

"Oh sure," Ana answered, somewhat befuddled by the invitation. "Sure, I'll follow you. I think that's a safe idea. Sure."

Ana moved behind Taylor and started pushing the wheelchair toward the parking lot. Nikki stared at the two of them and mumbled, "Taylor could turn on the power and wheel that thing herself."

Ginni put her arm around Nikki and gave her an affectionate squeeze, as she whispered, "She is turning on the power, my dear. Just not with the wheelchair."

CHAPTER 13

▼

Nikki leaned on Max's open car window and took a moment to catch her breath. She had just run several yards to flag him down before he left the parking lot. "I'm glad I caught you," she said between breaths. "I was afraid you already left for home."

"I've still got tons of paperwork to finish up before I head home," Max answered, the tiredness apparent in his voice. "So, what's so important that you break into a run this hour of the night."

"It was a dart..." Nikki was still panting. "The murderer tried to stab me with a dart." She paused and held up her bandaged hand. "Some guy lost control of a dart in Tailfeathers. When Ana and I saw it, we both realized my puncture wound was caused by a dart."

She stopped again, which gave Max time to put together what she was saying. "That's not all," Nikki started again. "Charity Daniels was at the bar kissing and making out with Bradley Davis not Bill Hanson...and both Ted Browning and his wife were in there too, competing on one of the dart teams."

Max rubbed the stubble of a beard forming on his chin and tried to put this new information in perspective. "So, this confirms our first idea that Tailfeathers is somehow involved in the murders. It also puts some of our suspects in the Saloon. We got Charity Daniels, the Brownings, and who is this Bradley Davis?"

"He's another student from St. David's," Nikki answered. "He's that football player who tried to get me fired because he doesn't like gays. He's nothing but trouble, Max. I told you about him last year. Picks fights with anyone he deems is different."

She took a breath, then went on, "Got in a fight with an Asian exchange student and two African-American students on a rival team...but he seems to always get away with his behavior. Somehow, his father, a high-powered lawyer, comes over to the college and talks or pays his son's way out of the trouble."

The name clicked with Max, and he jumped in, "He didn't get away with the charges he brought against you though, as I remember."

Nikki nodded. "No, he didn't win that time. My entire class went to the Dean and defended me. Bradley said I was recruiting women for the gay lifestyle...during my class yet."

"I remember now," Max added. "All fifteen students, guys and girls wrote out statements supporting your teaching and you. Then they went to the Dean and gave personal statements. You must be a good teacher, Nik."

"I don't know about that," Nikki was embarrassed by the compliment. "I was sure proud of those students though. Maybe Bradley did learn that he can't always get his way. The Dean was at least forced to reprimand him...and by mutual consent, he is no longer welcome in my classes."

"Looks like we have one more suspect to add to the list," Max said. "Where was Bill Hanson when all this smooching was going on?"

"I didn't see him," Nikki answered. "I do know that Bill Hanson and Bradley Davis were friends. I remember that, because I always thought they were noticeably different and yet close friends. Maybe there's something I don't know about Bill Hanson."

"Well, now there's definitely more that we know about Charity Daniels," Max interjected, as he made a few notes in his notebook.

He put the notebook back in his breast pocket and patted Nikki's arm. "I don't think we're gonna solve this one tonight. Maybe you should go home and try to get some of that rest you didn't get today."

Nikki gave him a big smile. "I'm on my way, Max. Call me tomorrow, okay?"

"You got it," Max answered, putting the car into gear.

Nikki backed away from the car, and Ginni stood next to her as they watched Max pull away. Then, Ginni took Nikki's arm again and led her back to her car. They got in and started for home.

*   *   *   *

Taylor unlocked the front door to her upscale, handicapped-accessible apartment. With the power to her wheelchair now switched on, she opened the door and wheeled down a shiny, hardwood floor ramp into her luxurious living room.

She turned and waved Ana into the room. "Please, come in. I'm so grateful that you followed me home. The least I can do is make you a cup of coffee."

Ana paused for a moment in the entranceway. She was slightly intimidated by the opulence of the furnishings. The living room was decorated in modern Scandinavian. Everything was light wood and white. An oversized white leather sofa took up almost one whole wall, and a matching chair was opposite the sofa. A plush, white, wall-to-wall rug was decorated with a full-size polar bear skin lying in front of a white marble fireplace.

As Ana turned to lock the door behind her, Taylor flipped a switch on the wall. Immediately, soft classical music floated through hidden wall speakers, and a subtle blue and gold fire materialized in the fireplace. Taylor flipped another switch and the lights in the living room dimmed to a mellow yellow glow.

Ana smiled at all the gizmos and walked slowly down the ramp to join Taylor. "This is a very impressive room," she said, as she finally reached the sofa.

"Thank you," Taylor replied. "I've always had well-paying jobs, and I received a very hefty settlement from the insurance company of the drunken bastard who was responsible for taking my legs."

She stopped and let the anger move through her. "Did that sound a little bitter?" she asked Ana.

"Maybe a little," Ana answered, as she sat at one end of the long sofa. "I think you might be entitled to a little bitterness, though," she added.

Taylor gave her a seductive smile and admitted, "I'm still working on that with my shrink...oh, they don't call them shrinks any-more...with my advisor. He doesn't have much hope for my mental well-being, because he doesn't think I make friends well. What do you think? Want to be my friend?"

Ana gave a little laugh. "I think you are very friendly. I have a great deal of hope for your well-being."

Now Taylor laughed. "While you're contemplating my being, would you like a latte or a little brandy? You are off-duty now, aren't you?"

"Yes," Ana answered in a very tired voice. "I am definitely off-duty for this day. I'm sure latte or brandy goes well with this room, but I'm really just a cold beer gal. Have you got any of those?"

"One cold beer coming up," Taylor replied, turning her wheelchair toward the kitchen. She stopped and turned back to add, "Of course, it's imported German beer. Will that do?"

"Beer is beer," Ana shrugged. "That'll be fine."

Taylor headed off to the kitchen, and Ana heard the sound of the refrigerator door opening, bottles clinking, and various rustling in the kitchen. Ana stretched her full length and unconsciously slipped off her loafers. She let the plush carpet massage her aching feet. Then she closed her eyes and let the warmth of the fireplace and the soft music release all the stress and stiffness of the day.

Taylor quickly returned, balancing a full tray on the arms of her wheelchair. She rolled up to the coffee table in front of the sofa and put the tray down. Next, she placed a cut-glass stein, filled to the rim, in front of Ana and a glass of red wine next to the stein. Then she lifted a platter of warm Brie and crackers onto the table and let the tray slide to the floor.

Taylor wheeled closer to Ana, just behind the glass of red wine. "Thought you might like some nourishment too," she said, as she raised the wine glass. "Here's to a relaxing evening for an overworked, albeit attractive, cop."

Ana raised the stein and clinked the wine glass. "Here's to a gracious, albeit attractive, Commissioner."

They both sipped some of their beverages, and Taylor broke into a wide grin. "So you just love me for my money and position."

"Not really," Ana replied. "I think you're very beautiful…and sexy." She took another drink of her beer.

"And I think you are a striking, hot-blooded Latino," Taylor said, leaning closer to Ana. She touched Ana's face with her left hand, while with her right hand, she released the comb fastener from Ana's long hair.

Ana's long, dark hair fell loosely to her shoulders. Taylor used both her hands to fluff Ana's hair. She took several minutes to stroke the loose strands. "I like your hair," Taylor whispered. "You should let it down more often."

"That wouldn't be very appropriate for my work," Ana said softly, as she took both Taylor's hands in hers and kissed each palm.

"Ohhh!" Taylor moaned. "Those little messages are going right to my answering machine."

Ana bent closer to Taylor. Their eyes locked onto each other. "You have the most beautiful color eyes I have ever seen," Ana said softly. "They're the color of lilacs on a warm spring day."

"I'm not even wearing my contacts with the sparkles in them," Taylor replied not breaking the eye contact.

"I would like to kiss you," Ana whispered and moved her head closer to Taylor's.

"I think I'd like that too," Taylor responded and moved her lips closer to Ana's.

They kissed long and passionately. Ana took Taylor in her arms, and Taylor hugged her back. They stayed in the embrace for several minutes and continued kissing. Their passion heated up even more, as their tongues searched and darted, mimicking a grand ballet.

Taylor started moaning softly again, and Ana felt the passion building in her own body. They were both getting lost in the moment, in the intensity of their touches. Ana broke slowly from the embrace and said, "I'd like to lift you to the floor...over by the fireplace."

"On the bear-skin rug...by the fireplace," Taylor stuttered and tried to catch her breath. "I've waited a lifetime for someone to take me on that rug."

She lifted her arms up to Ana, who was now standing. Ana wrapped her arms around Taylor and carefully lifted her out of the wheelchair. She carried her the few feet to the rug and gently put her down.

Ana sat next to Taylor, and they were immediately back in each other's arms, kissing and caressing. Tremors alternated down Ana's body, then down Taylor's. They were lying on the rug now, mixing the feel of soft skin with soft fur. Without breaking from their kissing, Taylor unbuttoned Ana's blouse. With help from Ana, she pushed the blouse off with the blazer, all in one move.

Ana quickly unbuttoned Taylor's silk blouse and peeled it off, only to find she was wearing a black silk camisole and no bra. She quickly lifted the camisole over Taylor's head. This involved a break from the kissing and a brief moment to catch their breath again.

In an instant, Taylor was back in Ana's arms. She reached behind Ana to unfasten the hooks, peel down the straps, and take off her bra. They were now skin to skin, and they moved further and further into their passion. They were hot embers like the blue and gold flames in the fireplace. They were heat and touch and flying planets, orbiting out of control.

They earnestly pulled off slacks and panties, each helping each shed the remnants of another life...another world. Now they were free, melting into each other, racing to a burning, damp Land of Oz. Wild, uncontrollable energy moved between them, first one, then the other. Blazing, stiffening explosions...forest fires burning out of control. Nothing existed but flashes of Nirvana. They tunneled together on a sensual run-away train that finally left earth and flew like a shooting star. First heavenward, and then back...falling with a last flicker, to earth.

Both Ana and Taylor rolled over on their backs and felt the damp bear fur under them. They stared at the strange shadows from the fireplace that danced on the ceiling. Finally, Ana found the strength to move. She leaned on her elbow and reached over to once again kiss Taylor. She kissed her chin, her throat, her chest. She moved to Taylor's right breast...and abruptly stopped.

Taylor had some writing tattooed just above her right nipple. Ana got on her knees to read the small print. "B-I-T-E-M-E. Bite Me! Bite Me!" Ana repeated, as she looked at Taylor. "You tattooed, 'Bite me' on your breast?"

Taylor rolled over to face Ana, "You probably won't believe this, but I was really wild when I was young."

They both started laughing and ended up back in another caress. The kissing and touching started all over again.

*   *   *   *

Nikki and Ginni dragged their weary bodies into the townhouse and greeted Fluffy with lots of petting. After this sufficient pampering time, Ginni went directly to the downstairs bedroom, leaving shoes, jacket, attaché, and coat strewn along the way. Nikki followed close behind, picking up after her. Halfway down the hall, Nikki took a slight detour to her office. There were two messages on the answering machine. The first was from Betsy Frank's mother, asking Nikki to officiate at the burial of her daughter. It seemed Betsy had talked to her mother about Nikki many times.

"Please call me as soon as possible. I'm staying at the Best Western just off the Thruway, room 310. Thank you. Just ask for Elizabeth."

Nikki wrote down the information and again felt the sadness of these triple murders sink into her very being. The heaviness of her sorrow forced her to sit on the chair next to the phone.

The answering machine clicked again, announcing the next message. Nikki readied her pen to jot down more information. A strange, mechanically-enhanced voice came on the machine. "I thought I got you this time, Professor Barnes. I was sure my last little fling was with your Doctor Clayton. What a great lay she was, but it turns out I got the wrong girl. Don't worry. I'll get it right next time, and then it's your turn again. I won't leave the room in such a hurry this time."

He hung up, and Nikki started to shake. Her whole body was trembling. She couldn't write or move. This phantom voice had invaded her home…had threatened the thing she cared for the most.

The full realization that the murderer wanted to kill Ginni sent such terror through Nikki's body that she felt physically sick. She wanted to jump up and run out of this room…out of the house…away from the danger that threatened Ginni and herself.

Ginni walked into the office just in time to hear the second phone message. She was only a few feet behind Nikki when the message ended. Controlling her own emotions, she moved closer to Nikki and took her hand. "It's okay, Nikki. I'm fine. He can't hurt us with phone calls."

Nikki looked deeply into Ginni's eyes. "I love you, Ginni," she said, her voice still shaky. "I don't want anything to happen to you, and now I've put you in danger. Someone is trying to kill you, and it's my fault."

"You're not responsible for some nut trying to kill me," Ginni tried to reassure her. "You were just trying to plan a funeral, and he hit you on the head." She paused, trying desperately to control her emotions. "He wants to kill you too, remember. He wants to kill both of us."

Nikki got up and wrapped her arms around Ginni. They held on tightly to each other, while big, wet tears started to streak down Ginni's face. "Poor Sheba. I'm so sorry for her. He thought she was me...because of the lab coat...he thought he was killing me."

She buried her face in Nikki's shoulder and wept softly. Nikki stroked Ginni's soft, dark red hair, trying to comfort her partner. Her own fear was beginning to dissipate. The touch of Ginni next to her, the feel of her hair, and the wetness of her tears on Nikki's cheek were changing her emotions.

Her fear was turning into something much stronger. It was becoming anger...almost rage. Nikki steeled herself for a fight. The most important fight of her life. She was going to get this guy...and she would get him before he got her or Ginni. "I need to call Max, right away," she finally said, gently breaking from the hug. "He needs to hear this tape."

She moved back to the phone and punched in Max's cell phone number. It rang twice and Max answered with an exhausted, "Hello."

"Max, it's Nikki. I just checked my answering machine..." Nikki waited for her words to sink in. "The killer left me and Ginni a message. He thought he was killing Ginni when he killed Sheba Reinstein. He says he's going to kill both of us...just like the others. I think you should come over and listen to this tape."

"That's what I was afraid of," Max answered, as he turned the car around and aimed toward Nikki's. "Is the patrol car still out in front of your place?"

Nikki took the phone down the hall with her and looked out the small window in the front door. "Yeah," she answered. "Thank God, you decided to send a car. It's still there."

"As soon as I saw Ginni's white coat," Max tried to explain. "I figured he was after her. I just never thought he had the nerve to call you. He's a real nut case, Nikki. I want you to be very careful…both of you. I'll be right there."

He hung up, and Nikki returned the phone to the office. She looked at Ginni and explained, "He's on his way. Max already sent a patrol car to watch the house. They're out in front. He thought the guy might be after you, when he saw your name-tag on the jacket."

Nikki moved closer to Ginni and held her in her arms again. "Max thinks he's a real nut case…and so do I."

*   *   *   *

Max was at Nikki's house in less than fifteen minutes. Before he walked up to her door, he went over to the patrol car and gave the patrolman on duty some instructions. The car took off and began circling the apartment complex. Then Max walked slowly and heavily up to Nikki's door. He surveyed the surrounding area for a second time, and Nikki opened the door before he had a chance to ring the bell.

"Thanks for coming right over," Nikki said in relief. "I don't mind telling you, this message scared Ginni…and it scared me."

"You're better to be scared than sorry," Max replied, walking toward the office. He moved right to the answering machine and played the messages. He listened to the first one from Betsy Frank's mother. Then he sat on the chair next to the phone and listened carefully to the mechanically-enhanced voice while it admitted killing Dr. Reinstein and threatened to rape and kill both Ginni and Nikki.

The machine clicked off, and Max opened the cover. He carefully lifted out the tape with his pen. He took a small plastic bag from his jacket pocket and put the tape in it. "Ya know, he means what he said," Max addressed both Ginni and Nikki.

"He's gonna try something. So I don't think either one of you should leave this apartment for any reason."

"Well, that's a nice thought," Ginni began. "But I do have some sick patients depending on me tomorrow. Not only at the Medical Center, but I'll need to help with Sheba's patients at the hospital too. I can't just stay home tomorrow."

"I need to arrange Betsy's funeral with Mrs. Frank," Nikki chimed in. "And my final grades are due by tomorrow evening. I have to get them over to the University."

"Whoa! Whoa!" Max shook his head for effect. "I know you are both busy people, but someone is trying to kill you. Is that clear?"

"He's not going to frighten me or control my life," Nikki stated defiantly. "Nobody's going to do that to me."

"My patients do come first," Ginni added. "I took an oath to serve them, and I live by that oath."

"You two are both unreal!" Max raised his voice. "This is very serious! I'm not sure I have the manpower to escort you both around. So, promise me...," he paused for emphasis. "Promise me you won't go anywhere without a cop following you or escorting you. Will you promise me?"

Ginni and Nikki raised their right hands and swore in unison, "We promise."

"Okay," Max grunted, as he got up from the chair. "I'm gonna run this back to the Sheriff's boys to analyze. They have to send it into Buffalo, so we probably won't have anything usable until late next week. Hopefully by then, we'll have a suspect to match to the voice. Then I'm going home for some sleep. I'm so tired, I can't think anymore."

He turned to Nikki. "I'll be back here bright and early, so have the coffee on...and no one leaves this house until I get here. Is that clear?"

Ginni and Nikki shook their heads at the same time and said, "Yes."

"Then Ginni, you and the day officer can go heal your patients," Max explained. "Nikki, you can spend some quality time with me...putting together the parts of this puzzle."

Max walked toward the door with Ginni and Nikki right behind him. He opened the door and put the lock on. "Good night, you two."

Nikki leaned over and planted a big kiss on his cheek. "Good night, Max." Her eyes met his and she whispered, "We're going to get this guy before he can hurt anyone else."

"That's the plan," Max gave her a little smile and closed the door. He walked to his car and gave the patrolman another wave.

Ginni and Nikki looked through the door window and watched him pull away. "I think we better try to get some sleep too," Ginni said, putting her arm through Nikki's. "How will that head of yours ever heal?"

Nikki leaned over and gave Ginni a gentle kiss on the lips. "There, it's healing already."

CHAPTER 14

▼

At exactly 7:30 the following morning, Max rang the doorbell to Ginni and Nikki's townhouse. He was wearing the same slacks and sports jacket he wore the night before. However, his wife Rosa made him change his shirt and tie. This shirt had a muted paisley pattern in a pale blue and pink. The pink was not Max's favorite color, but his wife bought the shirt as a present, and Max tried to be sensitive to his wife's feelings.

Max grunted a hello and moved right to the kitchen. Nikki had a mug of coffee already poured and placed in front of his favorite position at the table. She sat across from his place and cradled her own steamy cup.

Fluffy woke up slowly, stretched her full length, and sauntered into the kitchen. She carefully checked out the canned cat food selection of the day and the freshness of her milk, and then waited for her chance to jump on Max's lap.

Ginni gathered up her trench coat and attaché case and followed the cat into the kitchen. Maintaining her usual morning routine, she grabbed a granola bar from the kitchen cupboard and stuffed it into her attaché.

Max finished a big gulp from his coffee mug and on the exhale said, "Good coffee." He turned to Ginni and added, "You can leave any time now, Ginni. The day officer has his orders." Max took another gulp and finished his explanation. "He'll be like your shadow, so don't be too rough on him, okay?"

Ginni smiled and said, "I will try to protect him from all the blood and guts." She made her way around the table and leaned over to give Nikki a peck on the cheek. "Take care today and try not to run around too much. You do still have stitches, you know."

Nikki grabbed Ginni's hand and touched it to her own cheek. "You be careful too, okay? I love you, and I want you to stay safe."

Max gulped more coffee and tried not to be embarrassed by the show of affection between his two friends. Fluffy just let out a loud, "Meow!" and demanded some attention for herself.

Ginni bent over and gave Fluffy a parting pat on the head, then walked down the hall and out the door. She waved to the day officer as she got into her car and slowly pulled away from the curb. The officer followed close behind her.

By this time, Fluffy had made her morning leap into Max's lap. He distractedly petted the purring cat and got down to business. "I'm having Ramos call the A-One garage in Letchworth," he started. "Just want to make sure we check out everything…and everyone."

"What do you think of Charity Daniels?" Nikki asked, as she took some frozen sweet rolls out of the freezer and popped them into the microwave.

"I think she has too many boyfriends for a lesbian," Max answered sarcastically. "Makes me wonder about the sincerity of all those tears she shed over Talia Carter's dead body."

Nikki sat back down and took another sip of coffee. "I can't believe she was faking the sorrow. I'm sure they cared about each other," she added.

"Then what about this Bill Hanson and your favorite, Bradley Davis?" Max asked.

"The funny thing is," Nikki began. "When I was thinking about it all last night, I remembered that Hanson and Davis were close buddies for awhile. They were both on the wrestling team. Different weight categories but both wrestlers."

Max tried not to, but his eyes darted over to the microwave before settling back on Nikki. "So, ya think the good buddies share everything, like girlfriends?"

Nikki got his hint and retrieved the sweet rolls from the microwave. She put them on the table and sat back down. "Help yourself, Max." Then she picked one out for herself and without another word, took a big bite out of the roll.

The kitchen was full of silent thinking as she chewed and swallowed. "Charity was kissing Bradley like there was no one else in the world. She didn't even notice me when she walked past. I don't think Bill Hanson knows about Bradley and Charity."

"When was she going to tell him?" Max commented while he continued to chew his mouthful of roll. "Maybe when she got to his parent's cottage?"

Nikki just shook her head. "So what does all of this have to do with the killer? Do you think Charity is involved?" she asked.

Max reached into his breast pocket and took out his notebook. He flipped some pages and detached the pen from the spiral binding. In a very serious tone, he answered, "I think Charity is definitely a suspect right now."

Nikki held her coffee cup with both hands and let the warmth move from her hands up to her arms. "She could've been the female I saw, all dressed in black. But the guy couldn't be Bill Hanson. Like I said, he's too short."

"What about Bradley Davis?" Max asked. "Could he be the killer?"

Nikki thought long and hard before answering, "I'm not sure. He's the right height, but I think he's stockier, more heavy-set than the guy I saw. It was dark, and I was getting pretty fuzzy."

"So, a definite maybe," Max smiled and made a note in his little notebook.

"Fraid so," Nikki replied. "Any other possibles?"

"I'm adding Ted Browning," Max threw out while still writing. "Can't tell you why, yet, but I don't like him. He's hiding something. I just don't know what."

He looked up from his notebook and added, "As a matter of fact, that's why I left word for Ramos to check out their story about the rented car and all that stranded in the woods baloney."

A thick silence returned to the room. Nikki and Max both got lost in their own thoughts about the case. There was only one sound permeating the intense quiet. It was Fluffy purring away, as Max kept up the petting.

"There really aren't many clues for this one are there?" Nikki somberly asked.

"Not yet," Max answered, trying to be more positive. "We do have some important pieces, and we're working on others. We'll get this creep, Nikki."

"What important pieces do we have?" Nikki half-heartedly asked.

Max flipped back a few pages and checked his notes before he answered. "We're pretty certain your hand wound was caused by a dart, probably from Tailfeathers." He looked up at Nikki, "I told you at the beginning that Tailfeathers was involved. Look at the last murder...right in the parking lot next door. That's another thing. This guy is getting bolder, and he's going to make a mistake. Which reminds me, I'm having your answering machine tape worked on. The Sheriff's boys think they can unscramble the voice, and we just might recognize it."

"Why is he after me?" Nikki asked. "I mean, why go to all that trouble to kill Ginni just to get at me?"

"Maybe because you made a fool out of him," Max tried to find a reason. "Probably this guy hates women. He just sees them as sex objects. You almost caught him in the act, but he couldn't finish you off then, so now, he has to."

"That's getting a little too close for comfort," Nikki commented, as she got up to pour more coffee. "You mean, he would kill Ginni just to get to me, just to hurt me?"

"I don't think he'd stop with Ginni," Max continued. "I think he really wants to kill you. You messed things up."

"I didn't mess things up enough to stop him, though." Nikki sat back down again. "I wish I had the power he thinks I have." She sipped more coffee and added, "I'm not sure any of the people we mentioned is the killer."

"I'm running what we do have through the national computer," Max explained. "We may just have a visiting serial killer in our midst, but somehow I think he's a local."

Nikki respected all of Max's gut feelings. He was right too many times to count. "So, what do we do now?" she asked.

"*We* don't do anything," Max quickly answered. "As soon as Ramos gets here, I'm going to see the lab boys at the Sheriff's Department. They've been combing over Talia Carter's car. I told ya the car was parked right outside the motel room, didn't I? They haven't found much yet but her backpack. And that's what's interesting. She definitely wasn't planning a sleepover…in the park or at the motel."

"Why don't I just come with you, Max?" Nikki asked.

"Because you told me last night, you needed to plan a funeral and get your grades in," Max huffed. "Besides, I thought you just might rest a little."

"But Max," Nikki pouted. "I hate being babysat."

"You have no choice," Max said, softening his tone. "I'm not about to let a killer get my old Army buddy. I need you safe, so you can help me crack this one. Okay?"

"Okay," Nikki grudgingly answered, realizing her old pal was right again.

Ana Ramos arrived on cue, and Nikki let her in. Max gave her a cursory wave while he headed for the door. He turned back just before exiting and said, "Stay glued to her, will ya Detective? Nikki tends to get careless when there's too much on her mind."

He threw Nikki a big smile and added, "She's pretty precious to me. We got a history, ya know."

Nikki just shook her head and waved him off saying, "I told you, I'd behave…and I love you too." She knew this last remark, even though it was true, would embarrass Max enough to send him on his way. It did, and he quickly left.

Nikki showed Ana into the kitchen. "Help yourself to the coffee or anything interesting in the refrigerator," she said, pouring herself another cup of coffee. "I'll be in the office, making some calls and doing my paperwork."

Ana poured herself a cup of coffee, left it on the cupboard, and non-chalantly followed Nikki into the office. She checked the windows and even opened a closet in the corner of the room. Next, she moved up the stairs. Nikki could hear her checking the large bathroom and extra bedroom up there.

Ana came back down the stairs and made her way to the hallway. She checked the small bathroom and downstairs bedroom before walking back to the living room.

As she passed the office again, she poked her head in the door and said, "I'll be in the living room making some calls on my cell phone and going through my notes. Please, let me know if you leave the office."

Nikki was about to protest but stopped herself. She knew that Ana was doing her job and probably saving Nikki's life. Nikki just quietly said, "Okay…and thanks."

Her first duty for the day was to call Elizabeth Frank and discuss the funeral for her daughter. Nikki looked up the phone number for the Best Western Hotel and jotted it down on a piece of paper by the phone. Next, she paused and said a short prayer, asking God to guide her thoughts and words while she spoke to this grieving mother. She pushed the numbers and asked to be connected to room 310. A woman answered the phone.

"This is Reverend Barnes. Is Elizabeth Frank there?"

"This is Elizabeth Frank," the woman answered. "Thank you for calling Reverend Barnes."

Nikki found her words came slowly and painfully. "I'm so sorry, Mrs. Frank."

Mrs. Frank hesitated before responding. "I know you are, Reverend. The police explained the circumstances of Betsy's death. They told me you were almost killed too." Her voice started to crack. "I just can't believe this happened to my little Betsy. She never hurt anyone. She was such a kind, thoughtful girl. Never any trouble."

"Betsy was a beautiful person," Nikki felt a deep pain in her heart. "She was helping out a friend when this happened…trying to console someone else. That's what Betsy often did. She was loved by many people."

"I know. I know." Her mother tearfully started again. "Betsy was my right hand when her father died. She even gave up a year of school to stay home and help me get on my feet. Did you know she worked in a gas station, so I could go to secretarial school?"

"That sounds like Betsy," Nikki answered. "She was very kind and generous to everyone."

"Then why did someone kill her?" Elizabeth Frank broke into tears. "Why did someone hurt my baby girl? She never harmed anyone, never even said a bad thing about anyone. Betsy just wanted to live her life openly, as the person she was. Why is there so much gay hating, Reverend? Can you tell me why someone killed my baby just because she was a lesbian?"

Nikki felt for Mrs. Frank's grief, but also needed to set the facts straight. "I don't know why people hate, and I will never understand gay-bashing. I do know that Betsy was not killed because she was a lesbian. I'm not sure where you got that idea. If the police said something…or someone you spoke with led you to believe she was killed because of her sexual orientation, that wasn't the case."

There was no response from the other end of the line, so Nikki tried to explain. "There is a serial killer loose in Sheridan. He drugs young women with GHB, and then he…" Nikki searched for the kindest way to tell the facts. "Then he attacks and kills the victim. Three women have been killed in the last few days. Two of them were students at St. David University, and one was a doctor at the local hospital."

Nikki took a breath before continuing, "We think the killer was looking for Charity Daniels when he found Betsy…" Nikki hesitated, "I'm still trying to understand this senseless murder myself. We don't know why he killed Betsy. Maybe he thought she would recognize him. Maybe he thought she was Charity. The police don't have much worked out yet on this case."

Mrs. Frank's silence was over. "Why didn't the University warn people of this GHB killer," she shot back, angrily. "Betsy would have said something about the warning. I speak…spoke to her every night. They should have warned the girls."

"I agree with you," Nikki answered. "I think their reason was that they didn't want to start a panic. I don't agree with that reason."

"I'll be talking to that University…and so will my lawyer." Her anger was already calming back down and turning once again to sorrow. "Thank you for explaining those things to me. You see Reverend…" Mrs. Frank choked on her words again, and Nikki knew a confession was coming. "I'm a lesbian too," she finally said in a hushed voice. "I'm in the closet and always have been. I tried to change…with the marriage and the baby…not that I regret that part of my life. But when Betsy came out to me…well…I just blamed myself…for ruining her life. I just thought she would always be as hidden and miserable as I was."

Mrs. Frank stopped to compose herself again. "Betsy was never really miserable. She loved being who she was. She was never afraid or ashamed like I was. Do you know…I never told her…never told her about myself. My baby died never knowing that my fear of getting beat up or hated because I'm gay kept me from telling my own little girl that we were both lesbians."

Elizabeth Frank started to cry. Nikki could hear the heart-wrenching sobs over the phone. She wished she was there in person to console this poor woman. "Mrs. Frank, please don't blame yourself for any of this. Betsy knew you were a lesbian," Nikki added, as gently as she could.

"What?" Elizabeth Frank sounded shocked. "What did you just say?"

Nikki said another quick prayer for guidance and went on. "Betsy knew you were a lesbian. She mentioned that fact several times at different meetings of the Gay and Lesbian Organization. Betsy also knew it was difficult for you to admit that openly, and it didn't matter to her. She was very proud of you, and she loved you for who you were. She loved you, Mrs. Frank."

"So, she knew." Mrs. Frank gave a little laugh. "My Betsy knew all along. I'm so glad, and I'm so proud of her. She wasn't just a daughter, you know. Betsy was an inspiration to me...a brave and wonderful gay woman."

There was silence at both ends of the phone for a few minutes, then Mrs. Frank asked, "I would like you to do a memorial service here in Sheridan, Reverend Barnes. This is where most of Betsy's friends live. And I know she would like to invite the members of the Gay and Lesbian Organization. We don't have much family. Her grandmother and my brother are about the only ones who were close to us. I've already asked them, and they'll come down. I've reserved the University Chapel for next Wednesday. Could you officiate at the service?"

"I would be very pleased to lead the service," Nikki answered. "Perhaps we could get together tomorrow and plan what you would like?"

"Tomorrow won't be a good day," Mrs. Frank answered. "I'm flying home with Betsy's body tomorrow, but you can call me in the evening. My number in Canton is 456-786-9002. I would appreciate a call tomorrow, Reverend…I'm thinking I'll want to say something about Betsy being a lesbian. I think she'd like that from me. Maybe you could help me find the right words."

"I'd be glad to help," Nikki answered. "I'll call you tomorrow evening, and I'll remember you both in my prayers. Take care, Mrs. Frank. Goodbye."

Nikki hung up the phone and sat back in her chair. She closed her eyes in prayerful meditation, and that was when she heard something…almost giggling…coming from the living room. There seemed to be rather carefree giggling coming from the somber and serious Detective Ramos, as she made her business calls in the living room.

I'm just being nosy, Nikki thought as she leaned over in her chair in order to get closer to the short hallway separating the office and living room. She leaned so far; she almost fell off the chair and had to catch herself from falling over.

Since this approach didn't work, Nikki just got up and stood by the office door that led to the living room. She tilted her head like a radar dish, and Ana's softly spoken conversation came through loud and clear.

"Yes, the words, 'Bite me' have been flashing in my brain all morning," Ana laughed. "You can say that again…but *unbelievable,* that doesn't even begin to describe it."

Nikki stuck her head partially into the hall and tried to catch more of this interesting discussion. *Doesn't sound like a business call to me,* she thought mischievously to herself.

"I don't think that's possible," Ana went on. "I'm going to be tied up today and probably tonight. I can't promise anything until we catch this killer…or killers." She paused, then started to laugh again. "Yeah, and you're a killer too…but this one is a son-of-a-bitch."

Her tone turned serious. "I'm going to tell you again, be careful. Especially when you're around the University or Tailfeathers. Be *very* careful, because he's out there, and he shows no mercy. He's crazy, and he doesn't like beautiful women." With this last comment, she laughed softly again.

Too far away to see any facial expressions, Nikki just picked up bits and pieces of the hushed conversation. Frustrated by what she was missing and feeling foolish for listening in on someone else's conversation, she finally started walking down the hall toward the living room.

Ana heard her footsteps and quickly ended the conversation. "Have to go now," Ana said quickly. "Maybe it's possible. Maybe. I'll call later."

She flipped her cell phone closed and stood up so quickly that the sofa cushion rose underneath Fluffy, asleep at the opposite end.

"Catch up on any of those important police calls?" Nikki asked smugly, as she walked over and started to pet the sleeping Fluffy.

Not at all thrown by the remark, Ana answered in her serious, professional demeanor. "The last one was a personal call, but I have made some progress in the case this morning."

Nikki sat next to Fluffy and continued petting the cat. "Can you share anything with me at this point or is it confidential?"

Ana sat back down, at the opposite end of the sofa and picked her notebook up off the coffee table. "I don't mind sharing police information with you, Nikki. Sergeant Mullen has made it clear that you are an unofficial part of the investigation. He respects your insight, and because of that, I do."

Nikki was a little embarrassed by this confidence they both have in her, but her curiosity won out. "So what did you find out?" she asked.

"I called the A-One garage and spoke to the owner," Ana began. "He was the one working the night Talia Carter was murdered. He confirmed that two people walked to his garage that night, and that they rented a loaner car from him, because he couldn't fix theirs until the following Monday."

"Well, that gives the Brownings their alibi," Nikki remarked.

"Not completely," Ana said, still thinking about the call. "There's just something about that couple and the alibi that keeps bothering me."

Nikki shrugged her shoulders and commented, "You're the second one today, who's told me they don't trust Ted Browning. What's wrong with the alibi?"

"I know a little about cars," Ana began again. "My father and two brothers all sell cars; it's a family business. I learned a little about fixing cars when I hung around with the mechanics. Anyway, I tracked down the owner of the A-One garage when Ted Browning found his receipts and dropped them off at the station yesterday afternoon. I called the garage owner back and asked a few more questions, like what was wrong with the car.

He told me he was a little suspicious about the car trouble…but not at first. The car would crank, but it wouldn't catch. He thought the problem was the battery or a fuse, but eventually he found it. One of the wires to the distributor cap was broken. The thing is, the break was so neat and clean, it looked like someone had snipped the wire with a clipper. By that time, it was too late to send for the part he needed to fix the car. The auto parts store he buys from was already closed."

"So the car was deliberately sabotaged," Nikki said. "Now that is interesting."

"That's not the only thing that bothers me." Ana flipped another page of her notebook, before going on. "I asked him to describe the couple who rented the car. He said the first couple was dressed alike, jeans, dark jackets, and baseball caps. The guy had dark hair and dark eyes. Could very well be Browning. The girl had short dark hair."

Ana looked up at Nikki. "Lindsey Browning could have put her hair up under the cap, so it looked short, but it really isn't dark. Talia's hair was short and dark. Then the garage owner said to me that a different girl came back with the guy to pick the car up."

"What?" Nikki jumped in. "Did you say Ted Browning came back with a different woman?"

"That's what the garage owner said," Ana tried to explain. "He can't be sure of course, but he thinks the owner came back with a blonde woman. He said it was hard to tell because they came back all dressed up in business clothes. He thinks she might have been a different woman."

Ana stopped and looked at Nikki again. "He made a point of telling me, he wouldn't want to swear to it in court, but he thinks she was different."

"I'm not sure hair color is enough to kill Browning's alibi," Nikki said, as she got up from the sofa. "He's still not high on my list, but the distributor wire problem is interesting."

"Well, I'm just about to call the Sergeant and tell him what I found out," Ana said, flipping open her phone.

"And I'm off again to finish my paperwork and my grades," Nikki countered. "See if Max is available for lunch; otherwise, we order out."

With this last remark, Nikki went back to the office to hit the books.

CHAPTER 15

▼

Ana took a slow walk around Ginni and Nikki's bedroom. First, she pushed aside the curtains to look behind each one. Next, she opened the large walk-in closet and checked behind the clothes. Lastly, she got down on the floor and looked under the king-size bed.

Nikki was grateful for the Detective's vigilance, but all these precautions brought back the reality that someone was trying to kill her…and Ginni. Once Ana left the room, Nikki went to the closet and reached up to an overhead shelf. She took down an old, dented ammunition box and put it on her bed.

She looked at the padlock and moved to the metal, Army chest under a side-window. Nikki bent down and removed the Vietnamese lamp and oriental cloth that rested on the chest. Then she opened the creaking top and made a mental note to lubricate the hinges. As she fished around in the front right corner, she couldn't help but remember her tour of duty during the Vietnam War.

Most of her flashbacks were gone now…had been for almost three years. But she could hear the gunfire today…she saw the dense foliage surrounding the small dirt road to Xuan Loc. There was a tree down in the road…Max stopped the jeep…but before they could get out to move it, they were surrounded by Viet Cong…the enemy rising out of the underbrush…grass on their shoulders…on their hats.

Max was hit before he could reach his rifle…she dragged him out of range…grabbed the rifle…cracking of gunfire…sound of bullets exploding…shooting back…hold them off…firing at will. Firing again…spraying the whole area with bullets.

Nikki covered both ears with her hands and tried to block out the noise of the gunfire…she felt the three hits…first in the back…a searing pain…the second in the side…a fiery poker that goes in but never comes out…she fell on Max…tried to protect him…a third bullet, right in the chest…losing consciousness…more gunfire…behind us…our troopers…an American recon unit…pushing back the Viet Cong with more gunfire…bullets exploding everywhere…

The memory of passing out jolted Nikki back to the present. She pulled a key ring out of the Army chest and moved back to the ammunition box on the bed. Quickly unlocking the padlock, she opened the box.

Two guns and two boxes of ammunition were in the box. She took a long look at the two guns, her Army issue forty-five and the Twenty-five caliber Browning she bought on the black market in Saigon.

She took out the Browning and thought to herself, *this gun is too small for that maniac.* She put it back into the box and carefully lifted out her forty-five. She checked the clip. It was full, so she snapped it back in place and laid the gun on the bed. Methodically, she locked the ammo box again and returned it to the closet.

Still following a careful military routine, she returned the key to the chest and put the cloth and lamp back on top. That taken care of, she finally changed into a clean denim shirt and pressed chinos. But just before she put on her brown blazer, she took the forty-five, checked the safety again, and tucked it in her belt, behind her back.

She checked in the mirror for any telltale signs of the gun. Seeing none, she went back to the office for her briefcase. Ana was waiting for her at the back door. "Here's the plan, Nikki," Ana explained. "We walk out together, very slowly. Stay right at my side and look around as we get into the car. When we get to the University, I'll park as close to the Administration Building as I can. Again, we walk in together. Once we're around other people, I think we can relax a little. He never seems to strike with others around. He likes to get his victims alone."

Nikki knew the information Ana was giving her was important for staying alive, and she tried to make a mental note of all the warnings. Nikki locked the door while Ana scanned the parking area, yard, and street. Nikki turned and scanned the same areas, as they walked toward Ana's car.

Nikki tried to tap into her instincts. They hadn't failed her yet, but suddenly, a shiver ran down her back, resting right where the forty-five was tucked. She looked around and noticed nothing out of the ordinary…but something didn't feel right.

Turning around again, she thought she saw an upstairs curtain in her neighbor's townhouse move…ever so slightly. Her neighbors had already left on vacation…to visit a son in Texas.

Nothing was moving there now. Nothing was moving anywhere. Ana followed Nikki's glance, but she didn't see anything either.

"It must be the jitters. I'm just jumpy and probably seeing things," Nikki thought to herself. She made eye contact with Ana and they drove off toward the University.

*   *   *   *

An overcast day in early May meant that winter was still fighting spring for dominance. It also meant that many days were still hung with grey clouds. Winter was winning, as Ana and Nikki drove up to the back of Sterling Hall.

Grades were due before five, so Nikki was cutting the deadline close. They walked together into the building and finally heard sounds of life. Several extended semester classes were going on in the few classrooms located in this building, and a line of students had formed outside the

Dean's office. Each student seemed to be waving a probation letter they were trying to intercept before it was sent home to their parents.

Nikki and Ana walked around the line and made their way to the Record's Office. The Registrar and three staff members were holding down a busy fort. Both of the Boccomo sisters were ahead of Nikki. They turned in their grades with lengthy explanations about pluses and minuses, and their grand gestures and size once again impressed Nikki.

She and Ana took their place in line, and Nikki started to rummage through her briefcase for the needed papers and forms. "Joining the rest of us, are you?" A squeaky voice said from behind Ana. A wafer-thin skinned hand reached from around the Detective and tapped Nikki on the shoulder.

"Running late too, are you Professor Barnes?" Mr. Hinkleberry squeaked, but before he could continue, Ana had locked onto his wrist.

"Ouch! Ouch! You're hurting me young lady!" he responded, waving his umbrella at Ana.

"He's okay," Nikki interjected quickly. "This is Professor Hinkleberry. He teaches philosophy. Professor, this is Detective Ramos of the Sheridan Police Department."

"Oh, I see." The Professor sniped, as he rubbed his sore wrist. "So you're one of those liberated feminists," Hinkleberry directed this squeak to Ana. "Did you think I was butting in line? You aren't going to arrest me, are you?"

Before Ana could respond, Nikki jumped in again. "Why don't you just go ahead of me, Professor?" Nikki made room for the rather tottering old man to move up in the line. Then she whispered to Ana. "He retired about eight years ago but forgets he's not teaching. He was a well-respected scholar in his day. Not only that, he could recite in chronological order, all the Kings of England and their reigns, by heart."

By this time, Hinkleberry was tapping one of the Baccomo sisters on the shoulder "You look like a beautiful pair of Rubenesque bookends," he squeaked at the women.

Everyone within earshot laughed, and the sisters took turns squeezing the little man in their arms. Greetings finished, they left, and the registrar gave Hinkleberry some requested forms while reassuring him that all his grades were in.

As he turned to leave, Hinkleberry once more addressed Ana. "Did you know that historically women are the fiercest warriors of all? Feminist policewomen are nothing compared to Queen Boudicca. It was in 62 A.D. that Boudicca, a Celtic woman warrior, led the Britons against the Romans."

He threw Nikki a big smile and left the office. Nikki looked at Ana and they both laughed. "Maybe you're a throw-back to Queen Boudicca," Nikki said.

"Maybe you are," Ana responded dryly.

Nikki shared some friendly conversation with Trudy Millworth, the Registrar, while she turned in all the necessary papers. She and Ana then left the office to make their way back down the hall to the rear parking lot.

Just as they again reached the long line of students, a woman's voice screaming for help could be heard down the long hallway. The screams seemed to come from one of the side offices, further down the hall.

"Stay right here, by all these people!" Ana yelled at Nikki, as she snapped open her shoulder holster and ran down the hall toward the screaming.

Nikki did just what she was told. She moved to the wall across from the line of students and waited. A door next to where she was standing opened abruptly, and Nikki heard that now familiar power wheelchair buzz, as Taylor Fleming rolled into the hall.

Taylor looked toward the commotion, where a crowd had now gathered and didn't notice Nikki standing next to her. The screaming had stopped and the students were getting back in line.

"Hello Taylor," Nikki said calmly, trying not to frighten her.

Taylor quickly turned her wheelchair to face Nikki and smiled, "Professor Barnes...I mean Nikki. What are you doing here?"

"Grades are due today," Nikki said rather repentantly.

"How's your head?" Taylor asked in a sincere tone. "And how's Ginni? I finally realized that murdered doctor was the friend she introduced me to at the awards ceremony. Ginni must be very upset."

Nikki was taken somewhat aback by the change in Taylor. This must be the person Ginni was talking about, not the sexy, flirtatious Taylor that kept popping up when Nikki was alone with her. "Ginni's okay. You know…," Nikki tried to answer. "Ginni buries herself in her work. Then she can deal with things like this."

"That sounds like the Ginni I know," Taylor said, laughing. Then she pointedly asked, "Are you here alone?"

That seemed like an odd question to Nikki. "No," she answered carefully, watching all responses. "I'm here with Ana Ramos. She just went down to see what all the screaming was about."

"Oh," Taylor forced nonchalance. "Detective Ramos. How nice."

Taylor suddenly seemed almost nervous to Nikki. Nervous or giddy, something was rather strange in her behavior. "Well, maybe you and Detective Ramos could join me for a cup of coffee before you leave. Why don't you meet me in the faculty break room at the end of the hall?"

Then, she powered her wheelchair down the hall and entered an open door on the right. Nikki still looked puzzled when Ana returned with an explanation. "Someone took a girl's wallet. She thinks it happened while she was waiting in line, but it could've been anytime or anywhere. She started accusing everyone around her. The Security Officer is taking care of her."

Nikki thought this was a good time to play a hunch. "I just ran into Taylor Fleming," she said, smiling. "She wants us to stop in the break room for a coffee. What do you think?"

Ana tried not to show any emotion, but a small wrinkle of a smile escaped.

Aha! Nikki thought. *There is something going on between Ana and Taylor!* "Well?" Nikki asked again. "Shall we go to the break room and get some coffee with Taylor?"

"I...I...think that would be okay," Ana stumbled on a few words.

Suddenly, there was more screaming from the same end of the hall as before. "Detective! Detective! I think you better come and see this," the Security Guard called to Ana. "There's a woman down...in the lavatory," he screamed down the hall. "I think she's hurt!"

Ana turned to Nikki. "Go to the break room with Taylor and don't leave that room. Do you understand? Close the door, don't let anyone in and don't leave that room!"

Nikki nodded her head, "Okay, I'll stay with Taylor. We won't move, and we won't let anyone in."

Ana flipped open her cell phone and called for back up. She ran toward the guard, while Nikki walked quickly to the break room.

As Nikki got closer to the open door, she could hear two voices inside. She recognized Taylor's immediately, and the other voice also sounded vaguely familiar.

*   *   *   *

After Taylor powered her wheelchair into the break room, she noticed a tall, beefy, male student sprawled out on the leather sofa. His dirty jeans were rolled up once and his right leg was draped over the arm of the sofa. He spilled coffee all over the seat cushions, as he slurped from a stoneware mug.

Taylor was still several feet away from him and verbally took him to task for his bad behavior. "For the fourteenth time," Taylor repeated herself, showing she had reached the end of her patience. "Students are not allowed in the faculty break room. You will have to leave right now, or I will call Security."

"Should I be afraid of the old retards you call Security," Bradley Davis laughed back at her. "I've stood in that line for twenty minutes. I need coffee, and this is where the coffee is."

Taylor took another deep breath and started again. "If you were standing in that line, you are already in trouble. With your attitude, you're probably being tossed out of the University, so why not be a nice young man and leave? Don't make any more trouble for yourself."

With this last comment, Taylor pushed the power button on the arm of her chair and wheeled toward the phone, located on a desk in the corner of the room. She reached the phone and turned once more to face Bradley. "I am calling Security."

Bradley was on his feet in one quick movement. "You gimp bitch!" he snarled threateningly. "Who do you think you are? Just because they give you some parking tag, so you can take the good spots doesn't get any sympathy from me. You're a bunch of crybabies. Why don't you just die and make the world a better place!"

He was yelling now and moving closer to Taylor. "Where did you get that fancy chair? I suppose the government paid for it with my old man's hard earned money. You rag-doll bitches belong legless. Maybe it will keep you home. I think all women should have their legs cut off!"

Taylor was too shocked to move. She couldn't believe some of the things she was hearing. She picked up the phone and started pushing the 891 Security extension. Bradley moved his hulky six-foot-four frame next to her and stomped on the phone cord, instantly tearing it out of the wall jack.

Taylor spun the wheelchair around, so she was facing him. His dark eyes burred holes through her. She always felt she could handle anything, but this altercation had her speechless and frightened. Pushing the reverse button, she wheeled backwards toward the door.

At this point, Nikki had finally reached the doorway. She caught the tail end of this heated exchange.

Bradley hadn't noticed Nikki yet because she was too far into the hallway and still part of the background. His full attention was on Taylor. He watched her eyes follow his hand, as he deliberately poured the rest of his coffee on the floor. Then he forcefully threw the mug at the wall behind him and let it shatter into tiny pieces.

Taylor locked onto his eyes now and tried to figure out what he would do next. He took another step toward her and started again. "I bet you're a Jew, aren't you? You're one of those money-grabbing kikes. We tried to get rid of you once, now we have to do it all over again. Are you a gimpy hymie?"

He was almost next to her now, and Taylor's hand started to sweat so much that her finger slipped when she tried to push the wheelchair button. She was almost frozen by her fear.

Bradley bent over her and screamed into her face, "The world doesn't need any more crippled cunts!"

He was too close for Nikki's comfort now, so she stepped into the room and walked next to Taylor. "That's enough Bradley Davis!" she demanded, getting his full attention.

"You're one sick boy!" she added, causing him to stand up straight and finally take notice.

"I warned you once about your fascist bullying. No one likes a prejudiced pea-brain." Nikki gained strength with each barb she threw. "We don't like you...and we don't want your kind at St. David University."

Bradley gave Nikki a look she had seen before...in Nam. It was the look of one of the Grunts who spent too much time In Country. Someone who separated from their humanity and was now only a killing machine. In Nam, it would take four corpsman to hold these guys down...until they sedated him...she didn't have any sedation for Bradley.

Bradley surprised her by turning nonchalantly and heading for the door. This was really out of character for Bradley. Where were the snotty comebacks? Where was the threatening posture? What was going on?

Nikki got careless. She was thrown off guard by his behavior. Bradley got to the door and slammed it shut. Then he turned around quickly and faced her. "You dike bitch!"

Bradley started coming at Nikki. "I'm gonna show you just how hard a real man can punch, and you queer little piece of shit, you're gonna yell uncle by the time I'm done with you."

Nikki's body went on full alert. Her Army training clicked in, and she checked the perimeter for an escape route. Seeing none, she prepared to fight, but first she whispered to Taylor. "When I get his attention, get out of here fast. Get help."

Taylor was still frightened but moved out of the path of the two adversaries. Not wanting to bring any attention to herself, she manually wheeled the chair toward the door.

Bradley was only a few feet away from Nikki now. He swung his right fist with all the power of his two hundred and forty pounds, but Nikki was too quick for him. She stepped back and over to the left. The punch missed, and the power behind it caused Bradley to lose his footing and almost fall.

This was enough of a distraction for Taylor, she opened the door and powered through it into the hallway. She raced for the crowd of people gathered by the lavatory, and tried to scream over their chatter. "Help! Someone help me! Please!"

Inside the Break Room, Bradley paid no attention to the escaping Taylor. All his energy was directed on Nikki, who had to go through him to get to the door. "Don't even think about getting out, dike!" he threatened again, as he stood to his full height and hiked up his pants.

Nikki thought it might be time to try some diplomacy. "Now Bradley, you don't want to get yourself into any more trouble than you're already in."

Maybe she should have tried the priest line? "Violence never solves anything. Maybe we can talk this out...resolve our differences."

"Resolve this, bitch!" Bradley yelled and lunged at her again. This time he grabbed her by the jacket and lifted her right off the ground. He held her several inches off the ground with one hand and drew back the other into a fist. This gave Nikki just enough wiggle room. She drew back her leg and kneed him in the groin.

He was a tough one though and before he grabbed his injured privates, he smashed Nikki against the wall. She hit the wall with the back of her head...right on the stitches. Her cut opened up again and a streak of red followed her falling body down the white wall.

Bradley recovered before she did and leapt across the room to where she awkwardly tried to get on her feet.

"You like kicking so much," he yelled at her. "How do you like this one!" He aimed a kick right at her mid-section, but again her training instincts kicked in. She grabbed his foot and twisted it with every inch of strength she could muster. He went over again with a loud yell.

Nikki's head was beginning to remind her of her age and slower healing time. She also remembered the need to retreat from battle from time to time. This was one of those times. She was back on her feet, ran past Bradley, and made straight for the door.

Again, she underestimated Bradley's strength over his brains. He popped up like a jack-in-the-box and grabbed her leg as she passed. One quick twist and she was down on the floor again.

He used his old wrestling crawl and was next to her in a second. Then he was on top of her, sitting on her legs, pinning down her arms, and yelling in her face. "Thought you got away, didn't ya, Professor Dike Barnes?" He spit the words in her face.

Nikki could feel his breath on her face and smell a good supply of whiskey on that breath. Maybe he really needed that cup of coffee.

He lifted her up a few inches from the floor and slammed her back down, hitting that bleeding wound again. "You're not so smart now, are ya?" he yelled again. "How ya gonna get out of this one? There's no Dean or student dike fan club to help you this time."

Then he put his full weight down on Nikki. The heaviness almost caused her to lose her breath. She took short, shallow gasps, and he raged on, "I hate you faggot women. I think we should kill you all!"

Nikki couldn't move…could hardly breathe with all that weight. She could feel her gun cutting into her back, as he pressed her flatter onto the floor. *How ironic*, she thought to herself. *I have the gun and can't even use it.* That was another thing she was taught in the military. Don't rely totally on your weapon. Use your brain. There will be times when you can't use your gun. This was one of those times.

"I'm gonna give you an extra present now," Bradley snarled, flashing his lunatic smile. He let go of one of her arms, but still maintained the full body press. He reached into his back pocket and took out a four-inch gravity knife. With a flick of his hand, it opened.

Nikki's adrenaline went into overdrive. She took her now free hand, extended her fingers straight out into a Karate spearhand position and with all her focused strength, thrust the fingers into Bradley's eye…hitting him once…then again…in quick stabbing movements to his eye.

He yelled and tried to stab her with the knife. Again, she used her only free hand and grabbed his wrist. She knew she couldn't win this hand-wrestling match, but she put all her muscle into keeping the knife away from her chest.

"My eye! My eye! You bitch. You blinded me!" He grabbed at the bleeding eye with both his hands. *A fatal mistake!* Nikki now had another hand free and a few inches of twisting room. She arched her back, slid her hand under her back and pulled out her gun.

Nikki shoved the gun into Bradley's balls and yelled, "I'll blow you away in two seconds, if you don't get off me!"

Bradley dropped the knife. "You blinded me," he started to whine and caress his bleeding eye with both hands.

"I'm going to kill you!" Nikki yelled again. "If you don't move, right now!"

Bradley still held his eye with both hands while he heaved himself off Nikki. "I need to go to the hospital," he pouted in a childish whine.

"You need a mental hospital," Nikki growled, as she got to her feet. She kept the gun leveled at Bradley. "What were you going to do with that knife?" she demanded, moving closer to him. "Just what were you going to do?" she yelled again.

Defiant as ever, Bradley let go of his eye and stared right at her, as he threatened, "I was gonna cut your face up…and then maybe cut…some other parts."

"You bastard!" Nikki felt her control slipping away. "I should just blow your head off!"

"That's enough Nikki," Ana Ramos ordered, as she entered the room with her gun drawn. "I'll take it from here."

She deliberately moved in front of Nikki's gun. "Face down on the floor," she ordered Bradley.

"My eye is bleeding! She blinded me!" he started to whine again.

"We'll get you to a doctor," Ana said, pushing him down on the floor and pulling back his wrists for the handcuffs. "You have the right to remain silent…"

As Ana started to read Bradley his rights, Nikki felt all the energy drain from her body. She turned away and walked over to the sofa. She tucked her gun back in her belt and dropped down into a corner of the sofa. The bump on the back of her head was wet and sticky to her touch.

Taylor wheeled into the room and over to Nikki. "Are you okay, Nikki? Did he hurt you?"

"I'm fine," Nikki answered bitterly, as she let some of the anger return. "I'll be even better when that piece of garbage is in jail."

CHAPTER 16

▼

Nikki was sitting up on a cold examining table, staring at the bright stainless steel supply cupboard. Medical attention was not a favorite pastime for Nikki, and her constant wiggling sent this message out loud and clear.

"Ouch!" She grimaced and pulled away from Ginni, who continued to deftly stitch the head gash closed.

Ginni used her gentlest voice and said, "Sorry, honey. The opening isn't as bad as you think. Only a few stitches popped."

"Thank you, Doctor Clayton," Nikki responded petulantly. "The thought of any opening letting all my hot air escape is not a comforting one."

Ginni giggled at Nikki's joke and finished cutting the last stitch. "There you are, good as new." She went to pat Nikki on the back and felt the gun stuck in Nikki's belt.

"Just what is this?" Her tone changed immediately. "I thought we had a deal? No getting involved in dangerous missions and no guns."

Nikki twisted around and gave Ginni a weak smile. "Would you believe that's a widow's hump?" she said jokingly.

Ginni held back a smile and worked on her anger instead. "That's a little low for a widow's hump." She unconsciously tapped her right foot. "It has the shape of a Forty-five."

Nikki hunted for a comeback but decided some of her cleverness seeped out the gash with the hot air. "I can explain...," she began.

"I'm waiting," Ginni continued to tap her foot.

"I'm afraid of this killer," Nikki said. "He's trying to kill me...and you. I just decided not to take any chances. I only took the gun to protect myself, and...and...as it turned out, I needed the gun to save myself from being carved up by crazy Bradley Davis."

Ginni's foot fell silent. She moved a few steps closer to Nikki, took her in her arms, and planted a big, sensual kiss on Nikki's lips. "I'm worried about this killer too," she said softly, not breaking the embrace. "I'm glad you had the gun when Bradley came at you. Even Taylor thinks you're a heroine."

Nikki was embarrassed. "I'm not a heroine. I'm just lucky."

Ginni stepped back and crossed her arms. "Do you think Bradley is the killer?"

Nikki hopped down from the table. "That's just it," she tried to explain. "What Bradley did doesn't fit any of the behavior of the killer. Plus, he was alone. I still believe the killer works with someone."

"The girl in the lavatory had a bad reaction to GHB," Ginni continued. "She said someone in the student line passed her a soda that must have been drugged. Another student confirmed that Bradley was passing around free bottles of soda."

"I think someone laced that girl's drink after Bradley opened it," Nikki said. "I think the killer was there...waiting for a chance to get at me."

Ginni moved next to Nikki and hugged her again. "So you think the killer was in the hallway too?"

Nikki looked into Ginni's eyes and in a very serious tone answered, "I think the killer is watching both of us...all the time. That's why I'm keeping the gun close to me...and why I'm keeping you close to me."

"Unfortunately," Ginni broke the embrace and moved to her black medical bag on the counter. "We may have to be separated for a few more hours tonight. I need to cover for Sheba at Mercy Hospital. I feel

I owe it to her. I'm still feeling a little guilty about her death. She was wearing my lab coat."

"You're not responsible," Nikki quickly jumped in. "But I know I can't talk you out of working tonight. So...please keep the officer covering you in sight. Don't go anywhere in the hospital where you might be alone...and hurry home."

Three short knocks on the examining room door made both Nikki and Ginni jump. Max poked his head into the room and asked, "Hey Nik. Is it okay if I come in?"

"Sure, Max. Come on in," Nikki threw her old friend a little smile.

Max moved his bulky body into the room. "How ya doing?" he asked. "I heard this Davis guy gave you quite a workout."

"He broke open her head stitches," Ginni answered for Nikki. "She got her usual bumps and bruises...which to me signifies that she won."

"I'm fine, Max," Nikki said defensively. "That Bradley Davis is crazy."

"We know he's drunk, and we're running a blood test for drugs," Max explained. "Once he sobers up, we'll see if he's crazy too. Ramos booked him for assault with a deadly weapon, attempted battery, attempted rape and I think she has a few more to tag on."

Max moved closer to Nikki and gave her an awkward hug. "You sure you're doing okay?" he asked again. "I heard all about what happened."

Nikki broke from the embrace and self-consciously said, "I'm fine. I'm great, really, Max." Then she punched his arm and added, "I'm still in pretty good shape you know. Almost as fit as when I was in the Army."

With this last comment, both Max and Ginni burst into laughter.

"Okay. Okay." Nikki tried to quell the laughter. "Maybe I'm not in that good a shape, but I kicked his ass. Didn't I?"

"You sure did," Max replied, as he put his arm around his old friend. "And now, I'm going to drive you home. Ana is off for the evening, so I plan to leave Officer Carbone parked out front of your place…unless you want him in the house with you."

"No," Nikki answered quickly. "I could use a little down time with no one but Fluffy and myself. What about Davis? Will you get to question him before his parent's lawyer gets there?"

"I'm going right back to headquarters after I drop you off," Max explained. "I plan to find out if he's our killer before the lawyer gets there."

He gave Nikki his full attention. "What's your take on him, Nik? You think he's our serial killer."

Nikki shook her head. "I don't think he's the guy. I think he's a nut…and maybe capable of murder, especially when he's flying on some dope. But I don't think he's the killer. Like I told Ginni, I think our killer has an accomplice with him when he attacks women."

"I don't think he's our boy either," Max said. "That whole attack on you just doesn't have the same MO as the serial murderer. I'm looking at the drugged girl in the lavatory as a possible victim, but I'm not sure Davis drugged her either."

Max took a few steps toward the door, "For now, I'm getting you home. When I finish interrogating Davis, I'll check in on you and compare notes. Then we should know for sure if he's the one."

*   *   *   *

Max dropped Nikki off and walked her into the house. He cautiously checked every room, upstairs and downstairs, along with every window and door. He also stopped to give Officer Carbone some last minute orders.

Nikki watched Max drive away, and then closed the front window blinds and moved to the kitchen. Her growling stomach had been announcing it was feeding time for several hours. She opened the refrigerator door and hunted around for something edible.

There were the four-day-old egg rolls. They evoked an image of solidified grease and Chinese cabbage gliding through one's arteries. Last week's macaroni and cheese was sprinkled in greenish-blue, and Nikki knew it wasn't made with Roquefort. That just left a few table-spoons of the unnamed casserole. She popped the lid and one whiff told her the casserole shall remain forever unnamed.

She dumped the casserole contents in the garbage along with the egg rolls and macaroni. Holding her nose, she rinsed the bowls and quickly placed them in the dishwasher. Her work here was finished.

She plopped down into a kitchen chair and rested her elbows on the table while she cradled her face in her hands. "Do I have enough energy to think of something to eat? Do I really have enough energy to prepare the something I think of? Should I just eat those candy bars Ginni hid in the China cabinet?"

No answers came readily, so it appeared the candy bars won out. But as luck would have it, the doorbell rang just as Nikki got up. Her first reaction was alarm and her hand was already on the gun handle behind her back. Then she realized Officer Carbone would see anyone at the front door, but what if this was the two minutes it took him to drive around the building and check out the back?

She took no chances. Drawing the gun out slowly, she checked the clip, snapped it back in place, and took off the safety. She held the gun at arms length and made her way down the hall to the door. She peered through the peephole...and almost cried out...in happiness. Another prayer answered before it was said!

Nikki quickly flipped the safety back on and tucked the gun under her blazer again. Then she flung open the door and smiled warmly at a package-laden Barrett.

"Hi Nicolette. Heard you could use some food." Barrett laughed and threw Nikki a big smile.

"Come in! Come in!" Nikki practically pulled her in by the sleeve. "I can't believe you're here. I mean...I was just trying to think of something to cook...I mean...somehow cooking and you go together...I mean..." Nikki fumbled for the right words.

Barrett walked toward the kitchen with her bundles and bags. "It's okay, Nicolette. Ginni gave me a call from the hospital and said she wanted to order some food for you."

Barrett started placing the bags and packages on the table. "So I just told her, 'Leave it all to me-your personal chef.'"

She looked at Nikki and added, "I don't think she appreciates my sense of humor."

"Of course she does," Nikki lied. "She knows what a great chef you are, and how much I appreciate your talent."

Barrett just gave her an "Oh, yeah, right." look. Then she began her food magic. "It doesn't matter," Barrett went on. "When I heard you were hungry, I knew just what to do."

Nikki took her place at the table and clasped her hands together. She resembled a five-year-old, as she asked, "What's in the bags? What did you bring? So what are we eating?"

Barrett was fond of those who appreciated a good chef. In Nikki's case she was more than fond of this woman who loved her cooking. She opened the first shopping bag and brought out a small, French-white casserole dish. "First, we have fresh spring vegetables in a nutmeg-brie sauce."

She moved on to the next package, watching Nikki's eyes grow larger in anticipation. "Next, a small loaf of my home-baked, sun-dried tomato bread. Oh good, it's still warm, and I brought some herbed olive oil for dipping."

Nikki's mouth began to water, and she continued a silent litany of thank you prayers to the God who oversees all, including delicious food for humble servants and hungry, beat-up priests.

Barrett opened the last package. "Because I feel you need some vitamins that vegetables cannot provide, I brought a tarragon-roasted chicken breast...high in vitamin B-12...in paprika au jus."

Perfect! Nikki's brain screamed, while her eyes were fixed on the food. Any hope of speech or movement was lost in anticipation of the food.

Barrett was familiar with this response in Nikki, and although she appreciated a little chef-worship, she wished Nikki would sometimes see her as a woman too. Meanwhile, she accepted the situation and prepared the table for two.

Finally, Barrett served the food and joined Nikki at the table. They ate in silence for the first few minutes. "Oh, thank you, thank you, Barrett," Nikki mumbled, still chewing merrily. "This is heavenly...just wonderful...you are such a talent."

"You're welcome," Barrett answered, as she critically tasted each serving. "You're always welcome, Nicolette."

Nikki finally had enough food to satiate her hunger pangs and realized Barrett was in one of her "I'm mooning over my professor," moods. She tried to run interference and keep this a pleasant moment between friends.

She put her fork down and looked up at Barrett. "You're a very good friend to take the time to run all this delicious food over to my house." Nikki spoke sincerely.

"I don't mind doing things for you, Nicolette." Barrett smiled back at Nikki. "I'm always glad when we can share some time together...alone."

Oh! Oh! Warning signals were going up for Nikki. The time had come for a counter move. "How's your mother?" she asked in a voice higher than normal.

Barrett just smiled, knowing full well that Nikki was trying to change the subject. "She's fine. As a matter of fact, she's almost finished with her very long business trip in Vietnam."

The thought of Trang in Vietnam sent more memories speeding through Nikki's mind. It was hard for her to believe that the prostitute she almost killed and then paid to be her Mama San turned out to be Barrett's mother. She could still feel the attraction she felt all those years ago. That's why she gave Trang the money to escape to Malaysia with her Amerasian child.

"Did she succeed in getting visas for her uncle and her sister?" Nikki asked.

Relieved by the break in Nikki's long silence, Barrett answered, "Yes. She as usual, did get them both visas. She's waiting for the paperwork on my uncle's medical condition to come through, and once they're here she plans to work on getting them both citizenship." She caught Nikki's eye, "You know she'll succeed, don't you?"

"Oh yes!" Nikki didn't hesitate in answering. "Trang gets things done. Whatever she wants, she somehow gets."

"Wish I inherited those genes," Barrett remarked, as she started to clear the table.

Nikki ignored the comment and continued dipping her crusty, warm bread.

Even Barrett knew when it was time to change the subject. "I spoke with Carbone before I came in," Barrett said, scraping plates at the sink. "He stops in the restaurant quite a bit. He told me you and Ginni are under twenty-four hour watch." She stopped working and looked over at Nikki. "What's going on?"

Nikki got up and brought more dishes to the sink. "Two students and a doctor from the Mercy Hospital are now dead. There's a serial murderer loose, and he seems to be saving himself for Ginni and me. I think Ginni's in danger because he really wants to get me. That's why we have a police guard."

Just verbalizing the threat to her life sent another shiver down Nikki's spine. "I feel so helpless with this one," she thought out loud. "I feel like I'm sitting around helpless, waiting for them to strike."

Barrett wiped her hands on the towel tucked in her waistband. She turned and gave Nikki a big, consoling hug. Nikki accepted Barrett's concern. It felt good to be wrapped in the arms of this big, strong woman. She gave Barrett a hug back, and they stood in this holding pattern for several minutes.

Nikki was the first to push away. "Thanks, I think I needed that."

"Would you like me to stay for awhile," Barrett asked. "Petri is capable of running the restaurant without me."

This offer was very tempting to Nikki, but a little voice, which sounded a lot like Ginni's, whispered in her ear. "It's not a good idea to be alone too long with Barrett. She still loves you...and you need to be fair to her." Definitely, Ginni's words.

"Thanks," Nikki responded. "I'm fine with Officer Carbone out there. Actually, I'm pretty tired. I'm going to bed early, but thanks for the offer...and for all this food."

Barrett gave her a knowing look again and said, "I've put the left-overs in the refrigerator. There's enough for another meal for you...and Ginni." She made her way down the hall to the door, and bent down. She gave Nikki a kiss on the lips. Nikki tried not to kiss back...but she wasn't good at that.

Barrett let her off the hook. "Goodnight, Nicolette. I'm glad you liked the food. Call me if you need anything, and I'll check back with you tomorrow. Oh, and Nikki...be careful, okay? I care about you...I don't want anything to happen to you."

With this last comment, she opened the door and left.

Nikki checked the lock on the door and went back down the hall. With her mind still on the blueberry tart dessert, she passed the gold, seraphim bordered mirror on the wall. This was at least the fourth time she passed the mirror, but the first time she took notice of her reflection.

"Oh noooo!" she groaned. "My hair...my blouse...my jacket."

The realization finally hit her that she was still wearing the same clothes she had on when she rolled around the floor with Bradley Davis. The red spots on her blazer were not paprika sauce.

"Ohhhhh! Barrett must think I'm some kind of slob," she chastised herself and set off immediately for her bedroom. "Definitely time for a change," she muttered on the way.

She pushed the closet door open and picked out a clean denim shirt and a pair of jeans. As she turned to place the clothes on her bed, she froze. Gooseflesh rose on both arms and an alarm buzzer went off in her head. There was a white lab coat lying on the bed.

Nikki dropped her clothes where she was standing and reached for her gun. She brought it out and snapped off the safety. Scanning the room for any movement or signs of an intruder, she walked carefully around the bed. With her free hand, she checked the lock on the window. The lock was secure.

She took a few steps closer to the bed, got down on one knee, and with the gun leading peered under the bed. Nothing was there. She didn't let her guard down but stood up again.

She moved to the bed and got a good look at the lab coat. The large letters on the nametag were the first things to catch her eye. "DR. VIR-GINIA CLAYTON!" It screamed out at Nikki.

"My God!" Nikki exhaled. "This is Ginni's coat…the one she uses at Mercy Hospital! This wasn't here when Max and I made our sweep of the house."

Nikki verbalized her fear and her growing panic pushed her to grab the coat and run for the front door. Halfway down the hall leading from the bedroom to the living room, Nikki tripped over something that wasn't in the hall on her way to the bedroom. She lost her balance and tumbled foreword. Still on alarm, she went with the fall, rolling over twice and forcing her body back to a crouching position. She never let go of her gun and again scanned the hallway for the intruder.

She stood upright again, her gun at the ready. She bent back down to pick up the lab coat she dropped. Under the coat was the item she tripped over, Ginni's "Distinguished Women of Sheridan Award." The award they both hung in the living room was lying in the middle of the hall floor.

Nikki picked up the plaque and still not letting down her guard, noticed that some writing had been scratched onto the award. Just after the word "Distinguished" someone had scratched in "Dead", so the award now read, "Distinguished *Dead* Women of Sheridan Award."

No time to check any other room. There was screaming in Nikki's head, *Danger! Danger! Retreat! Get out of Danger!*

She scooped up the award and ran first to the living room. Sticking her head into the room, Nikki shrieked at Fluffy, "Go hide Fluffy! Go hide!" This was a game that Nikki and Fluffy had played for years. Fluffy ran and hid, and Nikki had to find her. In one leap, Fluffy was off the sofa and out of sight.

Nikki ran down the rest of the hall, straight for the front door. Once there, she flipped the lock and opened the door in one movement. She raced across the lawn to Officer Carbone's patrol car.

He saw her running toward the car...and saw the gun in her hand. This was enough for him to jump out of the car and draw his gun. "What's going on? What's wrong?" he yelled, as Nikki reached the car.

"Out of breath from the panic and the run, Nikki took a few minutes to breathe in some air. "Someone's...in...the house..."

Carbone didn't wait to hear the rest of her details. He grabbed his shoulder radio and called for back-up. He clicked off the radio and asked, "Where is he?" Again not waiting for an answer, he began moving toward the house.

"Wait," Nikki stopped him. "I don't know where he is. I don't even know who it is."

Officer Carbone stopped and took the few steps back to Nikki. Remembering some important police protocol he said, "You should wait in the car. Please lock the doors." With this, he opened the patrol car door for Nikki.

"He could be anywhere in there," Nikki tried to help the nervous young officer. "I think you better wait for some back-up. Whoever it is managed to put this in my bedroom." She held out the lab coat. "And he put this in the hall right after I walked there."

Officer Carbone stopped for a moment, unsure of what to do next. "If he's that good at hiding...and Ma'm...I don't know how he got past me. I swear, I've had my eyes glued to the house…well…maybe I better wait for the Sergeant."

Nikki was relieved to hear this new plan. She was also pleased to hear Max was on his way. She sank into the patrol car seat and glued her eyes to the front of her house. Her gun was cradled and ready in her hands.

CHAPTER 17

▼

Nikki looked at the lab coat and the Distinguished Women's Award in her lap and something suddenly clicked. She jumped out of the patrol car and yelled at Carbone, "Tell Max to meet me at Mercy Hospital...Ginni's in danger."

She didn't wait for a response but raced across the parking area to her car. She grabbed the keys out of her jacket pocket and clicked the door unlocked. Then she slid behind the wheel and squealed off for Mercy Hospital. Two Police cars, sirens blaring, whizzed past her as she hit Main Street. The third car, a ten-year-old, unobtrusive looking Cavalier with a magnetic flashing light attached to the roof, held Max. He was so intent on getting to Nikki's house, he didn't seem to recognize her car, as she passed him at full speed.

She tucked her gun back into her belt and pushed the gas pedal closer to the floor. Taking the hospital driveway at thirty-miles-an-hour, it looked like she was driving on only two tires. When her car landed back on all fours, she scooted into a No Parking Zone and jumped out.

She raced through the glass entrance doors and across the lobby, scanning the entire foyer while she waited for one of the two elevator doors to open. Finally, there was a ding and the second door opened.

Nikki jumped in, pushed six, and headed for the floor Ginni should be working on.

Nikki got off the elevator on the Post-Surgical floor. Everything was quiet, so she made her way to the floor desk. No one was there. "It's not unusual for a floor to be quiet at this hour," Nikki mumbled under her breath. "But it's rather unusual for no one to be at the desk…although I know Mercy is short staffed lately."

She kept up her monologue, as she checked up and down the adjoining halls. "There should be a secretary though…secretaries don't make rounds."

This last observation caused Nikki to reach back under her blazer and grab her gun handle. She kept her hand on the gun and moved slowly down the first hallway. Finally, giving in to better judgment, she started down the hall. "Anyone here! Hey! Charge Nurse! Secretary! Doctor! Is anyone on this floor?"

Several frail voices answered back, "We're…here!" "I'm okay Bella, go home." "I need water…and a bed pan." "I'm in pain, nurse. Can you give me something for the pain?"

That may not have been the right approach to this situation, Nikki found herself thinking.

"Who's doing all that yelling," an obviously tired Nurse asked, as she popped her head out of the third room. "Visitors are not allowed at this hour. You will have to leave," she finished instructing Nikki.

As the nurse came into the hall to make sure the unwanted and loud visitor left, Nikki saw the reason for her absence from the front desk. Almost the entire front of her white uniform pantsuit was covered with urine and feces.

"Is that you, Reverend Barnes," the nurse walked closer to Nikki. "Were you doing all that yelling? What else could go wrong tonight?"

She was within smelling distance, and Nikki's stomach took a nose-dive. "Yes, it's me, Reverend Barnes," she gagged out the words.

"My goodness, I didn't recognize you." The nurse started to hold out a hand but thought better of the unhygienic gesture. "It's me,

Carol Muldoon. I haven't seen you in about eight or nine months. How have you been?"

The friendly nurse was standing way too close, and Nikki's eyes saw only human waste. Carol followed Nikki's eyes and felt she must try to explain. "Isn't this a mess?"

Nikki could only shake her head in agreement.

"Some new orderly," Carol tried to explain. "First, he whips into several rooms...looking for something to mess up, I think. Anyway, before we can get him to the right wing, he dumps a whole bedpan on me." She looked up at Nikki for commiseration.

Nikki gave all the facial consolation she could muster.

"I couldn't very well finish rounds like this," Carol slapped her wet jersey. "I'm on tonight with Edith Farber. Do you remember Edith? She had the twins last year. They're all doing fine. Anyway, Edith went to fetch me some scrubs, so I can finish my shift."

"So, that's why no one's at the desk," Nikki put some of the puzzle together.

"Your back hurting you, Reverend?" Carol asked, staring at the hand Nikki's holding behind her back.

Nikki let go of her gun and brought her hand back to her side. "No, I'm just fine," she said meekly. "I really came up here because I thought Dr. Clayton was working this floor tonight."

"Oh yeah." Carol's tone changed to deep concern. "Wasn't that terrible about Dr. Reinstein? She was a good doctor. Makes you not want to trust anyone...like that orderly. I never saw him before, but I didn't have enough help to escort him to East Wing and find out if he really belongs there."

A familiar chill moved down Nikki's neck. Warnings appeared again, and her fear for Ginni gained new momentum. "Do you know where Dr. Clayton is?" she asked again.

"She's finished up here," Carol answered. "I imagine she's in the doctor's lounge on two, doing her paperwork."

Before Carol could finish her sentence, Nikki turned and ran for the elevator. Minutes felt like hours as she waited for the elevator to arrive. It was taking too much time, so she ran for the stairs instead. She took two stairs at a time, racing down to the second floor. Several thoughts kept her propelling down the stairs. The doctor's lounge was deserted at this time of night, and the orderly could be the killer...a killer who now roamed freely throughout the hospital.

Nikki reached the second floor and pushed open the fire door. This hall was also deserted, but since there were no patients on this floor, there was never much activity. She slowed down her pace and walked silently toward the Doctor's Lounge. Nikki tried to get her breathing back to normal, while she stayed on alert. She checked the hall behind her several times and scanned the adjoining hallways as she passed by them.

She listened for anything out of the ordinary, but all she heard was the thumping of her heart and her shallow breathing. She stepped in front of the closed Lounge door and automatically put her hand on her gun.

"Get the hell away from me! I don't need a sermon or a friend! My friends got me into this mess!" Someone was yelling from the Outpatient Services Office, down the hall from the lounge. "If you can't get it for me, then I'm outta here!" The voice yelled again.

Nikki was drawn to the voice...there was something familiar about it. Should she go into the office or check on Ginni first? She quickly pushed open the Doctor's Lounge door.

Ginni looked up from a stack of folders on the worktable. "Nikki, what are you doing here?"

The young officer sat on the sofa next to the worktable. He was on his feet in a flash. His hand moved to the handle of his gun, while he snapped open the holster with his finger.

"She's okay, Chet," Ginni yelled, giving the officer a wave. "This is Nikki Barnes, my partner."

Nikki's hand was still behind her back, as she stared at Officer Chet, whose hand was also on his gun. They appeared to be at a stand-off without the OK Corral. Nikki was the first to back down. She let go of the gun and reached out to shake hands. "Nice to meet you, Chet," she said in her friendliest voice.

Chet relaxed his hold on the revolver and offered his hand to Nikki. "Nice to meet you, too. So you're Ginni's business partner. Are you a doctor too?"

Ginni smiled. She loved to confuse the unknowing.

"No." Nikki relaxed a little. "I'm not a doctor...I'm a priest." She liked to tease too.

Ginni got up and walked closer to Nikki. "Just what are you doing here, at this hour...and without your police escort?"

Nikki tried to explain giving the short form. "Someone got into the house. They had your lab coat from here at the hospital, and they scratched a warning on your Women's Club Award. I was afraid he got in here too...or his accomplice."

Ginni took a deep breath and pushed back her fear. "Damn! I finally get an award and some shithead has to scratch it all up."

Nikki moved closer. "I was so worried," she whispered to Ginni.

Ginni kept up her bravado. "No need to worry, honey. I have officer Chet with me. He hasn't left my side."

With the lounge door open, all three of them could hear the continued yelling coming from down the hall. "I'm not fucking leaving until I get the results!"

Nikki looked questioningly at Ginni, who nodded knowingly. "She's been at that for the last half-hour. No one seems to know how she got left in Outpatient after they closed for the day, but Rita's trying to keep her happy. We've had a day of troubled patients. One guy got lose from the psych ward, dressed up like an orderly and was throwing bedpans at everyone."

Two mysterious strangers, Nikki thought to herself. "Why didn't Rita call Security?" she asked, her tone betraying her concern.

"For that girl? Rita didn't think she needed to," Ginni tried to explain. "She came down here and got me...and Officer Chet went too. The young woman only wanted to know if she was pregnant or not. She isn't married and very confused right now. I think Rita wanted to make sure she just calmed down, so she wouldn't do anything rash. Rita just wanted to do a nice thing by helping the woman and hurrying up the test. As usual, there's a hold-up in the lab."

"Why the hell is it taking so long!" Another barrage of yelling echoed through the hall. "I should've just pissed in a cup again and used another drugstore test. I wanted to be sure! I have to be sure!"

Ginni turned to Nikki again. "Actually, you know that screamer," she added. "She's Charity Daniels, the student who was getting it on with Bradley Davis at Tailfeathers. You said she was Talia Carter's partner.

Nikki didn't wait for Ginni to finish her sentence. She finally recognized the voice herself and raced down the hall toward Charity.

Charity Daniels was in the doorway of the Outpatient Services Office ripping a written report out of Rita Blair's hand. "Okay! That's all the fuck I wanted to know! Now let me get the hell out of here!" She turned abruptly, ready to leave and saw Nikki barreling down the hall toward her.

"Just a minute, Charity! I want to talk to you!" Nikki yelled at her.

Charity did a full turn and started running down the opposite end of the hallway. She made it to a stairwell and started down to the first floor.

Nikki was right behind her, getting better at skipping stairs all the time. Charity was faster and reached the first floor before Nikki could catch up to her. Charity pushed open the fire door and slammed it closed, just as Nikki approached.

The heavy door took Nikki by surprise, and the force of her running crashed her right into the door. Her face got the full force of the impact with her nose leading the charge.

It was only then, that she remembered how sensitive her nose was, having been broken several times. Nikki's nose showed its weakness by starting to bleed.

"Oh crap!" she said, wiping away the bright-red blood with the back of her hand.

This little setback didn't stop the chase. Nikki pushed the door open again, just in time to see Charity reach the hospital lobby. Nikki raced on, and so did her nose. She reached the lobby, stopped to look for Charity, and again wiped the flowing red stream on her blazer sleeve.

Nikki could see Charity almost at the exit doors. She could also see someone else, hastily entering through the same doors. It was her old friend Max, right on cue.

"Grab her, Max!" Nikki screamed from across the lobby. "Get Charity Daniels! Don't let her escape!"

Max did a quick double-take at Nikki. He couldn't help notice the bloody nose. Then he saw Charity. She was already through the first set of glass doors, so Max quickly backtracked and made it outside at the same time Charity did.

"I'd stop right there, Ms. Daniels!" Max yelled in his most authoritarian voice.

Charity stopped, looked at him for a split second, and decided to keep running. She turned and ran right into the arms of another police officer.

"Cuff her, Jones, and put her in the car," Max yelled to the officer. "I need to ask her some questions, and I don't want her running away."

Nikki made it to the exit doors in time to see Max and Officer Jones capture Charity. Smiling in satisfaction, she suddenly felt a bloody river flowing over her lips and onto her chin. She quickly put her head back and pinched her nostrils.

Max moved back through the entrance doors and went right to Nikki. "What happened? What's going on?" he asked, taking her by the arm and leading her to a chair in the lobby.

"Did she break your nose?" Max asked, as he took a clean hankie out of his pant's pocket.

Nikki gratefully replaced her hand with the clean hankie and unconsciously wiped the bloody hand on her blazer. "She didn't hit me," Nikki said in a full nasal twang. "She slammed the door, and I ran into it...with my nose."

By this time, Ginni and Officer Chet had traced Nikki's steps and were also in the lobby. Ginni was next to Nikki in a flash. "Did she hit you?" Ginni echoed Max's words.

"No." Max answered for Nikki. "She slammed the door on Nikki's nose."

"Ouch! Poor baby." Ginni said, tenderly feeling the nose for any breaks. "Nothing seems broken." She checked both of Nikki's eyes and continued her examination. "Just a bad epistaxis, I think."

Ginni took the hankie from Nikki and pinched the nose again. "A few minutes of this pressure should stop the bleeding."

Nikki felt a great sense of relief. She trusted her doctor. Heck! She loved her doctor, and she could feel the blood flow stop.

Max recognized a good time to jump in and asked, "So, what's going on with Charity Daniels."

Ginni spoke for her partner. "Nikki thinks someone was in the house. She found my lab coat in the bedroom, and someone ruined my new Award with some kind of warning."

"I have those in my car," Nikki nasally added.

"She came to warn me," Ginni went on. "Then we heard some yelling down the hall, and Nikki recognized Charity's voice. Next thing Chet and I saw was Nikki running down the hall after Charity. We chased them here."

"She tried to run away," Nikki tried to speak again with a hankie on her nose and her head still back.

Ginni made it easier by removing the hankie. "Now put your head up slowly," Ginni instructed. "And don't move around too much while you talk."

Nikki did as she was told. "I just wanted to ask her some questions," Nikki explained. "But she took off. I wanted to know why she's here at the hospital. I think she may be involved with the murders."

"Okay." Max asked slowly, trying to put everything together in his mind. "I can't arrest her, but I can question her. I do have to give her time to get a lawyer, so I'm going to ask her to come into the station at nine tomorrow. I want you there, Nikki. If you feel up to it."

"I'm fine," Nikki said sincerely, not realizing that everyone was staring at her tussled hair, bloodied nose and face, and ruined blazer. "I mean it." She tried to be more convincing. "Remember how they used to do blood letting for medicinal purposes. I feel energized."

"That wasn't proven to be very good medicine," Ginni said sarcastically.

"The guys are going over your house with a fine tooth comb," Max got serious again. "So far, they haven't found any sign of someone being there. Are you sure your lab coat was here at the hospital," he asked Ginni.

"I wore it this afternoon...around two," Ginni answered.

"So, I don't want you two to go back home tonight," Max added. "How about staying at my place? You know Rosa loves to see ya. She'll feed you good."

Ginni, who was usually the one to pick a motel over a friend's offering, took a long look at Nikki and said, "I think that's a good idea, Max. I have about another hour's worth of work to finish up. Nikki can stay with me and rest. Then Chet will drive us to your place. Are you sure it's not an imposition? What about the boys?"

"They love company," Max assured them. "They probably won't even see you though, cause they're already in bed. We added on that guestroom last fall for Rosa's mother, but she's still in Florida. That room is just like a motel."

"Wait a minute!" Nikki suddenly exclaimed. "What about Fluffy? I left her hiding...and she won't come out until I go find her. She needs to eat?"

"Don't worry," Max reassured her. "Carbone and Jefferson are still assigned to your house. They can check on Fluffy and report back to me. I'm planning to swing back there anyway...I'll feed Fluffy and make sure she's okay."

He turned to Chet and said, "See that they get to my place." Then he turned to Nikki and Ginni. "See you two later...with a full report on Fluffy."

Max walked back outside, while Ginni and Chet helped Nikki to the elevator. "There's a comfy sofa in the Lounge," Ginni said to Nikki. "You can rest that beat-up body while I finish my reports."

CHAPTER 18

▼

Max's in-law apartment turned out to be just the thing for a restful night. The bathroom was equipped with an oversized, whirlpool tub. A perk which Nikki and Ginni took advantage of immediately. They turned on all the water jets and sank down together into the tepid water. Both groaned in appreciation at the same time.

"This could be better than sex," Ginni cooed, snuggling closer to Nikki.

"For tonight, anyway," Nikki joked back.

They let the gurgling water soothe away the aches and anxieties of the day. In less than ten minutes, Ginni heard the familiar, syncopated breathing that signaled Nikki was asleep. She hated to, but she gently shook Nikki's arm.

"Wake up honey," she said quietly. "Let me help you wash your hair."

Nikki's eyes woke up before she did. "What? What did you say?"

Ginni stood and pulled Nikki up. "Come on, let's get the last of that blood out of your hair and fall into the mother-in-law bed."

The only energy Nikki could muster was enough to stand there, while Ginni lathered her hair and rinsed it with the shower. She dried herself on automatic pilot and pulled on the hospital scrubs Ginni borrowed for the evening.

As her head hit the lavender, dryer-sheet scented, hand-embroidered pillowcase, Nikki drifted off to a lovely dream garden filled with yellow tulips. She was holding someone's hand as she walked down the cobblestone path. Feeling calm and joyful, she stopped and turned to smile at her cohort. However, when she took a closer look at this paradise partner, she saw the black-hooded person who attacked her in Charity Daniel's apartment.

Nikki quickly dropped the hand she was holding and woke up with a start. Ginni had just climbed into bed next to her. "What's the matter, Nikki?" she asked. "Everything's okay? Try to get some sleep."

Nikki did manage to smile at Ginni, as she let her head slowly sink back into the pillow. This time, she was alone in the garden.

*   *   *   *

Max's wife, Rosa, lived up to her "World's Best Cook" reputation. She put her tray full of breakfast delights on the small cabaret table by the garden window. Then she gently woke the sleepy doctor and priest. As if the homemade sweet rolls weren't enough, there were scrambled eggs, turkey sausages, and toasted Italian bread.

The two guests dug into the food like they were eating their last meal. Rosa sat with them and caught them up on the antics of her two teenage sons, her mother's quest for a third husband, and Max's success in losing five pounds.

Nikki and Ginni nodded in conversational participation, but neither stopped eating long enough to speak. Rosa finally ended the small talk and got very solemn. "Max told me about the killer who is on the lose. He's worried about you two...and that makes me worry about you."

She stood and announced the day's itinerary. "Max says he's leaving for the station in thirty minutes. And Ginni, Chet will get here around that same time to take you to the Medical Center."

"Thanks, Rosa," Nikki gave her a big hug. "Everything is wonderful...the room...the food."

"We really appreciate your hospitality," Ginni added, also giving her a hug.

"What about clothes," Rosa asked. "Do you need any clean clothes?"

Nikki answered for both of them. "No, thanks. Ginni always keeps an extra outfit at the hospital, and I had my clerics in my locker over there, for when I do pastoral care. So we're all set."

Rosa left with the empty tray, and Nikki and Ginni made the thirty-minute deadline. Ginni gave Nikki a peck on the cheek and got into Officer Chet's patrol car. Nikki got into the Cavalier with Max.

*   *   *   *

Charity Daniels arrived at the police station right on time. Her lawyer wasn't present, but Bill Hanson was glued to her side. Ana Ramos escorted them to Max's office and motioned for them to sit in the two chairs in front of Max's desk. She took her place next to Max.

"I hope you don't object to Reverend Barnes being present at this interview," Max announced in his authoritarian voice. He motioned toward Nikki, who sat in the far corner of the room.

Both students turned in their chairs to look at Nikki. Charity promptly diverted her eyes when they came into contact with Nikki's. She turned back to Max and was about to protest, but Max stopped her with the first question.

"Just why were you at Mercy Hospital yesterday," he asked.

"I sent her to the hospital," the small Mr. Hanson answered back.

Max and Ana looked at each other, and Ana scribbled a note on the long yellow pad in front of her. "Would you like to elaborate on that?" Ana asked Hanson.

Charity quickly interjected, "This really isn't any of your business."

"It's all right, Honey," Hanson reassured her while patting her hand. "They think you're involved in those killings. We need to tell them what's going on."

Max stepped up to home plate again. "He's right, Ms. Daniels. We do think of you as a suspect in the murders."

"I'm innocent!" Charity started to protest again. "I was one of the victims. My best friend...two of my friends were killed. This is fucking crazy!"

Hanson continued patting her hand. "Now, now, Cherry. You mustn't get upset. Try to calm down. Do deep breaths...remember what I taught you. One, in, two, out."

Ana tried to get everyone back on track by asking, "Just what was your reason for being at the hospital?"

Hanson looked at Ana and then back to Max. "Cherry...I mean Charity, thought she might be pregnant. She went to the hospital to confirm the test she did at home. They aren't very reliable you know."

"They kept me there for hours," Charity was irate again. "First, they were closing. Then something in the lab broke down. Then this wacko nurse keeps talking to me about my choices and all that bullshit."

"There's only one choice for us," Hanson gushed back at her. "Isn't that right, Cherry?

We're going to get married and raise our child together."

With this last comment, Max choked on the gulp of coffee he just swallowed, and Nikki nearly slipped off her chair.

"You're going to get married," Nikki squeaked out, causing the two students to turn around and look at her again.

"That's right, Professor Barnes," Hanson spoke again. "I plan to do the right thing, and Charity has agreed to be my bride."

Finally finding her voice, Nikki asked, "When will this wedding take place?"

"We were going to make an appointment to see you today," Hanson continued on merrily. "Since you are the University Chaplain, we thought you could do the ceremony right in the St. David Chapel."

"Oh," Nikki tried to regain some composure. "That is part of my job...but I must tell you...I have some doubts about the motives behind this union."

"What the hell does that mean," Charity spewed her anger again. "I'm pregnant. Bill loves me and loves kids. I'm not a queer anymore, and his family has lots of money. We should all live happily ever after."

"My family does have lots of money," Hanson added meekly. "And everything else she says is true. So will you marry us?"

Nikki was at a loss for words. She looked to Max for help.

He coughed in order to get the attention of Charity and Hanson. "Ms. Daniels, we have reason to believe you are a close friend of Bradley Davis. Did you know we arrested him yesterday?"

"I heard about the arrest," Charity meekly admitted.

"Are you good friends?" Ana asked.

"They were," Hanson answered again for his betrothed. "That was until she found out he was spiking her drinks with drugs. Can you believe that? He was a friend of mine first. I introduced him to Charity, and I trusted him. When I was busy at meetings, he would take Charity out and drug her drinks. She thinks he even...well...you tell them Cherry."

"He raped me!" she suddenly blurted out. "I trusted him. We were just supposed to go out for dinner and stuff, and he drugged me and raped me. I think that's the only way he knows how to have sex."

"It's okay," Hanson put his arm around Charity. "He won't do that ever again. I'm here to take care of you now."

Max took a moment to assess the situation, and then he addressed Hanson. "Mr. Hanson, you realize that is a major accusation against Mr. Davis. Drugging a woman with the intent to rape is now a felony. I would like to ask you to wait outside while we take a statement from Ms. Daniels."

"But I came to speak for her," Hanson started to protest. "I'm here to protect her."

"You're doing a good job," Max tried to sound sincere. "But you were not present during the attacks. We need to get a statement from Ms. Daniels, if she doesn't object."

Hanson thought about what was in his best interest and turned to Charity. "You can give them a statement without me, can't you, Little Bug? I'll be just outside the door. Is that okay?"

"Okay," Charity answered in a flat monotone. "I'll give them the fucking statement."

Hanson gave her hand one last pat and stepped outside the room.

Nikki smoothly moved to Hanson's empty chair, right next to Charity. Charity kept her eyes fixed straight ahead. "Before you give your statement, Charity, I just want to ask you one question."

Charity turned her head and glared at Nikki.

"Did you kill Talia and Betsy?" Nikki asked bluntly. "Or did you help someone kill them?"

Charity's hardened facial expression started changing to deep remorse. Choking back tears, she answered, "How can you even ask me that, Reverend Barnes? I thought you were my friend. I thought you cared about Talia."

"I was your friend…and Talia's, but you're acting so weird lately." Nikki tried to keep the discourse going. "I saw you kissing Bradley Davis at Tailfeathers…and this marriage to Bill Hanson. I thought you and Talia were happy together…and why did you run from me at the hospital?"

Charity turned away from Nikki and stared at her hands. "My life is so fucked up. I was happy with Talia…even with all her problems. I thought we could overcome them together." She looked at Nikki again. "She broke it off, about a month ago. She just told me to get out. Oh yeah, she said it was for my own good. You know she had a premonition that something bad was going to happen to her. Still, where did that leave me?"

Charity went silent again and fiddled with the small diamond ring on her left hand. "I mean, I already told my family I was a lesbian.

They made it very clear, I wasn't welcome back home...or anywhere near the family. That was fine when I thought Talia and I were going to be our own family. Then, suddenly, it's all over."

Tears started to well up in Charity's eyes. "Billy Hanson was a friend of Talia's. He was always desperate for a girlfriend. So, I'm not proud of this, but I flirted with him. I led him on, and now we're engaged. His parents are thrilled that he's getting married...overjoyed with a future grandchild. He's the only child, and I'll have a built-in family...a home...money. Hey, everything a girl needs."

She started to cry. Nikki moved closer and put a consoling arm around Charity. "I'm sorry, Charity, but why didn't you come to me. We could have talked it out...found another solution for you."

Charity just as quickly stifled her tears and shook her head. "I was ashamed of what I was doing. Then, Talia called me and wanted to get back together. That was about a week before she got killed. I think she was scared. I think something her sister said, really scared her. That's the only reason she wanted me around. Talia was so pissed that I was dating Bill, but she was more scared than angry. That's why she wanted me back in the apartment. Her political sense of righteousness was offended by me being with a man."

Nikki chose not to comment on the pain and politics of being true to yourself. Instead, she focused on something else. "Did you say Talia saw her *sister?* I didn't know she had a sister."

Charity wiped her eyes with the back of her hand and composed herself before going on. "Talia never told anyone about her family. That whole scene was too painful for her. When her brother turned up, she had to tell me about him. Then one night...not too long ago...maybe a month, she gets a phone call from her sister. Well, she's a half-sister or something like that. She hits Talia up for some money. Wants to tell her some family secret or something. I tried to tell Talia not to go. That her family caused her enough grief, but she took about a hundred dollars and went to see her sister."

She stopped talking again and stared at Max's desk. Then she added pensively, "Talia never spoke about the meeting. Wouldn't tell me anything. Just told me to back off, it was her family and her problem."

Ana Ramos tapped her pencil on the legal pad in order to get everyone's attention. Then she addressed Charity, "Why did you run from Reverend Barnes at the hospital?"

Some of the hardness returned to Charity's face. "Billy is a very busy student this time of year with all his student organizations and crap. He didn't want me to get lonely, so he kept shoving me off on his wrestling buddy, Brad Davis. Like I said, I wasn't that happy about my life. When Brad offered me something to take away the pain…I took it. I felt great for a few hours. I loved everyone, and I was happy and popular. I felt like I was never alone. Problem was…I felt much worse the next day."

She broke eye contact with Ana, and her face softened again. She stared at the desk again, as she went on, "I've taken his pills almost every night. I don't even know what they are. Sometimes I forget what happens or where I am. I woke up a few times in Brad's bed…couldn't remember anything."

Turning to Nikki with a pained expression, she explained, "I heard about Brad getting arrested because of some fight with you. When you started running after me in the hospital…I just thought you were after me because of the drugs. I panicked and just ran. I've been running since Talia broke up with me. I'm just so tired of running."

Charity leaned over toward Nikki and started sobbing again. Nikki put her arm around the young woman and prayed silently for some way to comfort her. "I'm so sorry, Charity. I never knew any of this was going on. I'm just so sorry."

Nikki took a few minutes to let Charity cry out some of her emotions. Meanwhile, Ana and Max huddled together and whispered. When Charity stopped crying, Nikki gave her a tissue, and she wiped her eyes.

Max cleared his throat preparing to speak. "Ms. Daniels, if you feel up to it, Detective Ramos will take your statement concerning Bradley Davis. She will also explain some of the drug treatment services available here in Sheridan."

He paused and waited for the subtle suggestion to sink in. "Before Reverend Barnes and I leave, I need to ask you a few more questions that concern the murder case."

He picked up his little notebook and pen. "Can you tell me the name of Talia Carter's sister? And do you know where we can find her? You understand don't you, that she may be able to help us in this case?"

Charity looked puzzled but tried to answer. "I'm not sure where she lives. She was some place in Buffalo when Talia took her the money. Maybe a YWCA or traveler's place, something like that. The only name Talia called her was Kit or Kitty. I think I overheard Talia call her Kitty. I'm sorry, that's all I can remember. Talia only spoke to her once that I know of. That was the end of it."

Max thanked Charity and tucked his pen in the spiral wire of the notebook. Then he put both of them in the breast pocket of his jacket. He gave Nikki a quick look before turning back to Charity. "We're going to leave you with Detective Ramos. She'll take your statement."

He got up from the desk and went to the door. Nikki took her cue from him and followed him out into the hall.

Bill Hanson came right up to them and asked, "Can she leave now? Can we go?"

Max tried to explain why Charity didn't come out with them. "She's still giving her statement, but it shouldn't be long now. You can wait right here."

Max and Nikki made their way down the hall to the computer room. "I think we need to talk to this sister," Max said, opening the door for Nikki. "I'll ask Fred to do some searches, maybe he can come up with a lead that helps us find her. If not, I'll just get on the phone and call every YMCA or YWCA in Buffalo, and the motels, hotels, police stations, hospitals…"

"I get the picture," Nikki said. "We are definitely going to Buffalo today."

CHAPTER 19

▼

The police computer was not a winner this time, but Max's first call did make a connection. The main YWCA in the City of Buffalo maintained a short-term boarding house on the West Side of the city, and a Kitty Brown was listed as one of the tenants. This name was close enough to the name Charity mentioned for Max and Nikki to investigate. How many people with a name like Kitty and Browning could there be staying at a YWCA?

Max and Nikki drove the forty-five minutes to Buffalo mostly in silence. Then Max broke through the heavy thinking and offered Nikki a candy bar from the glove compartment.

Nikki took the candy bar and started munching along with her thinking. It occurred to her that if she ever really became Max's partner, they'd both need to be on diets. However, she didn't mention this hidden danger, just kept on munching.

Max tried not to think of diets, especially when he was eating a candy bar. Between bites, he asked, "You think girls still hook guys with pregnancy, just for the security?"

"I think Charity did," Nikki answered. "She got all her self-confidence from Talia and their relationship. She never found out who she really was when she was alone."

Nikki took the last bite of candy bar and chewed it slowly before she swallowed. "Charity was okay as a lesbian, as long as she was with Talia, who was very out, very political, fighting the world. I don't think Charity really knows if she's a lesbian or not. She wants someone else to do the work of self-discovery. Now, Bill Hanson can define who she is…or maybe his family can."

"We all want to feel secure," Max philosophized between bites.

"Sure we do," Nikki answered. "We usually find security by knowing who we are. Knowing who we really are is what leads to the confidence necessary to feel secure. But, you can't keep hooking up with different people, so they'll take care of your needs. You have to feel good in your own skin, then you can share your life with others."

Max opened the glove compartment for another candy bar, but Nikki decided to pass on a second one.

*   *   *   *

The woman at the reception desk escorted Max and Nikki up the winding staircase. She explained that the present building was originally the home of a Buffalo millionaire back in the 1800's.

The YWCA renovated the whole house and made seventeen apartments out of the many rooms. Each floor shared a bathroom, and each room was furnished with a bed, desk and chair, mini-refrigerator and microwave.

She stopped in front of room fourteen. "This is Miss Brown's room. I didn't see her leave, so she should be in." With this last bit of information and a friendly smile, she walked back toward the stairs.

Max knocked on the door. There was a short wait, and the door opened a crack, just enough for Max to notice that the woman inside was an obvious teenager. She gave the two visitors the once-over and hesitated a little longer on Nikki's outfit. Even though Nikki was not wearing her priest's collar, her black pantsuit and white cleric shirt were giveaways that she was a minister of some kind.

"Yeah. Whadda ya want?" the girl stayed half-hidden by the door.

Max showed her his badge and said, "I'm Sergeant Mullen of the Sheridan Police Department and this is Reverend Barnes. We'd like to ask you a few questions."

The girl didn't open the door but answered, "I told them before. I don't know what happened to the money, and I don't need any minister. I'm eighteen-years-old and that's legal."

"This isn't about stolen money," Max kept going. He was taking a chance that she was the woman they were looking for. "We need to ask you some questions about your sister, Talia Carter."

When she heard Talia's name, Kitty opened the door and then walked back to a chair placed next to the window where she sat down. Max and Nikki showed themselves in, and Max walked up to the chair, He took out his notebook, and Nikki sat on the edge of the bed.

Kitty Brown was wearing a tight, leather mini-skirt, about twelve inches long from waist to hem. Her short-sleeved top was ribbed-knit and too tight, with no bra underneath. She might be eighteen, but she looked like a fourteen-year-old who got loose with her mother's make-up.

"If Talia told you I stole money from her, she's lie'n" Kitty said, as she picked up one of the many fashion and movie magazines strewn on the floor around her chair.

Max looked to Nikki, who got off the bed and came closer to Kitty. "Your sister, Talia, is dead," Nikki said softly. "I'm very sorry. We thought you knew."

Kitty's mouth dropped open and the magazine in her lap slid to the floor. "My God!" she practically yelled. "I'm outta here."

She jumped up from the chair and reached under the bed for her suitcase. Without even looking at Max or Nikki, she put the suitcase on the bed and started throwing clothes from the dresser drawers into it.

Nikki took a few steps forward and moved directly into Kitty's path from the dresser to the suitcase. "We still need to ask you some questions," Nikki tried again.

"Look!" Kitty stared Nikki down. "I'm in a hurry. I'm outta here, or I end up like Talia."

Max stepped next to Nikki. "That's what we need to talk about," he said. "Why do you have to leave? Who or what are you afraid of?"

Kitty shook her head, like they should have known what was going on. Then she matter-of-factly said, "He killed her, and he probably knows where I am. He's not gonna kill me too. I've stayed away from him this long. I can disappear again."

"Who?" Max demanded. "Who killed Talia and who will try to kill you?"

"That bastard brother of hers!" Kitty shot back. "He's crazy! He always was. They all were, but he's the worst of 'em. Did you know he told her he was her father? Oh yeah! Plus, when she was fourteen, he got her pregnant and made her get an abortion."

Kitty walked around the two dumbfounded interviewers and threw more clothes into the suitcase. "Yeah, that's what I grew up with." She turned back. "That crazy bastard could be her father, ya know...he could be my father too, for all I know," Kitty went on. "Hey, I don't blame my old lady. She just tried to survive...tried to keep the peace...find enough money to feed us and buy booze. She was afraid of him too. I'd see him sneaking in her room after the John's left and she was wasted. He wasn't a kid either, he was in his late teens."

Kitty crossed her arms in a protective self-hug. "She didn't really know who my father was. I asked my mother once, but she said she couldn't remember." Kitty gave a sardonic smile. "Said she was on birth control pills at the time she got pregnant with me."

Kitty dropped her arms and again hardened her features. "I've forgiven her though, but that bastard, I'll never forgive him. They were both afraid of him, but I knew he was doing something weird in the basement. Keeping it locked, off-limits. I saw some of the girls, his dates, that he brought down there. I'm telling ya, I left home when I was twelve."

Nikki was first to find her voice. "Are you talking about Ted Browning?" she stammered. "The English Professor, Ted Browning?"

"He's Browning now," Kitty concentrated on her packing. "But he was Ted Brown, and she was Talia Brown. I don't know where she got that Carter from."

She threw a defiant look at Max. "Don't tell me you can protect me, because I saw him get away with murder over and over again. I heard that by the time they found those bodies in the basement, no one could remember who lived in that old rental house." She paused.

"You know, he used to talk to his invisible gang. That's what he called them…they were devils or something weird like that. He could be sweet and charming to all his girlfriends in school or on the phone, but as soon as he was alone…then he started those babbling conversations. Even his face changed when he was like that. I just disappeared a long time ago, and I'm disappearing again. He's some kind of murdering, pervert monster, and he's not gonna get me.'"

"You did contact Talia, didn't you?" Nikki asked. "Didn't you know your brother was here too?"

"I didn't even know Talia was around here," Kitty explained. "I was hanging with this guy, who was scoring some dope at the University in the city. I was just along for the ride, ya know. I was his Old Lady for awhile. We came up from Cleveland. Anyway, I see this campus paper and there was a picture of some Safe Night rally from last year, and I recognized Tally. She's standin' in the front row with this sign from St. David University."

The suitcase was full, so Kitty zipped it closed. She looked up again and continued, "I called St. David's, told'em I'm her sister from out of town, and they give me her number. I need money cause My Old Man got busted with the drugs. They took his money, and I didn't have any."

She gave another little laugh. "Tally really didn't have any either. All she could come up with was a hundred. That paid for this place and some food. She met me at a restaurant to give me the money. She wanted to talk about him, but I didn't. I could see she was scared…and then when she told me what she said to him…"

"What did she say to him," Max asked.

Kitty stopped for a moment and looked up at Max. "She was stupid. I told her that, but she said she had reached the end. She said she had hurt too much for too many years." Kitty looked back at her suitcase. "She told him she was going to the police about him. She was going to tell them about how he raped her, and he made her get the abortion…and about all the girls he took to the basement."

Kitty looked over to Nikki. "I told her she was being crazy and stupid. I told her if the police listened to her, and they just might not, they probably wouldn't believe her. They would believe the big-shot professor before they believed a dike nobody. I told her to just run…get away from him. But I don't think she listened to me."

Nikki was now worried about Kitty's welfare. "What will you do now?" Nikki asked.

"Don't worry, Reverend. I'm not going to any police. I know I can't prove nothin' and I'm not stupid." Kitty put on a tough front again. "I got some friends in New York City. They'll put me up…and keep me outta sight."

She stopped and patted her thigh with her hand. "What I don't have is the cash to get there." She looked up at Nikki and asked, "Hey. How ya fixed for cash? Got any fund for women who need to run from their wacko brothers?"

Nikki didn't even stop to think about the ramifications of what she was about to do. She threw Max a knowing look, and he nodded back. This was all she needed to pull out her wallet and hand all the money in it, and one of her business cards, over to Kitty.

The money counted out to sixty-two dollars. Nikki gave it to Kitty and said, "I'm sorry, that's all I have, but here's my card. If I can help you in some way, just call me."

Max stepped forward and in his most professional tone added, "I'd like you to stick around, but I can't force you to stay. So when you reach where you're going, give me a call, will you?"

He reached into his wallet and pulled out a business card. Then he took out his forty-dollar weekly allowance and gave it to Kitty.

She took the money without saying a word. Then she went to the closet and got out her black suede jacket. She slipped into the jacket and flipped her long black hair away from the collar.

Walking back to the bed, she picked up her suitcase and turned to Max and Nikki one last time. She looked at the money in her hand and quietly said, "Thanks."

Kitty walked out the door, letting it close behind her. Max and Nikki listened to her chunky-heeled shoes clomping down the stairs.

"Ted Browning is our serial killer," Nikki finally said.

"His wife, Lindsey, is probably the accomplice," Max echoed back.

Nikki shook her head. "I just don't believe these things when I hear them. He was the father of Talia's child and maybe even her own father. Ted Browning is more than just sick. He's crossed over the line from being human. He's evil…evil personified…and that black soul is dangerous to anyone who crosses his path."

"Like the sister said, he's a crazy bastard," Max offered. "I bet I can trace a string of killings back to his younger days too. We better get back to Sheridan and nail that lunatic."

Max took Nikki by the arm and led her out of the room and down the stairs. As they exited the building, they saw Kitty on the other side of the street, getting into a metro bus.

"I hope she gets away," Nikki said, silently offering a prayer for Kitty's escape.

"She's pretty smart," Max added. "Has enough self-confidence to make it."

They got into Max's car and headed back to Sheridan.

CHAPTER 20

▼

Halfway back to Sheridan, Nikki's cell phone started ringing and vibrating in her pocket. The vibrating feature was supposed to be a joke, since Ginni bought her the phone as a gift. Nikki, however, found the vibration a better incentive to answer the phone than the high-pitched buzzing that passed as ringing.

Once she flipped open the phone, a static-soaked voice started speaking. "Nikki? It's Ginni. Can you hear me all right?"

"Yes," Nikki spoke louder than usual to compensate for the fading in and out. "The signal isn't very clear, but I can hear you."

"I just retrieved our phone messages from home," Ginni started speaking at a rapid pace, probably trying to save minutes. "Dean Haslett wants you to call him about Bradley Davis. He doesn't sound happy. Mrs. Frank called to say goodbye, and Taylor called to see if we could get to the University welcoming reception for the new teachers. The reception starts at five, and I just can't get away. I'm doing a consult at Mercy when I finish with my last patient here. I'm sure I won't finish until around eight. Do you think you can stop in at Taylor's reception?"

Nikki took a minute to sort through what she just heard. A quizzical look came over her face and she responded, "I don't remember the

University giving welcoming receptions for spring or summer faculty. I never received any notice of it. Are you sure the reception is today?"

Ginni answered immediately. "I'm sure it's today. You know how precise Taylor is about everything she does. She repeated the date and time twice in her message. The reception is at Ted and Lindsey Browning's house at 414 Locust Street. Have you got that, Nikki?"

Nikki's face turned ashen, and her hands started to shake involuntarily. She turned to Max and repeated Ginni's message. "Ted and Lindsey Browning are having a welcoming reception for Taylor Fleming...at their house..."

She stopped speaking, looked at her watch and then at Max. "In less than fifteen minutes. Taylor wanted me and Ginni to meet her there."

Nikki turned her attention back to the phone and nervously demanded, "Ginni, don't go near the Brownings. We think they're the killers. Just stay away and don't worry. We'll get hold of Taylor and stop her from going over there. Just wait for me at Mercy Hospital tonight. Don't go anywhere and stay close to Chet."

Nikki didn't wait for an answer. She just flipped the phone closed and cut the connection. She turned to Max, who was already on his cell phone. "Ramos. Yeah, it's Max. Taylor Fleming is in danger. We have reason to believe the Brownings are our killers. She's just been invited to their house for some kind of welcoming reception."

He held the phone away from his mouth and asked Nikki, "What's the address of the Browning's house?"

"414 Locust Street," Nikki shot back. "Tell her to hurry."

"The address is 414 Locust Street. That's right off Main," Max continued his instructions. "Listen, she was supposed to get there by five, so you better hurry. Bring some back up because I'm not sure what you're walking into. The reception might be on the level, but my gut tells me something bad is goin' on. Check it out...and Ana...be careful."

He punched in "End" and put the phone back into his pocket. Then he grabbed the wheel with both hands and pressed the pedal to the medal. The car's speedy acceleration caused Nikki to fall back against her headrest. She said another short prayer for Taylor…and for Ana. *Help them in this time of need, dear Lord.*

*   *   *   *

Taylor looked around at the rental furniture living room and smiled at Lindsey Browning, who sat on the sofa across from her. *Typical Associate Professor's home,* she thought to herself. *Everything is temporary until they get that big break, a full professorship.*

She glanced around the room and made a mental note that the only things missing were the full bookcases. Every professor she knew had tons of books in every room. *They keep every book they read or borrow.* She thought to herself.

It was probably time to make some conversation with Mrs. Browning, who demurely sat across from her with her hands resting in her lap. Taylor couldn't help but chuckle at the Professor and wife's matching garb. Lindsay wore a mousy, grey wool jumper, which matched her husband's blazer. And her unattractive loafer-style pumps also matched her husband's. She was just missing the tassels.

Taylor struggled to find a subject of mutual interest. "I can't believe I'm the first to arrive," Taylor said cheerily. "I'm not the most punctual person around," she lied.

Lindsey Browning nodded her head and gave Taylor a strange plastic smile. "Your upcoming course sounds very interesting," Lindsey offered in an emotionless, flat voice.

"Yes," Taylor replied, already running out of things to say.

She took another sip of her Manhattan, thinking how unusual it was that Ted Browning had the drinks already mixed and waiting before the guests arrived. She wondered if hers came from some kind of grocery store Manhattan drink mix. It did seem a little sweeter than most Manhattans, but it was good…maybe a bit too strong. Taylor seemed to feel the effects of the drink almost immediately.

Her head was starting to spin…ever so slightly, and her hands and arms were getting a little rubbery. *Guess I'm out of practice with drinking Manhattans.* She thought again to herself.

"You know," she addressed Lindsey again and noticed a slight slur in her own voice. "I think I could use a cup of coffee. This drink was a little too much for me."

Without saying a word, Lindsey got up and walked into the kitchen. Taylor shook her head a few times trying to get rid of the fuzziness coming over her. A flush of heat started from her waist and made its way up her body, arms, and neck to her face. It felt like a full-body hot flash.

Taylor suddenly felt like she was going to faint. Her entire body was limp and would no longer follow her commands. *Where is Lindsey Browning, and where is her husband?* Taylor hadn't seen him since he handed her the drink.

Taylor didn't feel drunk anymore; she felt paralyzed. She was familiar with that feeling because of the car accident…after the amputation of her legs…the swelling around her spine caused paralysis. She had that same kind of feeling now. Her head was clearing, but her body was out of control, limp, and lifeless. The hot flushing continued to travel back and forth from her face down to her trunk, then back up to her face.

She saw herself slide out of her wheelchair and onto the floor. Her head actually bounced on the thin rug…but she felt nothing. She landed on her back, feeling like a disembodied spirit.

On some level, Taylor knew she should be frightened. Her mind was telling her that the drink was drugged. She was in grave danger, but she was experiencing an artificial calmness, a sense of euphoria…even elation.

Her intellect and emotions were in a battle for her life. She remembered this struggle too. All those weeks and months in the rehab hospital, where the anti-depressants wrestled with the painkillers…where the struggle to live was a constant battle to accept that she would no longer walk.

Someone walked back into the living room. *Maybe Lindsey came back to help her*, Taylor thought. No, the figure wasn't Lindsey. It was a man with a stocking mask over his face. He bent down and stared at her. Dark, dull eyes peered through her face to her very soul.

Try to focus…try to stay alive… This was the mantra in Taylor's head. The distorted, masked face moved back up and a brightly colored yellow dart fell to the floor. Taylor's eyes tried to follow the dart as it bounced slightly and rolled away from her face. This was when she recognized the masked man's shoes. They were Ted Browning's loafers, and he was next to her. Ted Browning was wearing the mask…He was the killer!

She refused to slip into the drug. Her body was already drugged enough to be taken, but she would not go without a fight. Taylor struggled to keep aware of everything going on around her.

Lindsey Browning kneeled next to Taylor. She leaned over her and unbuttoned Taylor's blouse. She slid it off her shoulders and then deftly slipped off Taylor's skirt…her half-slip…her bra and underpants.

Taylor was totally nude, but all she felt was the artificial heat of the drug. She couldn't feel the carpet under her…or Lindsey's touch on her skin. Lindsey got up, and the loafers were back…right in front of Taylor's face.

Ted Browning kneeled next to her now. The mask was gone, and his pants were unzipped and opened at the waist. He was smiling…laughing…saying something…but she couldn't hear anything. Taylor was deaf and paralyzed…but she knew she was about to be raped and killed.

Lindsey's feet moved quickly past Taylor's face. *Where's she going? Sick bitch! Can't even stay to watch!* Taylor's voice screamed inside her head, as she struggled to keep some kind of control.

Browning jumped to his feet and moved in the opposite direction of his wife. *What's going on? Something's happening!* Taylor didn't know what would happen next. She fought unconsciousness by focusing her attention on the wooden sofa leg.

"Open the door! This is the police!" Ana Ramos screamed the command a second time. She was not the only one who saw movement in the house. Officer Hewlett saw it too.

"Break the door down...now!" she screamed to Hewlett and Gerard, the other officer with them. Gerard swung the iron door-buster close to the lock, and with a loud "Crack!" the door smashed open.

Ana moved in first; her gun ready. The two officers pulled their weapons and followed her. The first thing she saw was Taylor's naked body lying next to her wheelchair. An invisible punch hit her stomach, nearly taking her breath away, but she didn't let down her guard.

"This is the police! Come out with your hands in the air!" She yelled another warning, as she forced her eyes away from Taylor's body. She signaled the officers to move toward the kitchen while she moved stealthily down the hall to the bedrooms.

The first room door was open. Ana entered slowly, moving her gun, which she held in both hands, back and forth across the room. She scanned for any signs of movement or life. Then walking deliberately toward the closet door, she let go of the gun with her left hand but kept her right hand index finger on the trigger.

She noiselessly turned the handle and inched the door partway open. Lindsey Browning forcefully pushed the door the rest of the way...aimed a .22 caliber pistol at Ana...and blasted away twice. Ana felt the burning bullets tear into her arm...her chest. She fell to the floor and dropped into total darkness.

Hewlett and Gerard entered the bedroom almost together. Their guns were aimed at Lindsey, but she didn't back down. She fired one shot between the two officers, and both fired back. The force of the spray of bullets from their .45 automatics threw her against the closet door before she slid down into death.

*   *   *   *

Max and Nikki arrived at Mercy Hospital shortly after Ana Ramos and Taylor arrived in separate ambulances. Officer Hewlett had already briefed Max on his cell phone. Now, he stood outside the Emergency Room waiting to report to his Sergeant.

"She's in bad shape, sir," the young officer stammered. "We were right behind her, but the woman came out of the closet shooting."

Realizing how upset the officer was, Max calmly said, "Everything will be okay. Just tell me what happened; where's Ted Browning?"

"We must have been right behind him when he slipped out the kitchen door," the officer tried to explain. "Girard saw his car pull away from the driveway, and he called it in to Traffic. That's when we backtracked to Detective Ramos, but we got there too late."

Max tried to snap the officer back to action. "You need to secure that crime scene and file a full report, as soon as possible. Then make sure you and Girard make an appointment with Dr. Cotter. There's no discussion on that, you understand?"

Hewlett shook his head in agreement and added, "They took Lindsey Browning's body over to the morgue. Now, we'll never really know what she did or why she did it."

Max put his hand on the officer's arm, "I'm sure you did what you had to do. She was an accessory to a murder, if not a murderer herself. The wives of serial killers often get threatened or sucked into the crimes. Their fear or their fascination with the awful brutality going on leads them into becoming part of it. They're just as sick and just as guilty as the murderer."

Max paused here for emphasis, "Remember Hewlett, there's nothing wrong with defending your life. We cops have to do that everyday. You had no choice, and you did the right thing."

At that moment, Ginni walked into the waiting room looking for Nikki. Max said goodbye to the officer and moved into the triage area with Nikki and Ginni.

"Taylor will be okay," Ginni explained. "She didn't drink enough to cause an overdose, but it'll take a few hours for the effects to wear off. They're cooling down her body and hydrating her. Thank God, Ana got there before she was raped."

"What about Ana?" Max asked, the worry apparent in his voice. "How is she?"

Ginni looked at Nikki before making eye contact with Max. "She doesn't look too good right now. There are two entry wounds, but we don't know yet if any hit vital organs. Her vital signs are strong, and they're taking her right up to surgery. Jeff Manheim is on tonight, so you know she has the best surgeon here."

"I haven't been very nice to that woman," Max said self-consciously. "She's a damn good cop, and she got a bad deal from those Buffalo boys."

Nikki felt his concern and stepped next to him, "Ana knows all about the blue line of silence, Max. She blew in her partner because he broke the law, but turning in a fellow officer, even if that's the right thing to do, leaves a person alone and unprotected. I'm sure she was grateful that you took her as your partner."

"I didn't really have a choice," Max answered, a touch of bitterness creeping into his voice. "If I find out that those two officers weren't covering her, they're gone. I'm not afraid of the Code of Silence. I never should have judged her."

Max stopped talking and his shoulders sagged noticeably. The weight of Ana's fate seemed to be on him. Nikki tried to help. "She's a tough cop, and I think she'll be okay. Just to be sure, I'm going to the chapel to say a few prayers. You coming with, Max?"

"No, I'm staying right here," Max pointed to the waiting room. "Gotta make some more calls, and I want to be here when Taylor Fleming comes around. I've got to ask her some questions too."

Ginni took Nikki's arm, and they walked down the empty corridor to the Hospital Chapel. Officer Chet politely walked several yards behind them. When Nikki knelt down in one of the short pews, Ginni sat next to her.

Nikki asked God to heal Ana and Taylor. She asked for forgiveness and justice for Lindsey. Then she asked for protection, guidance and comfort for Max and the officers. Her last prayer was for the capture of Ted Browning and an end to the suffering he had caused.

When she finished her prayers, she sat back in the pew, next to Ginni. She closed her eyes and meditated for another fifteen minutes, remembering the souls of Talia, Betsy, and Sheba. Looking for the lessons in all the destruction that had taken place in the last week, she was drawn back to the idea of evil.

She believed that evil can be personified, and that Ted Browning was that personification. Nikki took a few more minutes to remind herself that God had overcome all evil, and the spirit of God would give her the strength to keep fighting the evil in her life.

The two of them left the chapel and walked back toward the Emergency Room. "By the way Nikki," Ginni once again took Nikki's arm. "You better cancel that food order from Barrett."

"What food order?" Nikki asked.

"The one I placed this afternoon," Ginni tried to explain. "I think with Browning still on the loose, we better stay at Max's house again." She looked into Nikki's eyes. "Barrett's food was going to be another surprise for you, since I knew I had to work late again tonight."

That familiar fear-shiver ran down Nikki's spine. "You mean Barrett is delivering another meal to our house tonight?"

Ginni looked at her watch. "Unless you can catch her at the restaurant before she leaves."

Nikki took out her cell phone and punched in Barrett's restaurant number. "Is Barrett there?" There was a long silence, and then Nikki repeated into the receiver, "She already left...delivering an order. Thanks. Goodbye."

They hurried back to the Emergency Room, and Nikki found Max. "Barrett is delivering food to my house, and I think she may be in danger," Nikki said, all in one breath.

Max stood and yanked his phone out of his pocket. "Carbone is still on duty over there. I'll call and tell him to send her back to the restaurant."

He punched in the dispatch number and got transferred directly to the car radio. "Yeah, Barrett Fairburn from the restaurant. Just tell her Nikki and Ginni are staying at my house and get her out of there. They told you Browning is on the lose, right? Good. So be extra sharp...and phone in with any suspicion of trouble. Understand? Yeah. Bye."

"Carbone will send her back," Max related to Nikki, as he clumsily put his phone away.

At that moment, an Emergency Room nurse came over and whispered something to Ginni before she returned to the ER. "Taylor is coming around," Ginni announced. "She's asking for me, so I'm going in to see her. Why don't you come too, Max?'

Ginni, Max, Officer Chet, and Nikki all walked through the door to the ER. When they got to the line-up of beds, it was obvious that the crowded room wouldn't hold all of them. Officer Chet and Nikki went back to the Waiting Room.

Nikki sat by the exit door and aimlessly leafed through the old magazines on the table next to her. Suddenly, the same ER nurse ran back into the Waiting Room. She looked at Chet and yelled, "Security! I need help in here right away. I've got a man going off...he has a knife...C'mon, hurry!"

Officer Chet looked to Nikki for instructions. "Go ahead, help her. I'll be fine. I'll be right here," Nikki said.

The officer and the nurse went back into the ER. Nikki stretched her tired body and closed her eyes for a brief rest. She dosed off momentarily and an image of Barrett appeared in her dream.

"Nikki," Barrett sounded worried. "You promised my mother that you'd take care of me. I'm in danger, Nikki...and I love you."

Nikki's eyes sprang open! Something was very wrong! She needed to stop Barrett from going into her house. She knew Carbone was on duty, and that Max called him to stop Barrett. But this dream made her feel like she had to go herself...that only she could stop the danger.

Without thinking of anything but getting to Barrett, Nikki left the hospital. She found Ginni's Cadillac in the doctor's parking lot and used her extra key to start the car. She pulled out onto the street and sped home.

CHAPTER 21

▼

Nikki turned onto Center Street, took out her phone, and punched in Max's number. "Max, I didn't want you to get bent out of shape because I gave Chet the slip. I just had a bad dream about Barrett and needed to get over here and talk to her myself."

"What are you talkin' about," Max yelled back into the phone. "Aren't you in the Waiting Room?"

"I'm trying to tell you," Nikki went on in a calm, deliberate voice. "Chet was called into the ER for a security emergency. That's when I took Ginni's car. I'm on my way home. I'm just turning onto Center, and I can see Carbone in his car. Looks like Barrett's here too. Her car is parked in front of his. So don't worry. I'll be back before Chet knows I'm missing. Bye."

Nikki closed her phone and tucked it in her pocket. Then she glided the Cadillac behind the patrol car and parked. Officer Carbone was sitting behind the wheel…but he appeared to be very still.

Nikki slammed her car door shut, and Carbone still didn't move. She pulled out her forty-five and took a few steps toward the patrol car. Carbone was propped up in his seat, both eyes tightly closed. She opened his door carefully and checked his neck for a pulse.

"Thank God! He's still alive and breathing," she said, trying to shake him awake. His hat fell off revealing why he was unconscious. A small gash on the back of his head was still oozing blood.

She looked for his shoulder radio, but it was gone. Reaching over to try the car radio, she saw that someone had smashed it to pieces.

Fear started moving through her body. The thumping of her heart was beating in her ears. She took a few steps toward Barrett's car with her gun ready. She opened the driver's side door, but no one was in the car. She looked over at her townhouse and saw a light on in the downstairs bedroom and the front door ajar.

Nikki didn't want to go into the house. She didn't want to face whatever Ted Browning had waiting for her, but she couldn't let Barrett stay in danger. She used her fear to push her toward the door.

Once into the hallway, she silently moved toward the bedroom...her gun was ready...the safety was off...she held the handle with both hands. Her bedroom door was open, and she heard muffled noises coming from inside. *Barrett was inside and was being attacked!* The words were a reality hitting her over and over again in the chest.

She nudged the door halfway open, and saw a naked Barrett tied up on the floor. Her shoes, slacks, and blouse thrown all over the floor. Her underpants were stuffed into her mouth, so she couldn't scream. She was looking at Nikki...demanding her attention...trying to tell her something in her muffled cries.

*   *   *   *

Nikki was back in Vietnam...In-Country with a small group of grunts who requested a Sunday Service and Chaplain Gambino sent her.

"Just give'm a sermon and blessing and get your ass back here for supper." That was what Joe told her when he walked her to the chopper. She was only fifteen minutes from base camp...but something happened. Nikki didn't even start the sermon when Viet Cong soldiers began firing into the camp.

Someone grabbed her arm and dragged her into the jungle with the other grunts. "Stay close and keep your head down." That was all she was told, as they went deeper and deeper into a dark, vine-entangled unknown. She had her service revolver with her, but it seemed like a water pistol next to the automatic rifles.

The grunt ahead of her was hit, and he went down. Two behind her were hit, and she could feel the bullets whiz past her face. The Cong seemed to be all around them, so she fell down and played dead.

Three enemy soldiers walked warily up to her and the bodies around her. They were within two feet...when all the dead grunts rose up and opened fire.

"See ya know how to play possum, Rev," the first grunt said, as he pulled her to her feet. "Sorry I didn't have time to tip you off. Just hoped you knew about playing dead."

*   *   *   *

Nikki stepped into the bedroom with these thoughts in her mind. *Stay close and keep your head down.* She took a few cautious steps toward Barrett...the door slammed shut behind her. A stupid mistake, but she didn't have time to correct it.

Ted Browning was on top of her. He pushed her to the ground and grabbed her gun hand. She grabbed the hammer in his right hand. He was strong...crazy strong, with all the power of a madman. His strength got the better of her, and she pulled her head away just in time for the hammer to smash against the floor.

Nikki saw an opening and kneed him in the groan. This gave him enough pain, so that he dropped the hammer and for a moment grabbed the offended part of his anatomy. At the same time, he gave her right hand just enough twist to tear some cartilage. This caused her to drop her gun.

She held her throbbing wrist while he scooped up her gun. Browning used all his strength again and slapped Nikki across the face with his open hand. The force of the blow knocked her to the floor. He crouched over her now and laughed. Then he shoved the gun into her face.

"You stupid bitch," he hissed at her. "Here I thought you were super-soldier girl, and you turn out to be just another cunt. One that almost got away from me."

His face contorted into something that looked much less than human. "No bitch gets away from me. I get whoever I want."

He put the barrel of the gun into Nikki's mouth. "How's the taste?" he asked, laughing again. He roughly jerked the barrel out again, and said, "Don't worry. I've got better plans for you. Something with a nicer taste." He laughed again at his own joke.

"First, you have to rest." His voice was almost unrecognizable...almost as if another force had taken over this man. "I only do it to resting cunts," he went on, pushing Nikki onto her stomach and tying her hands behind her with a bathrobe belt.

Nikki tried to protest, but he stuffed her mouth with Barrett's bra. When he got back up, he kicked Nikki hard in the thigh. "You all talk too much. You know how distracting that is? I like cunts quiet...limp and open. That's how I like you bitches."

Nikki felt the pain from his kick travel up her leg. *Stay low and keep your head down.* She focused on the words and tried to think of a way out.

Browning dragged Nikki next to Barrett and dropped her on the floor. Then he walked toward the hall. He turned back and snarled, "Don't try to get away, or I'll make it hurt more."

Nikki tried to slide closer to Barrett, so she could touch Barrett's leg...make some kind of physical contact. Nikki turned and looked into Barrett's terror-filled eyes. She silently prayed for both of them.

Browning walked back into the room carrying a soda bottle and a glass. He still had the gun in his hand, as he poured some of the GHB laced soda into the glass. Carrying the glass over to Barrett, he bent down. "We can do this the hard way or the easy way," he threatened.

Then he roughly pulled the pants out of her mouth...and Barrett wasted no time, she sat up and spit at him, screaming, "You son-of-a-bitch! It won't be the easy way for you!"

Browning slapped her across the face and then held the gun to Nikki's head. "Okay, big, tough girl. I blow her brains out all over your body or you drink. Which will it be?"

Nikki knew she had to do something. She worked the bra out of her mouth and yelled, "Don't drink it, Barrett!" Next, she turned to Browning. "You'll never get away with this. They know where I am. The police will be here any minute now!"

Browning gave Nikki another hard kick, this time in the stomach. Nikki gasped for several seconds until she could finally inhale again. Then Browning put the gun into Nikki's mouth and turned back to Barrett, "Well, big girl, ready to drink?"

"Okay! Okay! Don't hurt her," Barrett begged. "I'll drink it!" And she took several gulps of the soda.

"No! No!" Nikki tried to stop Barrett, but the gun muffled her words.

Barrett seemed to feel the effects of the drug right away. She started moaning and dropped her head onto the floor.

Browning took the gun out of Nikki's mouth and snarled, "It's your turn," He poured the rest of the soda into the glass. "Don't try to fight me, because I really don't care if I waste this cow." As he spoke, he put the gun into Barrett's ear. "She isn't my reason for being here tonight. You are."

Nikki knew it was useless to fight him. He didn't care about who he killed...who he hurt. Barrett didn't mean anything to him. "I'll drink it," Nikki told him, raising herself on her elbows so she could sit up.

He took the gun out of Barrett's ear and brought the glass to Nikki. He started to pour it into her mouth, and she deliberately made it run out of the corners of her mouth. She started gagging, almost throwing up as fast as he poured it in.

"Stop the games!" he yelled and crouched down closer to Nikki, while he pushed the glass further into her mouth. She started to fight the swallowing again and her lack of cooperation drew his full attention.

Nikki and Barrett were back in Vietnam. They were playing possum...waiting for a chance to jump up and shoot the enemy. Barrett tried to jump up. She rolled over and gave Browning a forceful kick in the buttocks. This sent him flying across the room.

"You stupid bitch!" he yelped. "That just cost you your life!" He struggled to get back up.

But the soldiers couldn't get to their feet this time. They didn't have any weapons. They couldn't destroy the enemy. All Nikki could do was yell, "Noooo!"

She was more afraid than she had ever been. Playing possum doesn't always work. Sometimes the possum gets killed. Nikki scrambled awkwardly over to Barrett and fell backward on top of her. "Leave her alone, Browning. You want me. I'll drink the stuff. Just leave her alone."

"I should just kill you both and do you after," he growled, moving closer to them. "But that just isn't any fun." He was laughing that mad laugh again.

"She's dead, Reverend Nikki Barnes. Your friend there is dead." He pointed the gun at Barrett's head. Nikki knew she couldn't cover all of Barrett's body with hers.

A tear of resignation trickled down Nikki's cheek, as she tried fruitlessly to maneuver in front of the line of fire. "I'm okay, Nikki." Barrett whispered in a slurred voice. "Just stay close to me."

Browning readied his shot. He got close enough for a clean hit. "You don't seem to be enjoying this," he laughed at Nikki. "Wait for your turn, because that won't be as quick. I saved one of my winning darts for you. You'd be amazed at what I can do with a dart."

"Drop the gun, Browning!" Max yelled from the bedroom doorway. "Back away from the two of them! Drop the gun and put your hands on your head!"

Nikki couldn't believe what she was seeing. Her wonderful, Army buddy Max, was saving her life...Her joy, however, was short-lived. She realized what was about to happen. Browning had no intention of dropping the gun.

He swung around and fired at Max. In a split second, Max fired back but then fell backwards to the floor. Browning turned back to Nikki. His bloody chest indicated a mortal wound, but he rallied enough strength to keep standing. He pointed the gun at Nikki's head.

She closed her eyes and another gunshot exploded through the room.

Nikki's whole world froze for a few seconds. She opened her eyes, and her body was okay...she wasn't shot...she wasn't dead.

"That nut case ruined my belt buckle," Max said, struggling to get up on one knee, while he kept his gun aimed at Browning. He finished getting up and walked unsteadily toward Browning's body. He kicked Nikki's gun out of the way and nudged Browning with his foot. He finally reached down and felt for a pulse.

"He won't kill anyone else," Max announced, as he moved over to Nikki to untie the robe cord. "I told you this buckle was lucky," he tried to keep things calm. "Just look where his bullet hit."

He finished untying Nikki and stood up to point at the dent in his belt buckle. Nikki jumped up and threw her arms around him. "You really saved me this time, Max." She burst into tears.

"Okay. It's okay, Nik," Max held her in his arms and patted her back. "Everything will be okay. He's dead. He's not hurtin' anyone else. We may never know how many cities or states he's been in or how many women he really killed, but he won't be killing anymore."

Sirens filled the darkness outside, and police cars and ambulances quickly gathered at Nikki's door. Officers and paramedics waited for their orders.

"I called for backup before I left the hospital." Max explained. "Which is more than I can say about some of my friends."

Max gave Nikki another hug, and they held each other until the first officers ran into the bedroom. They were followed by Fluffy, who with her ears flat back announced a loud, "Meow!" Nikki translated this to mean, "The war is over."

Nikki broke from her hug with Max and grabbed the quilt from her bed. She draped it over Barrett, then moved aside for the paramedics, who hurried over to Browning and Barrett.

Fluffy came over to see what was going on, and Nikki scooped her up asking, "You smart cat; just where do you go to hide?" As soon as Nikki said, "hide," Fluffy jumped to the floor and disappeared with another, "Meow."

CHAPTER 22

▼

Nikki finished a prayer of healing and moved her thumb in the sign of the cross on Ana's forehead.

"I could use one of those," Taylor Fleming said jokingly, as she wheeled further into Ana's hospital room.

Nikki smiled at her and said, "I never took you for the religious type."

Taylor wheeled closer to the bed and took Ana's hand. "I wasn't sure about all that God stuff, until I was lying buck-naked on some couple-from-hell's parlor rug, with all the Queen's Army running and shooting around me."

She made a funny face at Ana and added, "It's the very first time I was glad not to be the center of attention."

Nikki moved closer to Taylor and made a cross on her forehead too. "Lord, continue to bless this most unusual and brazen woman."

Ana started to laugh first, and everyone joined in. "I'm really quite fond of this brazen woman," she said in a worn, hoarse voice.

Ginni appeared in the doorway. "Hey! I thought you were all told not to bother the patient. Detective Ramos has a lot of mending to do. She should not be talking but resting. This looks like some kind of party...and why wasn't I invited?"

Nikki could take a hint, even if it was given jokingly. She touched Ana's arm gently and said goodbye. Ginni gave Ana a wave and joined Nikki in the hall.

"Look who's waiting for the crowd to thin, so he can see Ana," Ginni whispered, as she pointed to Max, who stood a few feet away. He was almost hidden by a large flower arrangement in his hands.

"You can go in now," Ginni said, as she waved to Max.

Max lumbered over to the room and stopped for a moment to compose his speech. He entered just in time to find Taylor, who had pulled herself up onto Ana's bed, plant a big kiss on Ana's lips.

Max coughed and self-consciously stayed behind the flowers. Taylor gave him a bothered look and slid back into her wheelchair. "I thought she looked pale and needed some mouth to mouth," she quipped and glided her wheelchair out of the room.

Moving awkwardly through the small hospital room, Max reached Ana's bed and put the flowers on the table next to it.

"Thanks for coming, Sergeant," Ana struggled for the energy to speak. "The flowers are beautiful."

"I can't stay long," Max began. "I mean, the doctors won't let me. You need to rest…but you're gonna be fine." He fell silent for almost a full minute. "The flowers are from all the guys in the department. You did a brave thing…and they all respect you. I respect you."

He paused again, carefully searching for the right words. "I'm proud to have you as a partner, Ana. If you decide to stay with us here in Sheridan, any of the guys would be proud to work with you. If Henry just can't come back to work…well, I'd be happy to have you replace him. I better go now. Hope you feel better, real soon."

Max walked closer to the head of the bed and bent over. He planted the gentlest of kisses on Ana's cheek. Slowly, he stood back up and left the room.

*   *   *   *

Nikki strolled nonchalantly into the kitchen of the Fait Accompli Bakery and Eating Emporium. She stopped to breathe in the wonderful smells of spices and fresh baked bread. Smiling to herself, Nikki took a moment to admire the gleaming steel stovetops, freezers, and hanging pots and pans. She finally saw Barrett engrossed in a creative cooking project at the end of the room.

When Barrett realized someone was with her in the kitchen, she turned around and faced Nikki. "What are you doing here?" she asked in genuine surprise.

"You left the hospital in such a hurry..." Nikki began. "I didn't even get a chance to do an official pastoral care visit."

"I have a business to run," Barrett replied, as she returned to the piecrust she was working on. "Besides, that drug stuff wore off in a few hours. I was fine."

Nikki took a few steps closer to Barrett. "I wasn't fine. I was pretty scared. And...Barrett...I feel terrible that I almost got you killed. I'm so sorry that I put you through that."

Barrett stopped her work and wiped her hands on her apron. "You didn't put me in danger. It was my decision to deliver the food. When I saw Carbone had been attacked, I just got worried about you."

"You never should have gone into the house," Nikki tried to control the quiver in her voice. "You should've turned around and gotten out of there."

Barrett took a few steps closer to Nikki. Her five-foot-eleven inch height was made taller with her chef's hat, so she appeared to be a giant next to Nikki's five-foot-three height.

"I was worried about you, Nikki," Barrett said, softly. "I didn't want you to get hurt. I can take care of myself, but you need someone to take care of you."

Tears started to flow down Nikki's cheeks. There was no sense trying to stop them. Not many people have cared for Nikki as openly and sincerely as Barrett. The kindness in this moment touched Nikki's very spirit. All the fear, confusion, and darkness of the past week rushed up in her, and she started to sob, unable to hold back this needed catharsis.

"That's a lovely thing to say," Nikki finally choked out between sobs.

Barrett stepped next to her and enveloped Nikki in a big bear hug. She tried to console Nikki by rocking her back and forth. Barrett also started to cry. She may be big and strong, but she had gone through a frightening ordeal.

The tears washed away some of Nikki's doubt about what she should have done...maybe didn't do. Nikki felt better emotionally. Now, she was actually getting a little sea-sick from the rocking. "Barrett...Barrett...you need to let go of me now. I'm feeling much better."

Barrett slowly broke the embrace and started fumbling in her apron pocket for a hankie. Nikki reached into her blazer pocket and brought out two tissues. She handed one to Barrett, and they both wiped their eyes. They stood together in silence, until Nikki awkwardly said, "I better go now."

She fumbled for an excuse to leave. "I need to spend some time at home with Fluffy. She probably thinks I'm still playing Go Hide." Moving closer to Barrett again, Nikki leaned up on tiptoes and kissed Barrett on the cheek. "Thanks again, Barrett for caring...and everything."

Barrett gave Nikki another quick hug, and Nikki started walking toward the door. "How about I bring over some of my pasta marinara?" Barrett yelled to Nikki, who immediately turned around.

"That would be nice," Nikki answered. "But only if you plan to stay and enjoy it with me...and Ginni...and Fluffy."

"Does Fluffy like pasta?" Barrett asked with a big grin on her face.

"Are you sure you can get an evening away from the restaurant to share with old friends?" Nikki answered.

"Sure," Barrett smiled. "I'll be there with the marinara and all the trimmings...but Nicolette, someday...we won't be just old friends."

With this, Barrett turned back to her cooking, and Nikki started to smile. She thought about what Barrett was saying and shook her head. Definitely time to get home and find Fluffy.

*   *   *   *

Nikki carried on a conversation with herself while she walked down the familiar hallway of her home. "Fluffy did make a cameo appearance last night, so where would a good hiding place be?" She looked under the sofa, and then moved into the kitchen. She deliberately avoided checking her bedroom, because she was not yet ready to face the blood on the rug and the fearful memories.

On the kitchen table was a note from Max. "Nikki, I had a cleaning service come in and clean up your house after the Sheriff's boys got the evidence they needed for the case. Hope you're not too spooked to enjoy your home again. Your Bud, Max."

"Max, you are a down-right darling," Nikki yelled to the note. Then she noticed a P.S. at the bottom of the paper.

"PS. Fluffy is doing fine. She's not really hiding. That cat's trying to show you how Browning got into your house. I'll be over tomorrow to fix it, so no one can get in that way again. Just go down to the basement and look in the far left corner."

Nikki put the note down and headed for the basement. She opened the basement door and flipped on the lights. Then she took a flashlight from the shelf above the stairs and made her way down.

"Fluffy! Fluffy! Are you still playing 'Go Hide'?"

"Meow!" A loud cat-speak answer came from the rear of the basement. Nikki turned on the flashlight and walked back to the left corner. Fluffy sat on the empty shelf of an old wooden bookcase. As Nikki walked closer, Fluffy jumped to the floor and ran to where the bookcase met the wall. She started digging around the back leg of the bookcase. Nikki moved to where Fluffy was digging and used some muscle to push the bookcase away from the wall. There, in the middle of the concrete wall was a hole large enough for someone to crawl through.

"What's this?" Nikki asked, as she bent down and petted Fluffy on the head. "So that's how Browning got into the house."

Nikki flashed her light into the hole and tried to put it all together, "Browning dug a short tunnel from the large storm drain in the back parking lot to our basement wall. The hole in the wall and the tunnel are both large enough for him to crawl through."

She addressed Fluffy again, "This part of the basement is so far from the main rooms in the house, we couldn't even hear the tunneling."

"He smashed his way in, and we never heard him!" Nikki kept up her explanation to Fluffy. "All the plans for these houses and the surrounding development are still on view in the rental office. All Browning had to do to see the plans was pretend he wanted to rent a townhouse. He could've gone down a manhole two streets away from here and no one would have noticed. Those storm drains are all big enough for anyone to walk through."

She looked in the hole again, "So, he gets to our parking lot and smashes a hole through the drain tile. Then he digs a short tunnel and smashes through our cellar wall. He just pushes the bookcase in front of the hole, and no one sees anything out of place."

Nikki shook her head in disbelief. "Browning sure went through a lot of trouble to creep into our house unnoticed. He was an evil, ugly guy, Fluffy. His sister's threat to go to the police may have set him off, but who knows how many innocent women besides the three here in Sheridan, he was responsible for attacking. And when would he have stopped? When he killed Ginni and me? Or would he just move on to another city and get his equally evil wife to help him do the same thing there? Those two are what I call evil. Just plain evil."

She crouched down and got nose to nose with Fluffy. "You solved the biggest part of the puzzle and guess what? Barrett is bringing over pasta marinara."

Fluffy did not wait for any more acclaim, she ran up the stairs to the kitchen, and Nikki was right behind her. When Nikki reached the daylight at the top of the stairs, she stopped and took a deep breath. It was finally over. She could feel the light and goodness again. She would always wonder if she could have helped Talia in some way. If she should have known something horrible was behind her troubled life. And she would always miss Little Betsy.

She said a prayer of Thanksgiving, again realizing that Ginni and she had been saved. Maybe they were saved so they could do some good. There will always be evil but people can balance it, maybe even get rid of it, by doing good.

Nikki tried to shake away these negative, albeit philosophical, feelings and go with the buoyancy she was now feeling. "Disney World!" she practically shouted. "Oh yeah! We are definitely off to Disney World!"

"And Fluffy...," Nikki came back to the present. "You will have a lovely vacation too. Our dear friend, Max has a whole new in-law apartment that you can explore while we're away."

With this last remark, she finished following Fluffy into the kitchen. The detective cat stood next to her empty dish and let out another, "Meow!"

"Perhaps you can't wait for the pasta marinara," Nikki laughed and grabbed a can of cat food. Fluffy supervised, as Nikki opened it.

"You really are hungry," Ginni said facetiously, as she walked over to Nikki and pointed to the can.

Nikki smiled and said, "Barrett's bringing over pasta marinara." She gave Ginni a quick kiss, then bent down and spooned the food into Fluffy's dish. "I asked her to join us for dinner...is that okay?"

Ginni waited for Nikki to stand back up. Then she put her arms around her and smiled. "Of course that's okay. We are sort of her guardians, at least while Trang is in Vietnam."

She looked deeply into Nikki's eyes and added, "But I still feel like I have to keep my eyes on those two Fairburn women."

Nikki started to laugh...a little uncertain at first...but with more gusto as Ginni laughed too.

0-595-27303-3

Printed in the United States
1057000003B/184